Short Stories
from
Rabindranath Tagore

Short Stories
from
Rabindranath Tagore

Translated by

PRATIMA BOWES

First published in Great Britain in 1999
by East-West Publications
8 Caledonia Street
London N1 9DZ

Translation © 1999 Pratima Bowes

ISBN 0 85692 144 0
Printed in Malta by Interprint Ltd.

The short stories of Tagore— a selection

Contents

Preface

The stories translated here were written at various times between 1891 and 1917. They appear somewhat dated today, since they speak of manners and customs which no longer dominate the social scene in Hindu India as they did in the nineteenth and early part of the twentieth century, with which Tagore's stories are concerned.

As we know, the Hindu civilisation is a very old one, and its culture was moulded not only by the ethnic groups who inhabited the land since ancient times, but also by various peoples who penetrated into India at various times throughout its history and who were assimilated into its culture. No civilisation retains its creative impetus for ever but, apart from the forces that led to deterioration from inside, the culture received a major jolt when Islam – an unassimilable, proselytising and monotheistic religion – conquered India in the twelfth and thirteenth centuries. Hinduism – a polytheistic, decentralised and non-missionary faith was unable to offer much resistance. As was natural under the circumtances – centuries of domination by Islam followed by British rule – the culture went through a long period of steady deterioration, continuing to take a downward plunge in all spheres of its expression.

Having lost its creative vitality, possibly even before the arrival of Islam, Hinduism survived as a culture during those long centuries, when large numbers of people belonging to indigenous faiths such as Hinduism and Buddhism were converted to alien ways, by clinging on to those restrictive but integrative ways already present and by evolving in addition fresh prohibitions, often of a superstitious nature, in order to cast a protective net around itself. The result, as was to be expected in a patriarchal society striving to maintain itself under strain, was most severe in its effects on women, who were deprived of education and married off early – before puberty if the convention now established was followed – to avoid the possibility of their falling in love and exercising choice. Divorce was not allowed, nor remarriage of widows, but men could certainly take more than one wife, as they cannot now. The social pressure for the early marriage of girls was so intense that young girls had to be given in marriage to men old enough to be their fathers, if a suitable young man of the same caste was not available at the right time. Hindu women were not strictly speaking veiled, but they had very little freedom of association or movement. But not only women – men too suffered as the various restrictions built around the system of caste to which everyone, man and woman alike, was subject, became more and more pronounced, possibly thereby giving amorphous Hinduism a certain identity.

There restrictions and prohibitions had a tremendous hold on Hindu society and began to be taken as an integral part not just of Hindu culture but of the religion itself. But this belief is belied by the fact that some of the rules and customs with which the stories deal have disappeared, while others are in the process of doing so – including a great deal of the caste prohibitions – in the space of the last forty years of Indian independence, without that process imposing much strain on the religion itself, which is still going strong in its altered cultural milieu.

The contact with western civilisation and western education in the nineteenth century started the process of what became known as the 'Indian renaissance'. And in the movement for social reform that followed a large part was played by the Brahmo Samaj, a new religion that had sprung up, no doubt under the influence of Christianity, but with its roots in the ancient books called the *Upanishads*. Tagore's father was himself the founder of a particular sect within this movement. When later in his life Tagore no longer identified himself with the religious stance of the Brahmo Samaj, this freed him to accept a great deal of the culture and civilisation of ancient India that the Brahmo Samaj had set aside in its quest to modernise the faith, while at the same time he retained his inheritance of its liberal ideas on social reform. So although the subject of these stories is primarily human beings, their emotions and interactions within whatever social conditions these might be taking place, one can find in Tagore's tone a suggestion of the futility of many of the customs with which Hindu society had tied itself up. However, this protest – if protest is not too strong a word for what he was doing – constitutes only an undercurrent; it is neither loud nor vociferous, and it is the human interest of these stories, albeit that the people concerned move within the sphere of a particular cultural conditioning and none of us do otherwise, that gives them an interest beyond the confines of time and place. Tagore's main interest is people, the kaleidoscope of human emotions and their nuances as well as human behaviour when seized by these emotions, which, however they may identify themselves with different social conventions at different times and places, lie deep in human nature. But these stories certainly have an historical interest as well, especially in the context of the rapid social changes taking place in modern India.

Now a word or two about the problems facing a translator, especially a translator of someone as skilled as Tagore in the use of the Bengali language. Tagore was primarily a poet by natural inclination and even his prose style tends to display an abundance of poetic imagination. He was fond of using a great many metaphors and images, apart from a certain amount of repetition, to bring home his point, and he certainly had a predilection for using adjectives very liberally, sometimes three or four rather similar ones in succession to qualify a single noun. His sentences are often long and quite complex in structure, and when in addition these involve sentiments that are typical of the Bengalee character but alien to the western, it becomes difficult to transpose the matter into English without getting the language stilted. There is also the problem of general cultural differences which makes the resources of the one language not always adequate for the purpose of the other, and one has to get round this difficulty as best one can. But all these involve an agonising decision for the translator, whether to keep to the matter absolutely literally or in some ways to restructure the sentences and thereby to some extent their suggestive qualities, for the sake of clarity. and readability.

I have tried very hard not to take too many liberties and have in any case taken care not to change the meaning and intention of the original formulations even when their style of presentation had to be altered. My aim throughout has been an attempt to make the reading of Tagore's stories in translation a pleasure rather than a hardship.

Acknowledgements

I gratefully acknowledge the assistance given me for these translations by my daughter, Mrs Nita Clarke-Benn.

The Illusion of the Golden Deer

Adyanath and Vaidyanath Chakrovorty should have been joint owners of their family property. Of the two, Vaidyanath was the poorer. His father, Maheshchandra, having no business acumen, depended entirely on his elder brother, Sivnath, to look after the property. Sivnath offered his brother many affectionate words and in exchange appropriated all his share of the property. Nothing but a few Government securities were left as Vaidyanath's only support in his struggle for existence.

Sivnath made a lot of enquiries which enabled him to arrange marriage of his son, Adyanath, with Vindyavasini, the only daughter of a rich man, and this created further opportunities for an extension of his property. Maheshchandra married his son to the oldest daughter of a poor Brahmin burdened with six more daughters, and out of the kindness of his heart took no dowry. The reason why he did not take all seven as daughters-in-law was that he had only one son who had not put in a request for more than one wife. However he did help them financially over the marriage arrangements even beyond his means.

After his father's death, Vaidyanath was quite content with his few securities and altogether without worries. It never occurred to him to do anything to earn money. The only thing he used to do was to get branches of trees and sit and make them into sticks with great care. Young boys and men all around came for his sticks which he gave away as gifts. Over and above this he spent a lot of time making fishing rods, kites, and reels, entirely out of his impulse for generosity. Handmade things needing a lot of scraping and shaving, a lot of time and care - which were entirely unworthy of such an expenditure from the point of view of their usefulness to the family - greatly fired his enthusiasm.

By the grace of the goddess *Sasthi*[1], and defeating the wishes of his enemies, Vaidyanath became the proud father of two sons and a daughter. But his wife, Mokshadasyndari, was discontented, and getting more and more so. Why should Vaidyanath's household be bereft of the sort of opulence that prevailed in Adyanath's? The kind of ornaments and Benarasi sarees Vindyavasini there enjoyed, her demeanour and style of conversation, the haughty self-assertion shown in her dealing with everyone, all of these were beyond the reach of Mokshada. What could be more unreasonable than that? Didn't they belong to the same family? That side of the family was rolling in wealth through one brother misappropriating the property of the other. The more Mokshada heard of all this, the more disrespect and contempt she felt for her father-in-law and his only son. She failed to find any pleasure whatsoever in her own household where everything was inconvenient and contrary to the requirements of prestige. Their bed was not even worthy to bear a dead body; not even a titmouse orphan with nobody to call its own would be willing to live within the dilapidated walls of their house, and its decorations would bring tears to the eyes of a spiritual man who had renounced all. To protest against these exaggerations was however beyond the capacity of a member of the cowardly male sex. So Vaidyanath stayed on the verandah and doubling his attention to scraping, kept himself engaged with the sticks.

[1]Goddess of fertility

But silence was not enough protection against his troubles. There would be times when his wife would have him called indoors, forcing him to abandon for the time being his artistic endeavours. She would then look away from him and say with great solemnity, "Please ask the milkman to stop the milk." Vaidyanath would stay silent for a time and then ask in a most submissive manner, "How can we manage without milk? What will the children drink?" His wife would reply, "Rice water."

Sometimes she would display a contrary disposition. After having him called she would say, "I don't know, do what is necessary". Vaidyanath would ask, with a lack-lustre face, "Why, what needs doing, now?" The wife would say, "Go and get the marketing done for this month", and would then produce such a list as would be enough to perform the *Rajsuya*¹ sacrifice on a grand scale.

If Vaidyanath could summon up enough courage to ask if all these were really necessary, he would be told, "No, let the children die unfed and let me too go away. You could then manage very cheap'.

So as time went on Vaidyanath woke up to the fact that scraping sticks was not enough; some way must be found to earn some money. It was beyond his capabilities to find a job or start a business. So some short cut to the treasure of *Kuber*, the king of wealth, must be discovered.

One night he prayed in bed with earnest solicitude, "Dear mother, goddess *Jagadamba*, if you tell me in a dream of a patent medicine for some incurable disease I shall take upon myself the burden of having to advertise that in the papers."

He dreamt that night that his wife, very annoyed with him, had stated her intention of getting remarried as a widow. Vaidyanath was objecting to the proposal on the ground that there was no money to buy the necessary ornaments for the occasion. His wife was countering this

¹Ancient sacrifice performed by kings to declare supremacy over neighbours.
²One of many names given to the mother goddess.

objection with the argument that a widow did not need ornaments. Vaidyanath felt that the perfect answer was available against this, but what it was he could not quite get hold of; whereupon he woke up to find that it was morning. The right answer to the question why his wife could not be remarried as a widow occurred to him at once. Perhaps he felt a little sorry about it too.

Next morning he was sitting alone after breakfast and getting ready to make a kite when a *sannyasi*[1] stopped at his door with the traditional incantation of victory to God. Like a flash of lightning Vaidyanath at once saw in this the bright face of his future prosperity. So he welcomed the *sannyasi* with lavish use of endearing words and then supplied him with a befitting repast. After a lot of cajoling he was able to find out that the *sannyasi* knew how to make gold and wasn't unwilling to impart this knowledge to him either.

The wife was overjoyed; as a man with jaundice sees everything yellow she began to see gold everywhere. Like a craftsman her imagination studded everything – the bed, the house decorations, the wall – with gold; and then mentally invited Vindyavasini to come and see.

The *sannyasi* was fed every day with two litres of milk and a kilo of sweetmeat, drawing out of Vaidyanath's few Government securities a lot of silvery juice.

Supplicants for fishing rods, kites and reels now came to knock at Vaidyanath's closed door in vain. The children's dinner-time was not maintained and if they got hurt or cried aloud neither the master nor the mistress took much notice.

Vaidyanath and his wife sat still in front of the fire and without a flicker of their eyelids kept looking speechlessly at the cauldron. Through the constant reflection of the fire's glow in their concentrated, thirsty eyes, their pupils acquired, as it were, the properties of a touch-stone. Whatever came into view they overlaid with gold – shining like the path of the setting sun towards the evening.

[1]Man who has renounced all worldly goods.

4

After two of the securities had gone as offerings in this golden fire, the *sannyasi* assured them, "Tomorrow the gold will begin to take colour."

Nobody slept that night. The husband and wife together began building a golden castle. There were occasional disagreements and arguments but these were soon resolved in their glow of happiness. They did not shrink from giving up some of their own opinions for the sake of mutual adjustment – so deep was their conjugal unity that night.

The next morning the *sannyasi* was missing. The colour of gold vanished from everywhere and even the sunlight appeared dark. And after this their bed, their decorations and walls showed up their impoverished, worn-out state in a fourfold manner.

From now on if Vaidyanath tried to express an opinion on any domestic matter the wife stopped him in an apparently sweet but sharp tone, "We have had enough evidence of your cleverness. Now give it a rest for a while." This altogether flattened Vaidyanath.

Mokshada assumed a superior pose as if this mirage of gold had not taken her in, not for a moment.

Guilty, Vaidyanath began thinking of ways of pleasing his wife. One day he concealed a present in a square parcel and, presenting himself to his wife amidst a lot of laughter, cocked his head and asked, "Tell me, what do you think I have got here?"

The wife hid her curiosity and said in an apparently indifferent tone, "How can I tell? I am not a soothsayer."

Vaidyanath took a lot of unnecessary time over the undoing of the string, blew the dust away from the paper, then carefully unwrapped its folds to reveal a coloured picture of *Dashamahavidya*[1] from the art studio, which he turned towards the light for his wife to gaze at.

Instantly she thought of the foreign oil painting in Vindyavasini's bedroom and said with total contempt,

[1]Illustrates goddesses representing the ten principal branches of learning.

"What a to-do about nothing! You can keep this in your sitting room and gaze at it. I have no use for such things." Dismayed, Vaidyanath realized that among other things, fate had deprived him of the power to please women.

Mokshada now began to go to all the palmists she could get hold of, as well as consulting her horoscope with astrologers. Everyone said that she would die while her husband was still alive. But she was not particularly eager for this supposedly coveted and blissful end for a woman and her curiosity was not satisfied.

She was also told that good fortune awaited her as regards children with which her house would be full. This did not especially cheer her up either.

At last one fortune-teller was found who prophesied that if Vaidyanath did not find some hidden treasure within a year he, the fortune teller, would burn all his books. After such a promise Mokshada could hardly find any occasion for the least doubt about it.

The fortune-teller left well rewarded, but the prophecy made Vidyanath's life an absolute misery. There were in current use, some ways of getting money, such as agriculture, business, theft and cheating. But there was no recognized way of divining where a treasure, supposedly hidden, could be found. The more Mokshada encouraged and unbraided Vaidyanath, the more befuddled he became. Where to start digging, which pond to choose for diving, which wall of the house had to come down – he was totally unable to decide.

Extremely annoyed, Mokshada let her husband know that she had no idea before this that the skull of a man could contain so much cowdung instead of a brain. She urged, "Make a move. Do you think that if you just sit staring in front of you money will rain down the sky?"

Very reasonable – although it was Vaidyanath's earnest wish that it would! However, which way to move, what to ride on – why didn't somebody tell him that please? As nobody did, Vaidyanath carried on scraping sticks, sitting in his verandah.

In the meanwhile *Durgapuja*[1] approached with the month of *Asvin*.[2] For two or three days before the event boats began to arrive at the ferry station. Those living away from home were returning. In their baskets were various vegetables: aram, pumpkin, dried coconut; their tin boxes containing shoes, umbrellas, children's clothes and, for the beloved, perfume, soap, newly published novels and scented coconut oil.

The autumn sun in the cloudless sky had spread like laughter at a festive occasion. The newly ripe paddy fields were trembling in agitation. Trees and leaves washed and freshened by rain were shivering in the newly-arrived cool wind. Returning travellers were walking homewards through trodden paths in the fields wearing chinacoats made of tussore[2] with *chaddars*[3] on their shoulders and umbrellas over their heads.

Vaidyanath watched all this as he sat there and a deep sigh welled up in him. He compared his joyless home with a thousand other homes of Bengal full of the pleasure of reunion and he felt regret that the god of fate had made him so useless.

His children got up early and went to Adyanath's courtyard to have a look at the image of the goddess and the maid had to apply force to bring them back at lunch time. Vaidyanath was then seated, thinking about the fruitlessness of his own life, amidst universal rejoicing. He recovered his sons from the maid and drawing them close to his lap asked the older one, "Tell me Abu, what would you like for *Puja* this year?"

Abinash at once replied, "Give me a boat please, father". The younger son, not wanting to be left behind in any way,

[1] Festival when the mother goddess is worshipped under the name of Darga
[2] The month in autumn when Durapuja is held
[3] Cover for the upper part of the body

volunteered, "Give me a boat too, father."

Like father, like son. They did not care for anything other than some useless handmade thing. The father said, "All right."

Now an uncle of Mokshada had come back home from Benaras during the *Puja* holidays. He was a lawyer by profession. Mokshada began visiting him quite frequently. Then, one day she came to her husband and said, "Listen, you have to go to Benaras!" Vaidyanath thought that perhaps some fortune-teller had predicted that the time for him to die had arrived and having found that out, his wife was looking for some means of deliverance for him. But he heard afterwards that rumour had it that there was hidden treasure to be found in a house in Benaras. He was to buy that house and recover the treasure. Vaidyanath objected, "That's not possible. I can't go to Benaras."

He had never left home or gone anywhere. Authors of ancient treatises say that women have unlearnt expertise about how to make a man leave home. Mokshada's words often created heat and fume in the house, but, however much that made Vaidyanath shed tears, it did not make him wish to leave for Benaras.

A few days passed. Vaidyanath sat down to cut some wood into pieces, carve and join them to produce two toy boats. He added a mast, a sail of some cloth, a flag out of some red-coloured cotton fabric, and a rudder and oars. A toy boatman and a passenger were not missing either. The work showed great care and expertise and it would have been difficult to find a boy whose heart would not thud in great excitement to see it. So when Vaidyanath delivered the two boats into the hands of his two boys the night before the start of the *Puja* they began dancing for joy. The bare structure of the boat by itself would have been enough; the addition of rudder, oars, mast, sail and a boatman sitting in his place appealed to them as something most wonderful.

Attracted by the noise her sons were making out of sheer delight Mokshada arrived on the scene and saw their father's

8

Puja present. Inflamed with rage she began shouting and striking her own forehead; then, snatching at the toys she threw them out of the window. Not a gold chain, not a satin dress, not a silver-threaded cap – the wretched man had in the end gone to the extent of deceiving his own sons with mere toys. Even then they cost him nothing – just made by his own hands!

The younger boy began screaming at the top of his voice. Mokshada slapped him on the cheek, exclaiming, "Stupid boy!" A look at his father made the older boy forget his own misery. Feigning cheerfulness, he said, "Don't worry father, I shall pick them up tomorrow morning."

The next morning Vaidyanath agreed to go to Benaras. But where was the money to come from? Vaidyanath's wife sold her ornaments to get the necessary money together. The ornaments belonged to the time of Vaidyanath's grandmother; such heavy, real gold ornaments were not available these days.

Vaidyanath felt that he was going to Benaras to die. He picked up the boys, kissed them and left with tears in his eyes. Mokshada too began crying.

The owner of the house was a client of Mokshada's uncle. That was perhaps the reason why the house was sold at a high price. Vaidyanath occupied the house all by himself. The house was situated right on the bank of the river and the flow of its current lapped at the foundation.

At night Vaidyanath felt uneasy in the house. He lit a lamp at the head of the bed and lay down in the empty house covering himself with a sheet. But sleep refused to come. When at dead of night all noise had subsided Vaidyanath was startled to hear a clattering sound coming from somewhere. The noise was low but clear, as if in the underworld the treasurer in the storeroom of king Vali[1] was counting money.

Vaidyanath felt fear, curiosity and along with these an

[1]King of the underworld

9

unbounded hope. He took hold of the lamp in his shaking hands and moved from room to room – When he was in one room it felt that the sound was coming from the other and the same for the other room. So Vaidyanath moved around from room to room all night long. With daybreak that underground sound mingled with other noises and was lost.

When the world fell asleep late at night the sound started again. Vaidyanath was extremely disturbed. He could not make out which way to go to follow it. As if the babbling noise of water were being heard amidst a desert but it could not be ascertained which direction it was coming from: the traveller is afraid that once a wrong direction has been taken the hidden spring will forever go beyond his reach. Thirstily he stands still with ears alert, while his thirst goes on increasing – so stood Vidyanath.

Days passed in uncertainty. Sleeplessness and false hope made sharp lines of anxiety appear in his normally gentle and contented face. His flashing eyes in their sockets began to get a burning sensation like midday sand in a desert.

In the end, one noon he closed all doors and began sounding the floors with a crowbar. An empty sound came out of one small room by the side.

When sleep descended on the world at night Vaidyanath began digging the floor up all by himself. With signs of the approaching dawn the digging was complete. Vaidyanath found something like a room underneath. But he was afraid to set his foot there amidst the darkness that still prevailed. He placed his bed on top of the hole and lay down. But the sound was now so distinct that he had to get away from there in fear. Yet he was not inclined to leave the room unguarded and go further than the door. Greed and fear pulled him two ways by his two hands. At last the night was over.

Now the sound could be heard as clearly during the day. He did not allow the servant to enter the room, went out for lunch and then entered the room and locked the door. Invoking the name of God he set aside the bed from the mouth of the hole and heard quite clearly the noise of splashing water amidst the clatter of metal. With apprehension and timidity he placed his head in the hole and found water flowing through the low-ceilinged room underneath – he could not see much more in the dark. Then he pushed down a big stick and noticed that the water was just knee-deep. So he jumped into that low room with a box of matches and a lamp. His hands began trembling while he lighted the lamp, for fear that all his hopes might be dashed in a moment. He had to strike a lot of matches before the lamp was lit.

He found a huge copper pitcher tied up with a thick iron chain and when the current picked up the chain it fell on the pitcher and produced a sound. Vaidyanath went splashing through the water to that pitcher in a hurry – but found it empty.

Still he did not believe his eyes. He picked up the pitcher in his two hands and shook it vigorously – there was nothing inside. He held it upside down, nothing dropped out. He found the neck missing; it looked as if once it was filled up with something and somebody broke the neck. Then Vaidyanath began fumbling through the water with his two hands like mad. They touched something amidst layers of mud. He picked it up and finding it to be a skull held it near his ear and shook – nothing inside. He threw it away. A long search revealed nothing other than bones from a skeleton.

He noticed that the wall facing the river was broken down in one place; water was entering through the hole. Perhaps the person before him whose horoscope said that he would find hidden treasure had entered through the same hole.

In the end he gave up and crying 'Mother' let go a deep heart-rending sigh – the echo mingling with the sigh of many a hopeless person as it solemnly resounded throughout that underground cavern.

Vaidyanath came up with mud all over him. The noisy populated world around appeared to him totally false and empty like the broken pitcher bound in chains. It was unbearable to have to pack his things again, buy a ticket, get into a train, return home, argue with his wife and carry on living his days as before. He wished he could drop into the river, like its broken-down bank.

However he did pack his bags, buy a ticket and get into a train and one winter evening he arrived at the door of his house. Vaidyanath had seen many a man returning home in the month of *Asvin* and had coveted the pleasure of home-coming from abroad. Such a welcome was now beyond his dreams.

Entering home he sat down like someone simple on a wooden seat in his courtyard; he did not go into the inner quarters. The maid saw him first and started making gleeful noises – the boys came running, his wfie called to him.

Vaidyanath woke up as it were from a trance into his former existence. With a sad smile on his dry face he picked up one boy and holding the other by the hand entered the house.

The lamp had then been lit and although it was not yet night the winter evening was noiseless and silent like night. Vaidyanath said nothing for a time and then softly asked his wife, "How are you?"

She did not answer but asked instead, "What happened?" Vaidyanath speechless, just struck his forehead. Mokshada's face grew very stern.

The boys sensed the shadow of some great misfortune and quietly left. They went to the maid, asked for a story about a barber and lay down.

The night approached but the two of them said nothing. The inside of the house took on a somewhat uncanny atmosphere and Mokshada's lips tightened ominously. After a time she entered the bedroom and without a word closed the door behind her.

Vaidyanath stood outside in silence. The night guard cried at his appointed time to indicate the advance of the night, the tired world remained steeped in sleep. Nobody and nothing, from his own relations to the stars in the infinite sky, made any contact with this tortured, broken-hearted man.

When the night was far advanced the older boy, perhaps waking up from a dream, left his bed and quietly coming to the verandah called, 'Father'. But there was no response. Frightened, he went back to bed.

The maid prepared Vaidyanath's hubble-bubble ready in the morning according to the established pattern and looked for him. He was nowhere to be found. Later in the morning the neighbours came to have a chat with their friend who had just returned home; but no meeting with Vaidyanath took place.

At Night

"Doctor! Doctor!"

What a nuisance at this time of night... Opening my eyes I found that it was our landlord Dakshinacharan. I got up in a hurry, somehow managed to pull up a broken-backed chair, and looked anxiously at him. The clock showed the time to be 2.30 a.m. Wide-eyed and pallid Dakshinacharan said, "Tonight the trouble has started again, your medicine did no good."

I said with some diffidence, "Maybe you have exceeded your usual allowance of drink tonight." Dakshinacharan replied in a state of extreme irritation, "You are quite wrong. It has nothing to do with drink. You cannot guess why, unless you know the details."

In the recess of the wall a kerosene lamp was burning dimly. I gave a turn to the wick – the result was a lot of smoke and a somewhat brighter light. I sat on a packing case spread with newspapers and pulled a wrapping round myself. Dakshinacharan carried on:

"There can be few housewives as good as my first wife. But I was then quite young and well-read in poetry, so I was not particularly happy just with housewifely competence. Often I thought of this couplet from Kalidas:

'One's wife is a counsellor, a friend, one of a pair,
Also a beloved disciple in the matter of fine arts.'

But fine arts meant nothing to my wife and she would laugh it out of court, if I offered her love as a friend. As Indra's elephant, Airabat, was harassed and washed away in the current of the river Ganges, pieces of famous poetry and endearments I used were put to shame and borne away in the current of her laughter. She indeed had a remarkable capacity for laughter.

"About four years ago I became seriously ill – high fever with boils on my lips nearly took me to death's door and I hardly hoped for recovery. One day the doctor thought, in fact, that this was the end. But then a relative of mine brought along a young monk who treated me with some root or other mixed with clarified butter. I managed to survive; maybe because of the medicine, maybe it was just fate.

"My wife didn't rest at all whilst I was ill. During those few days a mere woman, with no more strength than belongs to a human being, fought with anxious desperation with the messengers of death at our door. She kept me covered with her two hands as a mother holds a child at her breast with all her heart, love and care. She forgot about food and sleep and indeed nothing else but my recovery meant anything at all to her.

"At last the king of death, like a tiger defeated of its purpose, threw me out of its grip and departed. But before going it struck her a forceful blow. She was then pregnant. Soon she was delivered of a dead child, and she became very ill herself with various severe complications. I began in my turn to look after her but my attentions embarrassed her very much. She objected, 'This is too much. What will people say? You shouldn't be attending on me day and night, like this.'

"If I fanned her at night whilst she had a high temperature, pretending that I was fanning myself, that led to a tussle with her. If ever my regular meal time was over by even a minute when I was busy nursing her that too became an occasion for appeals, requests and complaints. Any attempt on my part to serve her produced more ill-effects than good. Her reason – such overmuch solicitude was not for a man.

"You have probably seen my house in Baranagar. There was a garden in front and beyond that the river Ganges. Directly under our room, on the south side, my wife fenced off some ground with *mehdi*[1] and created a little garden after her own choice. That little piece, out of the whole garden, was quite simple and very "native." That is, colour had no preference over smell in it, nor many-coloured leaves over flowers, and there were no tubs of insignificant vegetation supported by sticks, with tags of Latin names attached. Instead one could find there such familiar flowers as bel, jasmine, gandharaj, oleander and tuberrose. A huge *bakul*[2] tree was there, underneath which was a cemented terrace with white marble on top. She used to have it cleaned twice a day in her days of health, and it was her place for rest on a summer's evening after work. One could see the Ganges from there, but people on boats couldn't see her from the river.

"After having been in bed for days, one evening of the bright fortnight[3] she requested, "I would like to sit in my garden, I feel fidgety, I have been in this room too long." I took hold of her very carefully, slowly led her to the terrace and made her lie down there. I could have rested her head on my knees, but felt that she would consider that strange, so I got her a pillow instead.

"One or two full-blown flowers began dropping from the bakul tree and through its branches shadowed moonlight came through to rest on her sickly face. The atmosphere was quiet and peaceful. My eyes filled with tears to look at her, as I sat silently to the side in that shaded darkness thick with scent of flowers. I came closer and took one of her fever-hot hands in mine; she said nothing. In a while, sitting silently like this, I suddenly felt my heart brimming over with

[1]Variety of bush used for fencing
[2]Evergreen tree bearing small star-shaped scented flowers
[3]Fortnight immediately following full moon

emotion and I declared, 'I shall never forget your love.'

"I realized instantly the superfluity of such a declaration. My wife laughed – there was some shyness in that laughter, some happiness, but a certain amount of disbelief as well as a certain sharpness born out of irony. She said nothing in protest but that laugh disclosed, 'It is impossible that you would never forget, nor do I expect such a thing.'

"It was her laugh, sweet but sharp, that always made me diffident about talking love to her. All the endearments I thought of when away from her, appeared nonsensical once in her presence. I don't know even now why the sentiments which, when appearing in a printed page, bring tears to one's eyes, should take on a laughable aspect when you utter them.

"One can argue with words, but not with a laugh, so I could do nothing but keep quiet. Moonlight became brighter and a cuckoo[1] nearby exhausted itself with repeated calls. I thought, how could its mate be so deaf in a night like this!

"My wife's illness showed no sign of abating and the physician suggested change of air. I took her to Allahabad."

Here Dakshinacharan abruptly stopped, looked at me rather doubtfully and then held his head between his hands as if in thought. I uttered no words to break the silence and the kerosene lamp in the recess continued burning, rather faintly. While the buzzing of the mosquitoes became clearly audible in that otherwise soundless room, Dakshinacharan took up the narrative again.

"There at Allahabad, Doctor Haran began attending my wife. At last when time showed no improvement the doctor said – my wife and I understood that quite well in any case – that the disease was incurable. She would always have to live the life of an invalid. Then my wife said to me one day, 'I am not going to get well, but I am not going to die in a hurry either. How long can you live with someone dead in

[1]Birds often sing in bright moonlight

17

life? You should marry again.'

"This was for her just a rational, well-considered proposition. She did not strike an attitude to suggest that it involved some greatness, courage or some other extraordinary quality on her part.

"This was my turn to laugh but I certainly did not know how to laugh like her. I began saying in a solemn and high tone, like the hero of a novel, 'As long as I live...'

"She stopped me: 'That's enough of that. You make me laugh.'

"Not yet ready to accept defeat I continued, 'I cannot love any one else in this life.'

"My wife this time laughed aloud. I was left with no choice but to stop.

"Whether I admitted this to myself or not I realise now that I had grown tired of this task of nursing a hopeless patient. The idea of leaving it never entered my head but that of having to live the rest of my life with an incurably ill woman did oppress me. In my forward-looking expectancy of youth, the temptation of love, the assurance of happiness, the illusion of beauty had once made the future take on a very cheerful appearance. It looked now like a hopeless stretch of thirsty desert all the way along, to the end of my days.

"She must have noticed that profound tiredness in my nursing of her. I didn't know then, but I have no doubt now, that she could read me like a simple Primer used to teach children. That is why when I talked romance, in all seriousness, simulating the hero of a novel, her response was laughter – laughter full of affection but inevitably also of irony. I die with shame today when I remember that my heart's language, unknown even to myself, was accessible to her like an open book.

"Doctor Haran was of our own caste and I was often invited for a meal at his place. After a while the doctor introduced me to his fifteen-year-old unmarried daughter. According to the doctor she was not married off for want of a suitable candidate but gossip suggested that there was some blemish attached to her birth. But nothing else was wrong with her. She was as good looking as well-educated. So now and again, engaged in discussions with her on various topics, I would return home quite late, when the time for my wife's medicine had passed. She knew that I had gone to the doctor's place, but never asked me the reason for the delay.

"I began to pursue a mirage amidst the desert. I was thirsty beyond measure, and right in front of me was clean, clear water overflowing its banks, and rippling in loveliness. My mind could not be turned away from it.

"The sick room now became doubly unpleasant and flaws began to appear in my nursing of my wife. Doctor Haran used to say at times that those who have no hope of recovery are better dead than alive; they only succeed in creating unhappiness for themselves and others. As a general remark this was unexceptionable, but he ought not to have aimed it at my wife. But a doctor's mind becomes so conditioned to death that he is hardly able to see how we, the others, feel.

"One day I heard, from a room next door, my wife saying, 'Doctor, why are you increasing the size of your bill with medicines that will do no good. My life itself is a disease, better give me something to end it soon.'

"The doctor protested, 'Please don't say such a thing.' The remark hit me hard. When the doctor was gone I went and sat by the side of her bed gently stroking her forehead. She said, 'It is rather hot here. Why don't you go out, it is time for your walk. You know you won't feel hungry at night if you don't take your walk.'

"To go for a walk meant going to the doctor's. It was I who told her that taking a walk was essential for my appetite. I know now that she was always aware of this deception on my part; I was such a fool to think that she was so stupid as not to know."

Dakshinacharan stopped again, resting his head on his palms. After a glass of water he took up the tale again.

"One day Monorama, the doctor's daughter, expressed a desire to visit my wife. I didn't much like the idea but didn't

19

know how to stop her.

"One evening she came to our place. That day my wife was in great pain. When in such a state she usually became still and silent. It was only her clenched fists and the bluish colour of her face that revealed the agony she was going through. There was no sound in the room and I was sitting silently by the bed. She probably was not even able to ask me to go for a walk or perhaps she did want me by her side at that time of acute pain. The kerosene lamp was put to the side, to avoid the light shining in her eyes. The room appeared dark and noiseless. Now and again all I heard was my wife sighing, at moments of lessened distress.

"Then Monorama appeared at the door. The light from the lamp opposite her fell on her face, blinding her for the moment, and unable to see anything she stood by the door, full of scruples as to whether to enter.

"Startled, my wife got hold of my hand and asked, 'Who is that?' That unknown appearance frightened her in her low state of vitality, and in her indistinct voice she asked a couple of times more as to who was there.

"Sudden folly took hold of me and I blurted out, 'I don't know.' Immediately I felt as if whipped and corrected myself, 'Oh, yes, she is the daughter of our doctor.'

"My wife looked at me but I couldn't look at her. Then she welcomed the newcomer in her frail voice, 'Do come in, please,' saying to me 'Hold the lamp for her.'

"Monorama came and sat in the room and some words were being exchanged between them when the doctor appeared. He brought with him from his chemist's shop two bottles of medicine. Taking these out he said to my wife, 'The blue bottle is for massage and this one is to take. Don't get these two bottles mixed up, for the other one contains poison.'

"He warned me too while placing the bottles on the table. On the point of leaving he called to his daughter, intending to take her with him.

"Monorama said, 'Why don't I stay here a while, father?

There is no woman here to nurse her.'

"Agitated, my wife objected, 'No, no, don't trouble yourself. I have an old maid, she looks after me like a mother.'

"The doctor laughed, 'She herself is like a mother incarnate and has always been busy serving others. So she finds it hard having to have others look after her.'

"The doctor was about to leave with his daughter when my wife said, 'Doctor, my husband has been sitting in this stuffy room a long time. Please take him with you for a walk.' The doctor replied, 'Why not, let us take a walk by the river.'

I objected a little but soon agreed. The doctor warned my wife again about the two bottles of medicine.

"I took dinner with the doctor that night and was a little late coming home. Back there I found my wife writhing in pain. Full of repentence I asked, 'Is it worse?' She said nothing, just looked at me. Her voice had failed by then.

"At once I called the doctor back. The doctor hardly knew what was wrong at first, then asked, 'So the pain is worse? Let us massage you with that medicine.'

"He took up the bottle from the table and finding it empty, asked my wife, 'Did you take it by mistake?'

"My wife nodded her head to let us know that she had.

"The doctor instantly returned home to fetch his pump. Half-fainting I fell on the bed. As a mother soothes a child who is ill she took my head to her breast and with the touch of her two compassionate hands conveyed this message, 'Do not grieve, this is the best way. You will now be happy and knowing that, I shall die happy.'
"When the doctor returned her life had ended, taking with it all her pains."

Dakshinacharan had another glass of water and said, "It is hot here." He rushed out for a walk on the verandah, then came back and sat down. Appearing reluctant to go any further he yet carried on – as if I was extracting the tale from him against his will.

"I married Monorama and came back home. Monorama married me according to her father's will. But when I caressed her or talked of love she remained very solemn, there never was a smile. It was beyond my understanding – this knot that had somehow occurred somewhere in her mind.

"I took to drink in a big way. One evening early in the season of *sarat*[1], I was taking a walk in our Barangar garden with Monorama. Darkness was gathering in. From the nest of birds came no sound, not even that of flapping wings. Only the rows of tamarisk trees along the avenue were shaking noisily in the wind.

"Tired, Monorama came to the marble-topped terrace under the bakul tree and lay down, supporting her head on her two arms. I too came and sat near.

"Darkness was even thicker there. The little bit of sky one could see was covered with stars. The cricket's call under the trees was adding a thin border, as it were, to the enveloping silence that appeared to have dropped from the bosom of the infinite sky.

"I had several drinks that afternoon and as a result was in a malleable state of mind. When my eyes got used to the darkness, the indistinct image of a tired woman – the end of her sari lying loose around her – drawn in pale colours under the shadowy woodland, brought about an inevitable passion in my mind. I felt as if she was just a shadow, not able to be caught up in my two arms.

"Then a fiery glow appeared on top of the dark tamarisk tree and the thin yellow moon of the dark fortnight[2] slowly ascended the sky above it. Its light fell on the face of the woman lying tired on the white marble, clad in a white sari. I could not resist it any more. I came near her and taking hold of her hand said, 'Monorama, you do not believe me but I love you. I could never forget you.'

"As soon as I said that, I was aware that I had said just

[1]The autumn season (September/October)
[2]Fortnight following the new moon

22

these words to someone else on another night. Right at that moment loud laughter blew like air, as it were, with speed, rushing over the branches of the bakul, over the heads of the tamarisk trees, under the broken yellow moon of the dark fortnight, from the east bank of the Ganges to the west. Was that laughter torn out of someone's innermost being, or a sky-piercing lament – I couldn't tell. I lost my senses and dropped down from the terrace to the ground underneath.

"When I came to myself, I found myself lying in my own bed. My wife asked, 'What happened to you?'

"Shivering I said, 'Didn't you hear that loud laughter blowing over, filling the whole sky?'

"She smiled, 'That was not laughter. Some flocks of birds in formation flew over, I heard the flapping of their wings. It does not, it seems, take much to scare you.'

"I realised in the daylight that what I heard was the sound of the wings of flying birds. This was the time when geese from the north came over, to frequent the sandy strip of land by the river. But I could not continue in that belief at the approach of the evening. Then it felt as if a dense laughter was amassed in the darkness all around, and on the slightest excuse it would break out and fill up the sky. In the end it came to such a pass that I was afraid to speak to Monorama when the evening approached.

"At last, I left that Baranagar house and went on a boat trip with Monorama. All fears left me in the soothing wind of the month of *Agrahayan*.[1] A few days passed in great happiness as the magnetism of the beauty all around her made Monorama gradually open her closed heart, after all that time.

"Leaving the river Ganges and Khare we reached Padma. The usually fierce river Padma was then in her winter sleep like a she-snake lying in her abode, emaciated and enfeebled. On the north the sandy strip, with no sign of man or grass on it, was stretched to the horizon and on the high bank

[1]Late November/early December

23

to the south stood the mango groves of the village trembling, as it were, with folded palms being so near to the mouth of this turbulent river. The sleeping Padma now and again turned on her side tearing up the land on her bank into shreds which fell into the river with a splash. Finding a suitable spot for walks I anchored the boat.

"One day the two of us walked a fair distance. The golden rays of the sun gradually faded away and in their place appeared the clear moonlight of the bright fortnight. When that boundlessly free and exuberant moonlight spread up to the horizon on that endless white sand it felt that there were but the two of us journeying in the infinite dreamland of this unpopulated domain of the moon. A red shawl, slipping from Monorama's head, had encircled her face and then wrapped itself round her body. When the silence became dense and nothing but a limitless whiteness and emptiness remained Monorama slowly brought out her hand to clasp mine, as if she had then come close to me and, surrendering her body and mind, life and youth, was standing by me in utter trust. With delighted heart filled with emotion I thought that it was not possible for love to blossom within four walls: nothing but this open, freely stretching, infinite sky could hold two human beings in love. I felt that we had no home, no door through which to enter anywhere, nowhere to return, that we would journey on hand in hand like this without a purpose on an unknown path over this moonlit emptiness.

"As we walked on we came to a spot where amidst the sand something like a pool had been formed – the water having been trapped there after the Padma had receded.

"Over that motionless, sleeping and still reservoir of water amidst the desert-like sands lay a long streak of moonlight as if in a swoon. We stood there together. Something made Monorama look at me when the shawl dropped off from her head. I took hold of that moonlight-washed face and kissed her.

"At that precise moment someone from that abandoned

and lonely desert land cried out in a grave voice three times in a row, 'Who is that? Who is that? Who is that?'

"I shuddered; so did my wife but we knew instantly that the sound did not come from a human being, neither was it something unnatural. It was the call of an aquatic bird now living on the sandy strip. The birds had been alerted by humans being so near to their isolated and safe abode at this time of night.

"Intimidated by this fright we hurried back to the boat. When we went to bed at night Monorama, tired, at once fell asleep. Then someone standing by my mosquito net in the dark pointed one of her thin boney fingers at Monorama and whispering in my ears as if in private kept asking in an indistinct voice, 'Who is that? Who is that? Who is that, tell me!'

"I got up in haste and striking a match, lit a lamp. The shadowy figure disappeared; instead a peal of laughter blew through the dark night shaking my mosquito net, rocking the boat and turning the blood of my perspiring body into ice. It went past the Padma, its sandy strip, then all the towns and villages beyond – as if it were going towards infinite distance through infinite time, on from country to country, from domain to domain, becoming gradually fainter and fainter. At last it went past the land of birth and death and the sound became thin like a needle point. I had never heard such a faint sound, nor imagined it, as if there was infinite space in my head, for however far the sound travelled it just couldn't go past its boundary. When the thing became unbearable I thought that sleep wouldn't come unless I put out the lamp. The moment the light was extinguished and I lay down the strangled voice, returning in the dark by my mosquito net, blurted out close to my ears, 'Who is that?, Who is that? Who is that, tell me!' The sound kept pace with the beat of the flow of blood in my heart, asking me without a break, 'Who is that? Who is that? Who is that, tell me!' At that dead of night in the silent boat my round clock too came alive and pointing its hand towards Monorama from above

25

the shelf began its rhythmic ticking, '*Who is that? Who is that? Who is that, tell me!*'"

Dakshinababu turned pale and his voice nearly failed him. Touching him I said, "Have a glass of water."

The wick of the kerosene lamp blazed up before it died altogether. I noticed light outside, a crow cawed, a *doel*[1] bird whistled. An on the road in front of the house a bullock cart made a creaking noise. Then the colour of Dakshinababu's face changed and it lost all traces of fear. He became ashamed, because he had disclosed his story under the spell of night and possessed by imaginary fear. He was very indignant with me and left abruptly without so much as a word of farewell.

That night there was a knock on my door at midnight, "Doctor! doctor!"

[1]Bengali magpie

A Nest in Ruins

Bhupati had no need to work. He was well-endowed with money and the country he lived in was hot. But his particular planetary influences meant that he was born with work on his brain, which is why he had to bring out an English newspaper – this saw to the complaints he had hitherto made about the tardiness of time in passing.

From his boyhood he fancied writing and lecturing in English. Even though there was no real need for it he used to send letters to English newspapers, and give lectures in meetings without having much to say.

Political leaders, eager to have a man like him on their side, used to praise him profusely and the result of this was that Bhupati conceived a high opinion about his English writing. Then, one day, Umapati, his brother-in-law, advised him, "Bhupati, why don't you bring out an English newspaper yourself. The kind of ability you have..."

This inspired Bhupati. There is no glory in publishing a letter in someone else's paper, much better to be free to use one's pen as one likes. So Bhupati became an editor at a young age, with his brother-in-law as co-worker.

He was at the stage when one can get caught up in the excitement of editorship as well as of politics, and there was no lack of people to further incite him. When he was thus engrossed with his paper his girl-wife gradually turned into a young woman. The editor of the paper was not particularly aware of this happening. The border policy of the Government of India was about to break its previous limits – this was the primary thing that captured his mind.

Charulata in her wealthy home did not have anything to do, nor was she in need of anything. Like a flower that blooms for no purpose, all she had to do was to let herself shine over a long, lazy day in an atmosphere of total purposelessness.

Usually in a case like this a wife – given opportunity of course – makes much of her husband and conjugal play tends to overstep the bounds of time and propriety. Charulata had no such opportunity. It was difficult for her to break through the barrier placed before her by the newspaper and claim her husband for herself. When a female relative reproached Bhupati, drawing his attention to his young wife, he said, suddenly becoming conscious, "You are right. Charu ought to have a companion, the poor girl has nothing to do."

He said to his brother-in-law, Umapada, "Why don't you bring your wife over here – there is no woman here of the same age as Charu, she must feel lonely."

The want of a female companion was what was bothering Charu. This was the editor's understanding, and when his brother-in-law's wife, Mandakini, came to live with them, he was relieved of all anxiety on Charu's score.

The time when love-play between husband and wife appears ever-fresh in its glory to the parties concerned, that golden dawn of conjugal happiness, passed away in unconsciousness without anyone's reckoning. Without any savouring of its freshness, these two, used to one another, developed a relationship that looked like one of long-standing familiarity.

Charulata had a natural urge for learning, so her days did not become altogether burdensome. Through her own effort she managed to find ways of engaging herself in studies. Bhupati's cousin Amal was a third-year student; Charulata enlisted his help towards her own end. For this she had to put up with a lot of pressure from Amal, such as finding money for meals in restaurants, and buying books on English literature. Amal would sometimes invite his friends for dinner and the burden of managing that was borne by Charulata herself, as something owing to a teacher. Bhupati himself made no demands on Charulata, but those of his cousin were endless. Charulata occasionally showed feigned annoyance and revolt against such pressures, but it was absolutely necessary for her to be useful to someone and undergo the disturbances that can follow feelings of affection.

Amal said, *"Bowthan*[1], the son-in-law of a royal family comes to College with boots made of carpet, woven by a special pair of family hands. I feel slighted. I must have a pair of carpet boots, otherwise I cannot maintain my status."

Charulata replied, "Oh, yes, that's what you think. I have no intention of making boots for you. Take some money and get those from the market." Amal refused, "That is simply not going to do." Charu did not know anything about making boots, but she did not want to confess that to Amal. Nobody wanted anything of her in this world, except Amal. So she started learning about carpet-making in the time when Amal was in college. Then when Amal had quite forgotten about the boots, Charu invited him over one evening.

It was Summer, and arrangements had been made for Amal's meal to be held on the roof. His plate was covered over with a brass lid. Amal changed after college and washed and dressed came up to the roof. Seated he took off the lid and found a pair of newly-made woollen boots inside. Charulata laughed out loud.

This gift of shoes encouraged Amal to ask for more. Now he wanted a muffler, an embroidered silk handkerchief, a cover for the back of the armchair in the lounge to prevent it from being soiled by his hair oil and so it went on.

[1]An address for wife of elder brother or cousin.

29

Charulata argued against his demands every time, nevertheless she continued fulfilling Amal's wishes with much care and affection. When Amal asked her, from time to time, how the work was getting on, Charulata lied with, "I did not remember to do it" or "Nothing at all has yet been done." But Amal was not one to give up. He reminded Charulata everyday, with childish insistence. Charulata feigned indifference on purpose and she liked to create arguments just to make pertinacious Amal pester her; then it amused her to suddenly let him have his wish.

Charu had nothing to do in a rich household and it was only Amal who made her work. It was through these little labours of pleasure that her emotions were engaged and satisfied.

There was a little piece of land in the inner quarters of Bhupati's household. It would be an exaggeration to call it a garden, as there was nothing much there except a hog-plum tree.

Charu and Amal got together to improve this piece of earth and the idea of a garden there took shape as these two, with great enthusiasm, made drawings and plans. Amal said, "*Bowthan*, you must water this garden of ours yourself, like princesses of ancient times." Charu said, "And we must have a hut made in the western corner for the young of a deer."

Amal added, "We must have a large pond for ducks."

This fired Charu's iamgination and she said, "We shall plant blue lotus there, I have wanted to see a blue lotus for a long time."

Amal said, "There has to be a bridge over the pond and a small boat by the landing stairs."

Charu said, "The stairs must be of white marble."

Amal ceremoniously made a map of the garden with paper, pencil, rubber and compass.

As these two revised their ideas or added to them, some twenty or twenty-five maps were drawn. When the map was ready, an estimate of the cost had to be prepared. The proposals was at first that Charu would create the garden, step by step, out of savings from her own monthly allowance. Bhupati took no interest in household matters and a surprise would be in store for him when an invitation would be issued for him to visit the completed garden. He would have to think that a whole garden had been brought over from Japan with the help of Aladdin's lamp.

But however economical the estimate, it was beyond Charu's means. So Amal sat down to change the map saying, "Well *bowthan*, let us give up the pond."

Charu protested, "No, no, that will never do, it will have my blue lotus in it."

Amal said, "What about giving up the tiles from the deer hut? Just thatch will do."

Indignant Charu replied, "Let me not have it at all then."

There was a proposal afoot to import cloves from Mauritius, sandalwood from Karnataka, and saplings for cinnamon sticks from Sri Lanka. When Amal suggested local native plants and foreign trees from nearby Manicktola instead, Charu went glum and said, "Let us not have the garden at all."

This was not the way to reduce the estimate. It was impossible for Charu to bring down her imagination along with the estimate and whatever Amal might have been saying he too did not wish for a reduction. So he suggested, "Why don't you then broach the subject to *dada*[1]. He would surely let us have the money." Charu protested, "No, there is no fun in that. We two should create the garden. He can place an order with a foreign firm to create an Eden here – but what use is that to us?"

Charu and Amal were enjoying in their imaginations the fulfilment of their impossible wish, sitting under the shade of the hog-plum tree, when Charu's sister-in-law, Manda, called from upstairs, "What are you two doing in the garden,

[1]Address for older brother or male cousin.

31

this late?" Charu said, "Looking for ripe hog-plum." Enticed, Manda said, "Bring some for me if you can find any."

Charu and Amal smiled. The greatest pleasure and pride of their imaginings together lay in the fact that these were solely confined to them. Whatever other things in her favour Manda might have, she had no imagination; how could she enjoy things like these? So she was left out of all the committees made up of these two.

The estimate for their beyond-reach garden could not be brought down. Ideas were not ready to come down either. But the committee under the hog-plum tree carried on somehow. Amal had the places in the proposed garden marked where the pond, the deer room, the marble terrace were to be.

Amal with a small spade in hand was doing the job of marking round the hog-plum tree where it was proposed to be paved, when Charu, sitting under the shade of the tree, said, "It would have been nice if you could write."

Amal asked, "Why so?"

Charu – "I would then have made you write a story about our garden, describing its deer room, the pond, the surround of this hog-plum tree. Nobody but we two could understand what it was all about, that would have been fun. Why don't you try? I am sure you can..."

Amal asked, "What are you going to give me, if I do write?"

Charu – "What is it that you want?"

Amal replied, "I shall make drawings of plants over the top of my mosquito net. You would have to embroider it all, with silk."

Charu – "How you revel in immoderation! Who has ever heard of embroidery on a mosquito net!"

Amal had a lot to say against the habit of treating the mosquito net as an ugly jail room, remarking further that this was proof enough that the majority of human beings did not have any aesthetic taste and were untroubled by ugliness

32

in their surroundings.

Charu agreed with this observation herself and was pleased to think that their committee of two was not included in that majority. She said, "All right, I shall do it, you write."

Amal asked, with an air of mystery, "Do you believe that I can't write?"

Charu was excited, "Then you have written something. Show it to me."

Amal said, "Not today, *bowthan*..."

"No, it must be today, go, get your writing."

Amal was in fact over-eager to let Charu listen to his writing. He was only putting up obstacles for fear that Charu might not understand or like it.

But he brought over his exercise book, flushed, coughed a little and then began to read. Charu leaned against the trunk of the hog-plum tree and with her feet stretched on the grass listened.

The subject of the essay was 'My Exercise Book'. Amal had written, 'My exercise book! You are empty and my imagination has not yet touched you. Like the forehead of a newborn child before the god of fate enters the lying-in-room you are pure and mysterious. Where is that day when I will write my conclusion on the last line of your last page? Your white, fresh papers cannot even dream of that end, when it will be inkstained, for ever', and so on.

Charu kept sitting in the shade and listening. When the reading was over, she was silent for a while, then said, "Who says you cannot write!"

That day, under that tree, Amal had his first taste of literature. The companion was young, the palate was fresh, and the afternoon light, with its long shadows, was full of a sense of mystery.

Charu said, "Amal, we must take some hog-plums, what to say to Manda, otherwise!"

She had absolutely no desire to tell ignorant Manda of their readings and discussions. So hog-plums had to be taken.

Amal and Charu did not notice when the proposal about their garden, like so many others of their fancy, got lost in the limitlessness of their imagination.

Now Amal's writings became the principal subject of their discussion and conference. Amal would come and say, "*Bowthan*, I have got hold of a grand idea."

Excited Charu would say, "Let's go to our north verandah – Manda will come here in a moment with her betel-leaf preparations."

Charu would sit in an old wicker chair in the Kashmiri verandah and Amal would stretch his legs sitting on the raised platform under the railings.

Amal's themes were none too definitely conceived and it was difficult to talk about them with clarity. What he said in rather a muddled manner could hardly be understood by anyone. Amal repeatedly apologized, "*Bowthan*, I can't clearly explain it to you."

Charu responded with, "No, no, I can understand a lot of it. You write it down, don't waste time..." She used to get something together in her own mind, out of half-understanding and half-incomprehension – some of it supplied by her imagination, some by the excitement generated by Amal's passion in trying to express the unexpressed – and happy with the result, she was eager and interested.

Charu would ask the same afternoon, "How is the writing going?"

"Can one write this fast?"

Next morning, a little querulous in tone she would ask again, "Haven't you written it, yet?"

Amal would answer, "Wait, let me think a little more."

Charu, irritated, would rejoin "It is no good." In the afternoon her mounting irritation would make Charu not speak to Amal any more. Amal would pretend to get his handkerchief from the pocket but bring out a little of his writing instead.

Charu's silence would be broken immediately and she would exclaim, "But you have written! What a tease you are.

Show me."

Amal would reply, "It is not finished yet, you will hear it when I have written a bit more." Charu – "No, I want to hear it now."

That is what Amal wanted too, but first he liked to make Charu fight for it. He would sit down with the papers, get them arranged, make some corrections with his pencil when Charu, like clouds heavy with water, would lean towards the papers with delighted expectation.

Whatever Amal wrote, even a paragraph or two, he had to let Charu hear it, fresh from the pen. Then the rest, the unwritten part, was churned through the imagination of these two, and in their discussions.

Up till now they had been busy with dreams concerning flowers, now the cultivation of the flower of literature made them forget all else.

One afternoon Amal returned from the College with his pocket heavier than usual. As he entered the house, from a window in the inner apartments Charu noticed his bulging pocket.

On other days, Amal did not take much time to come inside when back from College. Today he went to the outside lounge with his full pocket, in no hurry to go to the inner apartments.

Charu edged to the end of this part of the house and clapped her hands several times, with no result. Then, indignant, she sat down on the verandah with a book of Manmatha Dutta in hand, trying hard to concentrate.

Manmatha Dutta was a new author. His style was similar to that of Amal, the reason why Amal never praised him. On the contrary, he would make fun, reading from his writings with an odd intonation. Charu would take the book from him and throw it away with contempt. Today when she heard Amal's footsteps she held Manmatha Dutta's *Kalakantha* in front of her and began reading it with great perseverence. Amal entered the verandah; Charu did not deign to notice. He asked, "How are you, *bowthan*, what is it you are reading?"

When Charu kept silent Amal came to the back of her chair and remarked, "Oh, Manmatha Dutta's *Galaganda?*" Charu protested, "Don't disturb me. Let me get on." Amal stood at her back and started reading, "I am grass, insignificant grass. Dear *Asoke*,[1] red, royally dressed Asoke, I am mere grass. I have no flower, no shadow. I cannot raise my head sky-high. The cuckoo in Spring does not resort to me to sing his "coo" for the enchantment of the world. Yet, brother *Asoke*, do not look down on me from your flowered height. I am at your feet, mere grass, but do not slight me for that." Having finished reading he started a caricature, "I am a bunch of bananas, just green ones, brother pumpkin, resident high on the roof of the house, I am a mere bunch of green bananas." Charu, intrigued, could not continue with her anger any longer. Laughing, she threw away the book with the remark, "You are very selfish. Nothing but your own writing appeals to you." Amal replied, "And you are very liberal. You want to devour even grass."

Charu – "Enough of fooling. Bring out what is in your pocket.

Amal – "Guess what."

After teasing Charu for a while Amal produced a well-known journal called *Sororuha*. Charu noticed Amal's essay on *My Exercise Book* was included in it.

She remained silent. Amal had thought that *bowthan* would be mightily pleased, but seeing no sign of it said, "It is not every piece of writing that comes out in *Sororuha*."

This was rather an exaggeration: the editor accepted material of merely average quality. But Amal made Charu understand that the editor was very fussy and chose no more than one out of a hundred pieces for publication.

Charu tried to be pleased about it but couldn't quite manage it. She tried to understand what hurt her but found no justifiable reason. Amal's writing was, so far, a joint property of them both – Amal the writer and Charu the

[1] A flamboyant tree which produces flowers in clusters.

reader. The greatest enjoyment about it was its private possession. Now everyone would read and praise it. But she didn't quite comprehend why this hurt.

But no writer is pleased with only one reader. Amal started publishing his writings and received some appreciation too.

From time to time pen letters arrived and Amal showed these to *bowthan*. That pleased Charu but also pained her. Her interest and excitement were no longer needed to make Amal write. Amal even received unsigned letters from women. Charu teased him about that but it gave her no pleasure. Suddenly the reading public of Bengal had come between them, opening up the closed door of their secret committee.

One day Bhupati, finding some time in hand, remarked, "You know Charu, I did not think our Amal could write so well." This praise pleased Charu. Amal was Bhupati's dependant. But Charu was proud that her husband realized that he was very different from his other dependants. Her demeanour declared, "So you understand after all this time why I show such affection to Amal. I found out his real worth a long time ago; he is not to be treated with indifference." She asked, "You have read his writing?" Bhupati – "Yes, well, no, I can't say I read it. There wasn't time. But Nishikanta did, and thought highly of it. He understands Bengali writing."

Charu particularly desired that there should be a respectful attitude in Bhupati's mind towards Amal.

Umapati was advising Bhupati about giving away various gifts with his paper. Bhupati could not quite understand how a loss could be converted into profit through the giving of gifts.

Once, Charu entered the room, but seeing Umapada went away. Returning in a little while she found the two arguing about accounts. Charu's impatience made Umapati find some pretext to leave. Bhupati shook his head over the accounts. Charu charged, "You haven't finished yet? I wonder how you can spend all your time with this paper."

Bhupati smiled and set aside the accounts thinking, "Really it is too bad. I have no time for her. The poor girl has nothing to occupy her." He said affectionately, "No studying today? The teacher is absconding, maybe. Your school runs on a contrary principle, the pupil is willing – the teacher is absent. I don't think Amal teaches you regularly, these days."

Charu said, "Why should Amal waste his time teaching me? Do you think he is an ordinary private tutor?"

Bhupati pulled Charu by the waist, saying, "Is this ordinary private tutoring? If I could teach a sister-in-law like this."

Charu – "You can talk. You can't manage just being a husband, something else is out of the question."

Bhupati, a bit hurt, said, "All right, I shall teach you from tomorrow. Bring your book, let me see what you are doing."

Charu – "Enough, you don't have to teach me. Can you just leave your accounts for a moment and attend to something else?"

Bhupati – "Of course, my mind will turn to whatever you want."

Charu – "Fine, then read this piece of Amal's writing and see how excellent it is. The editor says that Nabagopalbabu has given him the title "Bengali Ruskin", for this piece."

Bhupati shrank a little at this but took the paper. The writing had the title *"Ashad Moon"*. For the last two weeks Bhupati had been busy doing various sums over his criticism of the Government of India's Budget. All those sums were running around the crevices of his brain like so many centipedes – he was hardly ready at this moment to read from beginning to end a Bengali essay on the moon of the month of *Ashad*.[1] The article was not a slender one either.

The essay started thus – "Why is today the Ashad moon hiding itself amongst the clouds all night long, as if it has stolen something from the heavens, as if there is nowhere else

[1]A month in the rainy season (June/July).

to hide its stains? When in the month of *Falgun*[1] there was no cloud in the sky at all, it revealed itself shamelessly in that sky open to everyone's gaze. Today that bubbling smile, like a child's dream, like the memory of one's beloved, like the pearl necklace round the loosened hair of the heavenly queen Sachi..."

Bhupati scratched his head and said, "It's fine. But why me? I understand nothing of such poetic imagination..."

Embarrassed Charu took away the paper from his hands, saying, "What do you understand then?"

Bhupati – "I am a man of the world. I understand human beings."

Charu – "Are human beings not talked about in literature?"

Bhupati – "In a wrong vein. Besides, when human beings are available in the flesh why seek them in literature?" Caressingly he held Charu's chin and said, "Like I understand you. But do I have to read the whole of *Meghnath badh*[2] or *Kabikankanchandi*[3] for it?"

Bhupati took pride in not appreciating poetry, yet without reading Amal's writings with any attention he admired them. He thought, "There is nothing to say, yet such a flow of words poured out with perfect ease. This is something I could never do. Who could tell Amal had this power?"

Bhupati denied having any aesthetic predilections, but he was not close-fisted where literature was concerned. He would bear the expense of printing if a poor author approached him, on this special condition, that it must not be dedicated to him. He used to buy all Bengali weekly and monthly magazines, great or small, and all published books, even if not famous or readable. His reason was, "I do not read these, so if I do not buy them either there will be sin of both omission and commission." He had no objection to even bad

[1]A month in the Spring – (February/March).
[2]Bengali setting of Sanskrit epic 'Ramanaya', by Dutta.
[3]Medieval poetry concerning the goddess Chandi.

books, just because he never read them – his Bengali library was big.

Amal used to help Bhupati over English proof-reading. At that moment he entered the room with a bundle of papers to consult about some illegible handwriting on a copy.

Bhupati laughed, "Amal, write as much as you fancy on the moon of the month of Ashad or the ripe palm of the month of *Bhadra*,[1] I have no objection – I do not wish to interfere with anyone's freedom, but why interfere with mine? Your *bowthan* is bent on my reading them all. This is tyranny."

Amal laughed too, and said to Charu, "Indeed *bowthan*! If I knew you would find a way to oppress *dada* with my writings I would never have written them."

Amal was annoyed with Charu for bringing such disgrace to his precious writings by forcing them on aesthetically disinclined Bhupati. Charu sensing it, was pained. To turn the direction of the discussion she said to Bhupati, "Arrange a marriage for your cousin, then there will be no more of this torture for you from his writings."

Bhupati replied, "Young men these days are not foolish like us. They may wax poetical in their writings, but are shrewd in practical matters. You know you tried and failed to make him agree to a marriage."

After Charu left, Bhupati said to Amal, "I am busy with the paper, poor Charu is lonely. She has nothing to do, so she looks in here now and again. I cannot help it. You Amal, if you can engage her in studying, that will be a good thing. If you translate English poetry for her she will benefit from it, but also enjoy it. Charu has taste in literature."

Amal replied, "That is true. If *bowthan* studies a little more I believe she can write quite well herself."

Bhupati laughed, "I do not hope for that much, but Charu can distinguish between good and bad Bengali writing better than I do."

[1]A month after the rainy season – (June/July).

Amal - "She has a good imagination, not common amongst women."

Bhupati - "Nor men either. I am a witness to that. Well, if you can build up your *bowthan*, you will be rewarded."

Amal - "What are you offering?"

Bhupati - "I shall find you someone like your *bowthan*."

Amal - "So, I shall have to start all over again with her. Must I spend all my life in this business of building up?"

The cousins were modern, able to discuss all topics.

Amal became important, having gained popularity amongst his readers. He used to be like a schoolboy before, now he was someone to reckon with. From time to time he was asked to read his articles in meetings; editors and their messengers awaited him in his room, he was asked to dine out, requests came for him to become the member or President of various organizations and so on. So his status rose in the eyes of the servants and dependants in Bhupati's household.

Mandakini had not considered him to be one worth noticing so far. The laughing exchanges and discussions between Charu and Amal she would ignore as childishness, keeping herself away with betel leaf preparations and other household chores. She considered herself superior, being someone necessary for the running of the household.

Amal was addicted to dressed betel leaf. Manda was in charge of it and she used to be annoyed with Amal for his excessive consumption of the stuff. Amal, in league with Charu, would often in fun burgle her store. But Manda did not find their thieving particularly amusing.

In fact no dependant looks upon another with favour. Manda felt somewhat humiliated if she had to do any extra household work for Amal. Not that she could openly protest, since Amal was Charu's protégé, but she certainly inclined towards neglect where Amal was concerned. Whenever an opportunity arose she said things against him to the servants in private, in which they too joined.

But when Amal began to rise Manda was taken aback. He was no longer his old self, no longer hesitant or humble and he seemed to have acquired the right to be disrespectful to others. A man who has been acclaimed in the world and can with confidence assert himself, easily draws the attention of women. When Manda found that Amal was receiving respect from everywhere she too began looking up to him, as he held himself high in pride. And fascinated by this pride, shining bright with newly acquired fame in Amal's young face, she discovered him anew.

No longer was there any need to steal betel leaf which now came to him unasked. This meant another loss for Charu brought about by Amal's fame – the conspiracy of fun which had bound them together came to an end.

The pleasure she had in skillfully keeping Manda away from their party of two was about to be lost as well; it was now hard to keep Manda away. Manda did not any longer like the idea that Amal should take Charu as the only one to appreciate him or worthy to be friends with. She was ready to make up, with interest, all her former neglect of Amal. So whenever Amal and Charu got together she found some pretext to come between them and cause an eclipse. It was becoming difficult, even in Manda's absence, to get the opportunity with Amal to make fun of this sudden change on her part.

One can take it for granted that this uninvited entrance of Manda was not as irksome to Amal as it was to Charu. He was finding it interesting that this hitherto antagonistic woman was getting attached to him.

But when Charu, seeing Manda from a distance, said in a sarcastic but low voice, "Here she comes," Amal too joined in saying, "Yes, she is a pest." They had established a convention of being impatient of all other company but their own and Amal found it hard to discard it, suddenly. When Manda was near he would say, as if forcing himself to be polite, "So, Manda *bowthan*, anything missing from your store of betel leaf today?"

Manda – "Why steal when you can get it for the asking?"

Amal – "It is much more fun, that way."

Manda – "Why don't you carry on reading, as you were. You don't have to stop, I like to hear too."

Up to now Manda had made no attempt to acquire the distinction of being interested in readings. How times change!

Charu did not wish that Amal should read to an unappreciative Manda, but Amal wanted Manda to listen too.

Charu – "Amal has written a criticism of *Kamalakanter Daptar*.[1] You would find it..."

Manda – "Maybe I am ignorant, but surely I would get something out of it if I listen."

Amal was reminded of another day. Charu and Manda were playing cards when he entered with his writing in hand, eager for Charu to hear and impatient of the play that was going on. In the end he stood up, "Well then, you carry on, I will go to Akhilbabu and read to him."

Charu got hold of Amal's shawl, "Wait a minute, don't go away." She finished the play early by managing to be defeated.

Manda said, "Are you going to start reading? I shall have to go then."

Charu, wanting to be civil said "Why, you can listen too."

Manda – "No, I don't understand anything of this meaningless stuff, I feel sleepy." She went away, annoyed with them, as the game was brought to an end before its proper time.

The same Manda was today eager to listen to the criticism of *Kamalakanta*. Amal said, "this is fine, Manda *bowthan*. It is my good fortune that you want to listen." So he turned back the pages ready to begin again at the beginning. He was disinclined to read his material to Manda without her enjoying the special flavour he had introduced at the

[1]Book by 19th century Bengali novelist Bankimchandra.

43

beginning of the piece.

Charu said with haste, "*Thakurpo,*[1] what happened to the books you promised to get from the Janhabi Library?"

Amal – "That was not for to-day."

Charu – "It was for to-day. Well, you have forgotten."

Amal – "I haven't. You said . . ."

Charu – "All right, you don't have to get them. You two carry on reading. I will go and send Paresh to the Library." She got up and went.

Amal sensed trouble. Manda understood Charu's behaviour and her mind was immediately poisoned against her. When Amal began hesitating whether to read or not after Charu's departure she smiled a little saying, "You go, my dear, and pacify her, she is angry. You will be in trouble, reading to me."

It was difficult for Amal to stop after this remark. Somewhat irritated with Charu he replied, "Trouble, my foot," and got his papers ready to start.

Manda covered his writing with her hands and said, "No, don't read, my dear." Then she went away, as if controlling her tears.

Charu had been invited out. Manda was busy dressing her hair when Amal entered, calling, "*Bowthan!*" Manda knew that Amal was well aware that Charu was out. Smiling she said, "Poor Amal finds only me when in search of someone else. Bad luck!" Amal said in reply, "The hay on the right is just as good for the ass as the hay on the left." He sat down.

Amal – "Manda *bowthan*, tell me about your home and village. I would like to hear."

Amal had started listening carefully to whatever anyone had to say, to collect material for his writing. So he no longer disregarded Manda as before – her psychology and history were now of interest to him. He began asking questions – her birth place, the sort of village it was, how her childhood was

[1]Address for brother or cousin-in-law.

spent, when she was married and such details. Nobody had shown such curiosity about Manda's very humdrum life before. Highly pleased, she went on talking, interspersing her talk with remarks like, "Maybe I am talking nonsense..." Amal encouraged her, "No, no I am enjoying it. Go on."

Manda's father had a one-eyed employee who used to quarrel with his second wife and sometimes take to fasting in protest. But hungry in the end, he had been known to come to the house of Manda's parents to eat in secret. Once by chance he was caught by his wife. Manda was relating this story and Amal, attentive and laughing, was hugely enjoying it all, when Charu entered the room.

The thread of the story was lost. Charu sensed quite clearly that her arrival had broken up a meeting in which the two were deeply engrossed. Amal asked, "*Bowthan*, you are back early?"

Charu replied, "So I see, I have come back much too early." She was about to leave when Amal said, "Thank goodness you are back. I was worried, thinking you would be late; I have got Manmatha Dutta's new book, *The Evening Bird*, to read to you."

Charu – "Leave it. I am busy."

Charu had known that Amal would buy the book that day and come to read it to her. Charu would praise the book inordinately and Amal would ridicule it by reading it with distorted intonation. These were the thoughts which made her override all requests to stay longer and come home early on the pretext of not feeling well. Now she thought, "I was better off there. It was wrong of me to have come away."

And how shameless was Manda, sitting alone with Amal in a room and laughing with her teeth showing. What would people say? But it was difficult for Charu to chastise Manda for it. For Manda would throw her own example in her face. But surely the two cases were different! She provided inspiration for Amal to write, and discussed literature with him. But Manda had no such purpose. All she was doing was

throwing a net to attract a simple young man. It was her duty
to save Amal from this terrible danger. The problem was
how to make him understand the plan of this temptress; any
word to this effect might fan his temptation rather than put
an end to it.

"My poor brother Umapada", thought Charu, "he is
working day and night for the sake of my husband's paper
and Manda, quietly sitting in a corner is plotting the
seduction of Amal. My brother, full of trust of Manda, feels
no anxiety. But how can I, seeing it all with my own eyes,
remain unperturbed? All this is highly improper."

Amal had been perfectly safe before. All these impro-
prieties had started since he had made a name for himself
with his writings. But wasn't Charu at the root of his
writings? It was an evil moment when she encouraged him to
write. It would no longer be possible for Charu to have the
same kind of right over him. And Amal having tasted the
respect of other people would not be worried if one person
dropped out of his life.

Charu surmised that Amal was in great danger having
gone out of her protection into the wide world. He no longer
thought of Charu as his equal and had left her behind. Now
he was a writer, Charu only a reader. All this must be put
right, somehow. She felt sorry for simple-minded Amal, in
the clutches of the temptress Manda, and for her poor
brother.

The sky was overcast that day with the fresh cloud of *Ashad.*
As darkness had gathered inside the room, Charu sat by the
window, leaning forwards and writing.

She did not know when Amal entered and stood behind
her. Charu kept on writing in the soft light of the rainy-
season evening and Amal was reading as she wrote. A piece
or two of Amal's writings were by her side, open. For Charu
these were the ideals to be followed.

Amal – "Why do you then say you cannot write?"

This gave Charu a start, to hear Amal's voice, and she quickly covered up her exercise book saying, "This is very naughty of you."

Amal – "Why? What have I done?"

Charu – "You were looking at my writings, like a thief."

Amal – "Only because they are not available otherwise."

Charu was about to tear up the exercise book when Amal quickly snatched it away from her. She exclaimed, "I shall never talk to you again if you read these."

Amal – "If you forbid me to read, I shall never talk to you again."

Charu had to accept defeat. As a matter of fact, she was anxious to show her writings to Amal but found herself overcome with shyness. When Amal, after a lot of cajoling, got the right to read, Charu's hands and feet became like ice in apprehension. She said, "Let me get something" and abruptly left for the next room on the pretext of dressing betel leaves.

Amal finished reading, went to Charu and said, "This is excellent."

Charu forgot to put catechu in her dressing and said, "You don't have to pull my leg. Give it back to me."

Amal replied, "No, not now, let me first copy it and have it sent to a journal."

Charu – "Publish it! You can't do that?"

Charu protested noisily but Amal was adamant. When he assured her, repeatedly, that her writing was worthy of publication, Charu feigned disappointment saying, "You are beyond correction, whatever you get hold of you must see to the end."

Amal – "I have to show it to *dada*."

Charu, letting go of whatever she was doing, instantly stood up and tried to force the book away from Amal saying, "You must not read it to him. If you tell him of my writings I shall stop them altogether."

Amal – "*Bowthan*, you are under a misconception. Whatever *dada* says, he will be highly pleased to see your

47

writing."

Charu – "May be, but I don't want him pleased."

What Charu had promised herself was that she would write and surprise Amal, determined to prove the difference between herself and Manda. She had written a lot over these few days but torn most of it up. Whatever she wrote looked like a piece of Amal's writing and comparison revealed some of it to be an exact copy. Those bits were good, the rest immature. Amal would laugh to see this, this was the thought that made her tear up the pieces in bits and throw them away in the pond; not even a fragment must come into Amal's hand.

To start with, she wrote about "Clouds of the month of *Sravan*[1]" and thought of it as an original piece, full of emotional appeal. But suddenly she became conscious that this was, as it were, just the other side of Amal's 'The Moon of the Month of Ashad'. Amal had written, "Dear moon, why do you hide yourself like a thief, amidst clouds."
Charu – "Dear *Kadambini*,[2] where have you come from suddenly to steal the moon under your blue garment . . ." and so on.

Unable to rid herself of Amal's influence, Charu changed the subject of her writing. She gave up the subject of the moon, clouds, *sefali*[3] flower, the *bowkathakao*[4] bird and the like and finally wrote about "The Locality of the *Kali* temple". In their village was a temple of the goddess *Kali*,[5] by a shaded pond. Her childhood imagination, fear, anxiety centering around the temple, her various memories about it, the old tales widespread in the village about the greatness of that "alive" goddess – these provided the subject-matter of her story. Its introduction was "poetic" after the manner of Amal, but soon her writing took on the simple style of village language, idiom and innuendo.

[1]A month after the rainy season (June/July).
[2]An endearing name for a cloud.
[3]Scented white flower with orange stalk.
[4]Bird whose calls sound like 'speak beloved' in Bengali.
[5]The mother goddess in her terrible aspect.

This was the writing Amal read and took away. He found the beginning aesthetically pleasing the poetic quality of which, however, could not be maintained to the end. Never mind, for a first attempt the writing was commendable.

Charu said, *"Thakurpo,* Let us start a journal. What do you think?"

Amal – "We need a lot of money for that."

Charu – "Not for our paper. It won't be printed, just handwritten; it will have no other writing than yours and mine, and nobody else will read it either. There will be only two copies, one for you and one for me."

There was a time when a proposal like this would have enthused Amal. Now he did not care for secrecy and there was no pleasure in writing without aiming it at a lot of people. But he showed interest, just to maintain an old convention, saying, "That will be fun."

Charu – "You must promise not to write for anything other than our journal."

Amal – "Then the editors will lynch me."

Charu – "Don't you think I too could have weapons?"

So it was agreed to set up a committee of two editors, two writers, two readers. Amal proposed a name for the journal *'Charupath'.* Charu turned it down. "No, we shall call it *Amala".*

One day Bhupati appeared with , "Charu, there was no such agreement that you would become a writer!"

Charu, surprized and flushing said, "A writer? I? Who says? Never."

Bhupati – "Caught red-handed, proof positive!" He brought out a copy of *Saroruha.* Charu found in it writings which were being stored in their monthly journal as their own hidden treasure, with the names of the authors.

She felt as if someone had opened the door of a cage and let the pet birds fly out. She forgot about being shy in front of Bhupati about the writings; instead she felt great consternation because of Amal's treachery.

"See this one." Bhupati opened before Charu the journal *Visvabandhu*. It contained an article on the style of modern Bengali writing.

Charu pushed it away, "What use is it to me?" She was unable to attend to anything else, her sensitive mind being hurt by Amal. Bhupati persisted, "Why not give it a read?"

Charu was forced to look at it. The author had written a sharp essay abusing the sentimental prose of some writers; particularly jeering was his criticism of Manmatha Dutta and Amal in comparison with whom the new writer Charulata Devi was praised for her unadorned simplicity, easy grace and descriptive skill. It said further that Amal and company could be saved only if they succeeded in imitating this style, otherwise they would completely fail – no doubt about it. Bhupati remarked, "This is what is called a disciple beating the teacher."

Charu's feelings were ambiguous, faced with this praise. Inclined to be pleased for a moment she was depressed the next. Her mind, refusing pleasure, wanted to throw away the tempting nectar that the praise represented.

It was clear to her that Amal wanted to surprise her by publishing her writings. And then after a favourable review in some paper or other he would have shown the two together to Charu to appease and encourage her. Why was it that Amal did not come to show it to her when her writing was praised? Amal was hurt by the criticism and he had kept quiet because he did not want Charu to know about it. Charu was creating a tiny literary circle entirely in private for her own pleasure when a hailstorm of praise was about to demolish it. She did not like it at all. After Bhupati's departure Charu kept sitting quietly in her bedroom with *Saroruha* and *Visvabandhu* open before her. When Amal, exercise book in hand, entered from behind to surprise Charu, he found her absorbed in her own thoughts with the *Visvabandhu* criticism open in front of her. Quietly he went out, "So Charu is beside herself because the paper has abused me while praising her." At once he felt bitter and angry with Charu as he was sure she was considering herself greater than her teacher, all on the basis of a criticism made by a fool. Charu ought to have torn that paper into bits and burned them.

Angry with Charu, Amal came to Manda's door and called in a loud voice, "Manda *bowthan*."

Manda – "Do come in, please. What good fortune that you have come of your own accord."

Amal – "Would you like to hear some new writing of mine?"

Manda – "You have been talking about it a long time with no action to follow. It is best that way, you will be in trouble if somebody takes exception to your reading to me."

Amal answered rather sharply, "Who is going to take exception and why? We shall see about that. For now, you listen."

Manda got ready with great eagerness. Amal, with some ceremony, started reading in a sing-song voice.

Amal's writing was entirely foreign to Manda; she could find no sense in it at all. That is why she had to show extra eagerness to hear him read, filling her face with a pleasurable smile. Amal's voice became louder and louder in enthusiasm.

He was reading – "As Abhimanyu, while in the womb learnt how to enter a battle formation but not how to come out of it, a river's current, born in the stony womb of the mountain had learnt how to go forward, not how to retrace its journey back. Alas, a river's current, youth, time, this world, all of you can only go forward and not return on the path you have left behind, strewn with golden pebbles of memory. It is only a human mind that looks backwards, the rest of the world cares nothing about it . . ."

Just then a shadow fell near Manda's door; she saw it, but pretended not to, and keeping her gaze fixed on Amal continued listening with seemingly rapt attention.

The shadow slunk away.

51

Charu had been waiting for Amal, to abuse the journal *Visvabandhu* in his presence and chide him for breaking his promise in publishing her writing.

The time for him to appear was over, still he hadn't come. Charu had kept a piece of her writing ready for reading to Amal. Then she heard his voice, maybe in Manda's room. She got up as if struck by an arrow and with silent footsteps came to stand by Manda's door. Charu had not yet heard this piece of writing. Amal was reading to Manda – 'Man's mind keeps on looking back, the rest of the world cares nothing about it.'

Charu could not be as silent in going back as she had been in coming. Hurt after hurt in one day made her lose patience. She felt like shouting at Amal, "Manda does not understand a word of it, and it is utterly foolish of you to take pleasure in reading to her." She said nothing but her angry footsteps declared her mind. She entered her bedroom and noisily closed the door.

Amal stopped reading for a moment. Manda smiled indicating Charu with her gestures. Amal thought, "This is an outrage. Does *bowthan* believe I am her slave, that I cannot read to anyone but her? What sort of tyranny is this?" He raised his voice even higher.

His reading finished, he went away by Charu's door. While passing he looked and found the door closed.

Charu knew from the footsteps that Amal passed by without stopping. Anger mixed with grief made her unable to cry; instead she tore up every page of her new exercise book in a heap. It had been an inauspicious moment when all this writing started.

It was evening and the scent of jasmine came wafting from the tub on the verandah. Through torn clouds one could see stars in the soft sky. Charu had not dressed her hair, nor changed her dress. She was sitting by the window in the dark, with her hair blowing in the gentle breeze.

She did not understand why tears kept flowing in such profusion.

Bhupati entered the room, his face very pale and his heart burdened. Normally, Bhupati would not be expected there at such a time. He was usually late, through having to write for the paper and correct proofs. Today he had come to Charu in the evening, searching for consolation somewhere.

There was no lamp in the room. Through the feeble light of the open window Bhupati saw Charu there, an indistinct figure. He came and stood behind her. Charu heard footsteps but did not turn. She sat there hard and motionless like a statue.

Somewhat surprized Bhupati called, "Charu". Startled Charu got up in haste. She had not considered that it could be Bhupati. Bhupati, gently stroking Charu's hair with his fingers asked in an affectionate voice, "Why are you alone in the dark Charu, where is Manda?"

The whole day through things had turned out otherwise than Charu had hoped for. She was certain that Amal would come and apologize, and she was waiting, ready for it. When instead she heard Bhupati's voice she could contain herself no longer, she broke out in tears. Bhupati, concerned and worried asked, "What's the matter Charu, do tell me."

But telling was difficult. Nothing much had happened. How could she complain to Bhupati that Amal had read his new material to Manda instead of to her. It would only make Bhupati laugh. It was impossible for her to work out why she was so aggrieved over this triviality. Her unease was the greater for not fully understanding herself why she was suffering so much over nothing. Bhupati persisted, "Tell me Charu, what's wrong. Have I been unkind to you? You know how busy I am with the paper. If I have hurt you with that it was quite unintentional."

Charu was agitated by these questions to which she had no answer. She wished Bhupati would leave her alone.

Unanswered a second time Bhupati said affectionately, "I

53

feel guilty that I cannot come to you often, but that phase is over. From now on, I shan't be busy with the paper that much. You will get me as much as you want."

Disturbed Charu replied "It isn't that."

Bhupati – "What then?" He sat down on the bed. Charu, unable to conceal her irritation, said "Leave it for now, I shall tell you at night."

Bhupati went silent for a moment, then said, "All right, as you wish." Quietly he went away. He had had something to say himself. It remained unsaid. Charu was aware that Bhupati went away in distress. She thought to call him back. But, then, what to say? She was full of repentance, but saw no way out.

At night Charu took special care over Bhupati's dinner and sat down fan in hand ready to attend him. Then she heard Manda calling out loud, "Braja, Braja." When the servant answered she asked, "Has Amalbabu taken his dinner?" When Braja said, "Yes" she began chastizing him, asking why then did he not take to Amal his after-dinner dressed betel leaf. Bhupati came just then and sat down for dinner. Charu began fanning him.

Charu had promised herself that she would talk a lot, gently and cheerfully, with Bhupati today. She was even ready with topics of conversation. But Manda's voice put to naught all her elaborate arrangements and she did not manage to say a word to Bhupati as he ate. Bhupati too was depressed and absent-minded. When he didn't eat much, Charu just asked, "Why aren't you eating?" Bhupati protested, "Why, I have eaten my fill."

When together in the bedroom Bhupati asked, "You were going to tell me something tonight?" Charu said, "You see, for some time Manda's behaviour is getting objectionable. I don't think it is right to keep her here any more."

Bhupati – "Why? what has happened?"

Charu – "The way she behaves with Amal, it is quite shameful."

Bhupati laughed, "Are you crazy? Amal is only young,

born the other day..."

Charu – "You are not interested in what happens at home. All the information you are after concerns the world outside. However, I am worried about my poor brother. Manda couldn't care less whether Umapada eats or not but when it comes to Amal the slightest lapse makes her shout at the servants and create a scene."

Bhupati – "I must say you women are of a suspicious nature."

Angered Charu replied, "All right, have it as you wish, but I tell you I shan't allow shameless behaviour in this house."

Bhupati was amused with all this uncalled-for suspicion, but pleased too – there was something full of grace and sublimity in a chaste wife's concern over the purity of her home, in her alertness that even an imaginary stain might not mark the felicity of conjugal relationship.

Bhupati kissed Charu's forehead with great respect and affection and said, "It won't be necessary to worry about this any more. Umapada is going to Maimansingh to work, Manda is going with him." Then to allay his own depressing thoughts and to put an end to this unpleasant discussion, Bhupati got hold of an exercise book from the table and said, "Why don't you read something to me, from your writing?"

Charu took away the book from his hands, saying, "You won't like it, you will just laugh." The remark pained Bhupati but concealing his feeling he smiled, "I promise you, I shall not laugh. I shall listen, remaining so still that you might believe I have gone to sleep."

But Charu did not encourage Bhupati. Soon the exercise book disappeared under her bedcover.

Bhupati had not been able to tell Charu everything. Umapada was in charge of Bhupati's paper. Collecting donations, paying the printers and other accounts, seeing to the wages – he was responsible for all this.

Suddenly one day Bhupati was surprized to get a solicitor's

letter from the paper merchant. It said that Bhupati owed them two thousand and seven hundred rupees. Bhupati called Umapada and asked what it was all about, as he had already paid the sum to Umapada and his outstanding debts ought not to be over four or five hundred rupees. Umapada said that it was a mistake, but the real state of affairs could not be kept concealed for long. Umapada had taken out a lot of loans from the market in Bhupati's name. He was having a brick house built in his village the materials for which had been debited to Bhupati's account and most of it had been paid back with money from the paper. When he was finally caught he said in a rough voice, "I am not going to disappear. I shall pay you back in time, through work. Don't call me Umapada any more if I default even by a penny."

Bhupati found no consolation in the thought of a change in Umapada's name. He was less upset by the financial loss than by this sudden breach of faith, which made him feel empty inside.

That day he had gone into his room early, eager to feel for a while that there was a firm place for faith in this world. Charu was then seated in darkness, near the window, full of her own grief. Umapada was ready to leave for Maimensingh the next day, eager to slink away before the creditors in the market found out. Bhupati, in disgust, did not speak to him, which Umapada considered his good fortune.

Amal came and asked, "What's all this Manda *bowthan*, why all this packing?"

Manda – "My dear, we have to go, we can't stay here for ever."

Amal – "Why, what was inconvenient here?"

Manda – "Nothing for me. I was very happy with you all here. But somebody found it inconvenient." She indicated towards Charu's door.

Amal became silent and grave. Manda kept on, "How shameful. Who knows what the master could have thought."

Amal did not discuss the matter further. He understood that Charu had said unpalatable things about them to

Bhupati. He went out and walked the streets, not feeling like returning to the house. If *dada* believed *bowtham* and considered him guilty, he must go, the same as Manda. Driving Manda away was a way of commanding banishment for him as well. That command had not been delivered verbally, that was the only difference. His duty was clear, he must not stay there another moment. But he could not allow *dada* to harbour a wrong impression about him. *Dada* had maintained him in his house for so long with complete trust. He could not go away without making him understand that he, Amal, had done nothing to break that trust.

Bhupati was sitting with his head in his hands, weighed down with thoughts of the faithlessness of his relative, the pressure of creditors, chaotic accounts and his empty purse. There was nobody to share his distress and dismay, and he was getting ready to fight alone with his pain and his debts.

Amal stormed into the room. Startled, Bhupati looked up emerging out of his bottomless thoughts and asked, "Why Amal, what is the matter?" He suddenly felt that Amal was bringing news of some dire misfortune.

Amal asked, *"Dada,* do you have cause to suspect me in any way?"

Surprized Bhupati asked, "Suspect you?", thinking to himself that the world was such that he could probably suspect even Amal, one day.

Amal – "Has *bowthan* complained about my character to you?"

Relieved, Bhupati thought, "Oh, that matter, what a relief, this is only hurt pride." He had anticipated some great disaster. But one had to listen to this insignificant nonsense even in the midst of a grave crisis. The world insisted on shaking a make-shift bridge while demanding that he must pass over, with his goods.

Another time Bhupati would have had a joke or two with Amal. But he lacked the necessary cheerfulness for it today. He only remarked, "Are you mad?"

Amal asked, *"Bowthan* has said nothing?"

Bhupati – "If she had said anything out of affection for you, there is nothing to take umbrage in that."
Amal – "I ought to go away and look for a job."

Bhupati scolded him, "Amal, this is very childish. Get on with your studies now – there will be time for a job later."

Amal came away, his face full of gloom, and Bhupati sat down to settle the accounts of the last three years, by comparing the list of his contributors with income and expenditure.

Amal decided that the matter must be thrashed out with *bowthan*, it could not be left in mid-air. He reheared all the embittered words he was going to say to Charu.

After Manda's departure Charu resolved to call Amal and pacify him. But he could only be called on the pretext of some writing to be heard. She wrote an article on the light of the night of the new moon, after the fashion of Amal as she could tell that Amal did not appreciate her independent style.

Charu, in her new writing was calling the full moon to account because it reveals all its light. She wrote – "Within the deep darkness of this night the light of all the sixteen parts of the moon are contained, layer over layer, not a ray has been lost. So the darkness of the night of the new moon is more complete than the brightness of the full moon . . .' and so on. Amal revealed all his writings to all and sundry, but not Charu – did the analogy of the full and new moon contain this suggestion?

In the meanwhile the third member of this family, Bhupati, went to his dear friend, Motilal, with the object of freeing himself from the impending pressure of debts. Bhupati had given a loan of a few thousand rupees to Motilal at the time of his urgent need – so he went there under duress to ask for it back. Motilal, his bath taken, was fanning his uncovered body and was writing the thousand names of the

Goddess *Durga*[1] on a piece of paper, resting on a wooden box. Seeing Bhupati he said with great cordiality, "Do come in, you are a rare bird these days."

When asked for the money back Motilal thought hard and said, "What money, have I taken anything from you lately?"

When Bhupati reminded him of the date and year of the loan he exclaimed, "Oh, yes, that is no longer legally recoverable. It has lapsed."

Bhupati saw everything change before his eyes. He was fearful to see this unmasked face of the world. As a person rushes to reach the most elevated place when faced by a sudden flood, Bhupati entered the inner apartments in haste, flying from the outer world of doubtful value. He thought, "Whatever happens, Charu will never cheat me."

Charu was seated on the bedstead with a pillow on her lap on which was placed an exercise book. She was leaning over and writing something on it. Only when Bhupati came and stood by her did she become aware of him, and then hastily put the exercise book under her feet.

When one is already wounded, it does not take much for the pain to become acute. Bhupati was hurt to see Charu hiding her book with such unnecessary haste. Slowly he sat down by her. Charu, unexpectedly obstructed in the flow of her writing and embarrassed by the anxiety she had shown in hiding the book could find nothing to say. Bhupati that day had nothing himself to say or offer. Like a pauper, he was a supplicant to Charu. What he needed to assuage his wound was some anxiety shown out of love by Charu, some tender concern in asking him something. But Charu just could not find the key to the store of her love for a need that was suddenly born. The heavy silence between them made the silence of the room ever deeper.

After sitting quietly for a while Bhupati got up with a sigh and went out.

Amal was quickly approaching Charu's room with a lot of

[1]The most important mother goddess in Bengal.

hard words in his head. But he stopped on the way seeing
Bhupati's worried, shrunken and discoloured face. He asked,
"*Dada*, are you feeling ill?"

Amal's gentle question made suppressed tears swell up in
Bhupati's heart, and for a while he could say nothing. Then
controlling himself with an effort he said in a shaky voice, "I
am all right Amal. Is any writing of yours coming out in the
magazine this time?" All the bitter words Amal had amassed
in his head to say to Charu disappeared. He hurried to her
and asked, "*Bowthan* what is the matter with *dada*?"

Charu – "I didn't think there was anything the matter.
Some paper may have criticised his."

Amal shook his head.

Charu was greatly relieved that Amal had come of his own
accord and his tone of conversation was natural. She started
with the matter of writing, "I was writing something today
on the light on the night of the new moon – he nearly saw i "

Charu thought Amal would pester her to show him the
writing. With that in mind she kept handling the exercise
book. But Amal looked at Charu once with burning eyes,
and what he gathered or thought from that look only God
knew. He got up abruptly. As if a traveller going through a
mountain path suddenly found – with the lifting of the
cloud-mist – that he was about to step into a thousand feet
deep canyon, Amal went out of the room, without a word.
Charu could not interpret Amal's unusual behaviour.

Bhupati next paid another untimely visit to the bedroom,
called to Charu and said "Charu, there is a good marriage
proposal afoot for Amal." Charu was absent-minded and
asked, "What is afoot?"

Bhupati – "A marriage proposal."

Charu – "Why? Am I not likeable?"

Bhupati laughed aloud, "I haven't asked Amal if you are
to his liking. Even if you are, I have a little claim myself, I
can't let that go, that easily."

Charu, flushing, "What a thing to say! you said there was a marriage proposal for you." She was red in the face.

Bhupati - "Would I have run to you in that case? I could hardly hope for a reward."

Charu - "A marriage proposal for Amal? That's good, there is no need for delay."

Bhupati - "Raghunathbabu, a lawyer from Burdwan, wants to give his daughter in marriage to Amal and then send him to England."

Surprised Charu asked, "England?"

Bhupati - "Yes, England."

Charu - "Amal's going to England? That's great. A very good idea. You may put the proposal to him."

Bhupati - "Wouldn't it be better if you talk to him before I do?"

Charu - "I have, already, hundreds of times. He does not listen to me, I can't talk to him about it."

Bhupati - "Do you think he is going to refuse?"

Charu - "Well, we have tried before. He did not give his consent."

Bhupati - "But he must not let go of this present proposal. I am heavily in debt. I cannot continue maintaining him."

Bhupati had Amal called and told him, "There is a marriage proposal for you with the daughter of Raghunath -babu, a lawyer from Burdwan. His plan is to send you to England after the marriage. What do you have to say?"

Amal - "If you find the idea agreeable I have no objection."

The were both rather surprised to hear this from Amal, not expecting him to accept as soon as the subject was mooted.

Charu ridiculed him, saying acidly, "So, you agree if *dada* agrees! What an obedient younger cousin! Where was this devotion to *dada*, all this time, *thakurpo*?" Amal just smiled a little, but did not answer. His silence made Charu wish to provoke him and her tone was severe, "Why don't you admit it's what you wish. What was the need, all this time, to pretend that you do not wish to marry - just feigning

61

disinclination while hungry all the time." Bhupati said in jest, "Amal kept his hunger in control for fear of you, lest you became jealous, to think of a sister-in-law."

Charu, red in the face, vigorously protested, "Jealous, never. You mustn't say a thing like that."

Bhupati – "Why, can't I even joke with my own wife?"

Charu – "Not this kind of joke."

Bhupati – "All right. I was in the wrong, forgive me. Anyway, so Amal, the proposal is accepted?"

Amal replied with, "Yes."

Charu – "Can't you even wait till you see the girl and find out whether she is desirable or not?"

Bhupati – "If you want to see her, I can arrange it. I am told she is beautiful."

Amal – "No. I see no need to see her first."

Charu – "Don't listen to him. How can this be? You can't fix a marriage without seeing the girl. If he does not want to see her, we do."

Amal – "No *dada*, don't waste time over this unnecessary detail."

Charu – "I see, the least delay is unbearable. Start right now then, with the bridegroom's headdress on you. Who knows, your treasure may be stolen by someone else."

Charu's jeering tone did not move Amal in the least.

Charu – "So, you are anxious to run away to England? Why? Were we beating you up here or something? Young men these days are not happy until they don a suit and a hat and become a sahib. *Thakurpo*, would you be able to recognize us, black people, when you return?"

Amal replied, "Going to England will be wasted if I do."

Bhupati laughed, "Well, crossing seven seas is for the purpose of forgetting black beauty. Don't worry Charu, we shall be here. There will be no dearth of people who are devotees of the colour black."

Pleased, Bhupati sent a letter to Burdwan immediately, fixing the marriage date.

In the meanwhile the paper had to be closed down, as Bhupati was no longer able to carry on the expense. In a matter of a moment he had to give up what had occupied him, eliciting his wholehearted and serious devotion, over a long time, something that was itself indifferent, called "the public". All his efforts during the last twelve years, his uninterrupted, habitual track suddenly ended as if in the midst of nowhere. Bhupati was not in the least prepared for such a happening. Where could he turn with all his past efforts thus suddenly obstructed, efforts which looked at him like starving orphans? – Bhupati brought them to the woman at home, someone who would be compassionate; ready to soothe and heal.

The woman was busy with her own thoughts. She was thinking, "This is astonishing; it is a good thing that Amal is getting married, but how could it be that he felt not the least compunction at the idea of going away to England, leaving us all? We have looked after him with affection all this time and the moment he gets an opportunity to leave, he is ready, bag and baggage, as if he had been waiting for just this. He is so sweet-tongued, seemingly so full of love – well, it is hard to know any one in their true colours. How could I tell that a man who can write as he does has no heart?"

Charu tried to look with disdain on Amal's lack of heart, as compared with its abundance in her own person. She did not succeed in this attempt. And a passionate pain like a red-hot skewer kept constantly probing her hurt pride, in secret. "Amal is going to go away, yet he never comes to see me. He does not even have time to settle the differences that have cropped up between us." "Amal is going to come," Charu kept thinking all the time – their relationship which had lasted for such a long time could not end thus. But Amal stayed away. The day of his departure by now had come very near and Charu had to have him called. Amal let her know that he was coming in a while. Charu went and sat down in a chair on the verandah. The day was close and had been thick with cloud since morning. Charu put up her loose hair in a bun and, feeling tired, began to use a hand fan.

She sat there a long time and her hand began to tire. Impatient with anger and grief she began seething inside. Charu said to herself, "What does it matter if Amal doesn't come", and yet the least sound of footsteps drew her mind to the door.

The church bell at a distance struck eleven. Bhupati would soon be here for lunch, after his bath. There was still time for Amal to arrive – half an hour. By whatever means this silent quarrel of the past few days must be brought to an end today. The brother-in-law/sister-in-law relationship between them, two people of the same age, was something full of sweetness – like a shady retreat, full of the light and shade of affection, and its claims – memories of many leisurely, happy discussions. Could Amal treat these of no account and just go away, for such a long time? Would there be no repentance at all, not a tear, to water for the last time, the well-established tree that was their relationship?

The half hour was nearly gone when Charu let loose her hair and began twining it round her fingers. It became very hard to keep back her tears. Then the servant appeared and said "*Mathakurun*[1] – green coconut for the master." Charu took out the store key and threw it at the servant's feet with a clatter. Surprised he picked it up and was gone. Something was pushing itself upwards from her chest to her throat.

Bhupati came in with a smile for his lunch at the accustomed time. Charu, fan in hand, went to attend him and found Amal there too. She could not look at him.

Amal asked, "*Bowthan*, did you ask for me?"

Charu replied, "It doesn't matter any more, it's not important."

Amal – "In that case, I must go, there is a lot to be packed." Charu looked at him once, with fiery eyes, and said, "All right, go."

---

[1]Address for the lady of the house by the servants.

Bhupati usually rested with Charu for a while, after lunch. Today he was particularly busy with payments and accounts and so a little mortified that he couldn't stay long. He said, "I can't be here for long today, there are a lot of things to be settled."

Charu replied curtly, "You may go."

Bhupati thought that her response meant that Charu was hurt – so he said, "I don't have to go right now, I can rest a while." He sat down. But he found Charu depressed. Repentant, Bhupati stayed for a long time, but couldn't get a conversation going. After some futile effort he remarked, "Amal is going away, you will feel lonely."

Charu got up without a word, and on the pretext of getting something, went out of the room. Bhupati departed after waiting for a while.

Charu had noticed, when she looked at Amal, that he had become thinner in these few days – his face did not show its former glow of youth. Charu was happy at this, but pained too. She did not doubt that what was troubling Amal was their coming separation. But why was he behaving like this – why did he keep himself at a distance? What was making him turn his departure into bitter conflict?

While thinking this way, lying in her bed, Charu abruptly sat up with a start, when she remembered Manda. Suppose Amal was in love with Manda? No, no, how could Amal be like that, so mean, so sinful, to fall for a married woman. Impossible. She tried hard to push this suspicion away but it remained, clinging to her.

So the time to go away arrived, but the cloud did not disperse. Amal came and said in a shaky voice, *"Bowthan*, it is time for me to go. You must look after *dada* from now on. He is going through a crisis and there is no one but you to console him."

Amal, having found Bhupati in a depressed mood, had inquired and come to know of his distress – how he had been fighting alone with his problems and troubles, without any help or sympathy from any quarters and yet he had not in

65

any way disturbed his dependent relatives while going through ruin himself. Thinking of this Amal could not find any word to express his feelings. He thought of Charu and of himself, flushed, and uttered with force "To hell with the moon of the month of Ashad and the light of the new moon. I am no man unless I help *dada* when I return as a barrister."

Charu had kept awake all through the previous night thinking of what she would say to Amal at the time of farewell. She had sharpened those words in her own mind, until they became bright and piercing – delivered with a hurt pride that was yet cased in a smile and with cheerful indifference. But no words came to her when the time for it actually arrived. She could only say, "Will you write, Amal?"

Amal did his *pranam*,[1] touching the ground with his head. Charu ran into the bedroom and closed the door.

Bhupati went to Burdwan, and having sent Amal off to England after his marriage, came back home. Knocks from many quarters had made trustful Bhupati somewhat indifferent to the world. He could no longer take pleasure in meetings and associations. He considered, "I have deceived myself all this time with these – the days for happiness have gone past, wasted, as I have thrown the best of it onto the rubbish dump."

Bhupati thought, "It is a good thing that the paper is closed. I am now free." As birds come back to their nest in the evening when it gets dark, Bhupati came back to Charu, leaving behind his pasture of long-standing. He decided not to go anywhere any more, he would rest here, at home. The playboat that was his paper had sunk; nothing for it but to go back home.

Bhupati returned home from Burdwan in the evening. He had a quick wash and then took his food early. He hurried,

[1] An act of respect shown to elders by bowing down and touching their feet.

thinking that Charu was waiting eagerly to hear about Amal's marriage and his departure to England. So he went to his bedroom and lying down began smoking his hubble-bubble. Charu did not appear. Perhaps she was still busy with some housework. His smoking finished, Bhupati felt sleepy. From time to time he woke up with a start from his drowsiness wondering what was keeping Charu. At last, unable to wait any longer he had her called and asked, "Charu, why are you so late tonight?" Without anwering his question Charu just replied, "Yes, it is rather late."

Bhupati waited for her anxious questionings, but they did not come. This aggrieved Bhupati somewhat. Did that mean that Charu did not care about Amal? As long as Amal was here Charu found him entertaining and the moment he was gone, such indifference! This unbecoming behaviour made Bhupati wonder, did Chru then lack depth of feeling? Could she indulge only in playful pleasures, but did not know how to love? Such indifference on the part of a woman was undesirable.

Bhupati had taken pleasure in the friendship between Amal and Charu. Their relationship of closeness, punctuated by not being on speaking terms, their play and conferences were things of sweet curiosity for Bhupati. He was pleased at Charu's gentle-heartedness, expressed through her constant care and affection for Amal. Astonished, he thought today, were all these just skin deep with no roots in Charu's heart? If Charu had no heart where would Bhupati find his refuge?

To test her, he began slowly to introduce the topic and asked, "Charu, you have been well, I presume?" Charu answered in brief, "I am quite all right." Bhupati said, "Amal is now married", and then kept quiet. Charu tried hard to find something relevant to say but couldn't. She sat there, benumbed.

Bhupati was by nature unobservant, but because he was himself touched by Amal's departure, Charu's indifference troubled him. What he desired was to lighten his own heart's burden through discussing Amal with Charu whom he took to be equally pained.

Bhupati – "The girl is good-looking. Charu, are you asleep?"

Charu – "No."

Bhupati – "Poor Amal went off alone. When I saw him to the train he was crying like a child and even at my age that brought tears to my eyes. There were two Englishmen in the carriage, they were amused to see men cry." Charu first turned around in the bed in the darkness – the lamp was out – then abruptly leaving the room went outside.

Taken by surprise Bhupati called after her, "Charu, are you feeling unwell?" and then got up at her lack of response. The sound of muffled crying from the verandah made him hurry there, to find Charu lying face down trying to control herself.

Such an irrepressible outburst of grief astonished Bhupati. He figured that he had misunderstood Charu. Her personality was so repressive that she was unwilling to express her feelings even to him. People whose nature was like this, loved deeply and they suffered deeply too. Her love was not outwardly apparent, as in the case of ordinary women, Bhupati realized that. He had never seen any passionate manifestation of love in Charu. This was because Charu's love was an inner and secret affair of her own heart. Bhupati himself was inept where self-expression was concerned and he felt a certain comfort, finding this in-dwelling depth of heart in Charu. He sat by her and without a word began stroking her gently, not knowing how else to offer consolation. He failed to understand that when one is trying to kill grief in the dark by choking it, a witness is not welcome.

When Bhupati retired from the newspaper business he had drawn a picture of his future in his own mind. He promised not to go for ambitious and difficult projects. He would live a domestic life, fulfilling its everyday responsibilities with Charu, and with studying and loving. He thought that domestic pleasures which were easy to come by, beautiful, in constant use and yet pure and clean, would now light up his life and confer on it peace in retirement. Laughter, conversation, jokes, minor everyday preparations to please each other, not much more would be needed to bring happiness – and quite a lot of it at that.

In real life he found it otherwise. Whatever cannot be bought at a price, cannot be obtained unless it offers itself to one, of its own accord.

Bhupati failed to make things right with Charu and blamed himself for the failure, thinking, "Busy with journalistic writing for twelve years I have altogether lost the knack for a tête-à-tête with my wife." The moment the evening lamp was lit Bhupati went to the inner apartments with eagerness and tried to get a conversation going with a few words, to which Charu responded with equal brevity. Then Bhupati did not know what else to say. He felt shy with Charu because of this inability of his. He had thought that it was easy to talk with one's wife, but to an ignoramus like him it turned out to be very difficult – it was far easier to lecture at a meeting.

The evenings, which Bhupati imagined would be rendered full of charm with laughter, amusement and lovemaking, became a problem for them to spend together. Bhupati, after a period of enforced silence, felt that he should go away, but he could not even do that for fear of how Charu would take it. If he asked Charu if she would like to play cards Charu, finding no alternative, would say, "Yes" and bring down the cards with reluctance. She would lose the game through wilful mistakes – the play offered neither of them any pleasure.

Bhupati after a great deal of thought once asked Charu, "How about getting Manda down here; you are lonely."

Charu, incensed at the mention of Manda, replied, "No, I don't want her."

Bhupati laughed and was inwardly pleased. A chaste wife was naturally impatient with the least flaw in wifely virtue.

After the first impact of resentment was over Charu thought that Manda could perhaps bring some amusement to Bhupati's life. She was oppressed with the thought that she could not in any way offer Bhupati the happiness he craved. Bhupati, abandoning all else, was trying to draw all his joy of living from Charu; his earnest endeavours and her own poverty of heart made Charu very apprehensive. How long could they carry on like this? Why didn't Bhupati attach himself to something else? Why not another paper? Charu had never had to cultivate the habit of pleasing Bhupati all these days of their married life. Bhupati had never asked for any service or desired any pleasure from her; he had not made Charu a necessity in his life. She felt bewildered that suddenly he was demanding the fulfilment of all his needs from her. Charu was not even properly aware what Bhupati needed, what pleased him, and even if she had been, these things were not within her control to offer on demand.

If Bhupati had proceeded slowly perhaps things wouldn't have been so difficult for Charu. But suddenly bankrupt, Bhupati approached her with an empty bowl and this embarrassed Charu.

Charu said to him, "All right, let us have Manda. She can look after you."

Bhupati laughed, "Look after me? I don't need that." Aggrieved he thought, "I am devoid of savoir-faire, I just cannot make Charu happy."

So he involved himself with literature. If friends ever came they were surprised to find Bhupati busy with Tennyson, Byron, Bankim[1]. They began making fun of him, at this untimely devotion to poetry. Bhupati's laughing reply was, "Even the bamboo plant may get flowers, one never knows when."

[1] A 19th century originator of the Bengali novel.

70

One evening Bhupati lit a big lamp in the bed-room and though feeling diffident through shyness said to Charu, "Would you like me to read to you?"

Charu said, "Why not?"

Bhupati – "What would you like to hear?"

Charu – "Whatever you like."

Finding Charu not much interested Bhupati got somewhat discouraged. But finally he made himself bold enough to say, "Let me read something from Tennyson in translation."

Charu said, "All right."

But to no avail. Bhupati's reading did not acquire any flow because of his lack of self-assurance and Charu's indifference. Bengali words refused to fall with a proper cadence and Charu's empty look revealed that she was not listening. Their leisure in privacy that evening in the small lighted room somehow did not fulfil its promise.

As a nerve gets deadened through a severe blow and one doesn't feel much pain to begin with, Charu hadn't quite realized what Amal's absence meant at the start of their separation.

But as days went by Amal's absence began to make Charu feel the emptiness of the world around her more and more acutely. Charu was dumbfounded at this terrible discovery, as if she had been thrust out of a flower garden into a desert – and day by day the extent of that desert kept increasing. Charu hadn't known anything like this before.

The first thing she felt on waking in the morning was a thump in her heart – Amal was no longer there. When she sat down in the verandah to dress betel leaves a thought constantly kept coming back to her – Amal wasn't going to come for it. Sometimes, absent-minded, she would prepare more than was necessary and would then remember with a start that there was nobody to consume so much. Whenever she went to the storeroom the thought would arise in her mind that no snack had to be made ready for Amal.

71

Inpatient, she would sometimes come to the edge of the inner quarters, only to remember that Amal was not going to come back from College. Nobody to expect new books, writings, news or amusements from. There was nobody to sew or write for, or buy any fancy goods.

Charu was dismayed at her own unbearable pain and restlessness, and, fearful of this constant mental pressure, she kept asking herself, "Why, why this much suffering? Who is Amal to me that I have to suffer like this for him? What has happened? Why this, after all this time? Everybody, the servants, the daily labourers on the road are moving about in peace. Why then am I in this state? Oh God! Why have you thrust me into this dangerous situation?"

She asked and wondered but the suffering continued. All the space around her, inside and outside, was full of the remembrance of Amal; there was nowhere to escape.

Bhupati ought to have rescued her from these attacks of Amal's memory. But that stupid, affectionate man, himself concerned by the separation, kept constantly reminding her of him.

At last Charu had to give up the struggle, tired of the fight within her own self. She accepted this, without further opposition. Amal's memory was carefully given a secure place in her heart.

Gradually thinking about Amal with single-minded concentration became a matter of secret pride for her – as if this memory was the greatest glory of her life.

She fixed a time in between her household chores. She would then close the door and in the privacy of her room retraced, in minute detail, every happening of her life with Amal. With face down on the pillow she would cry, "Amal, Amal, Amal." Then, as if a response came from beyond the sea *"Bowthan*, what is it *bowthan?"* With eyes wet and closed she would ask, "Why, why did you go away with such disagreement? I have done nothing wrong. If you said "Good bye" with a smiling face I wouldn't have suffered so." She uttered the words in the same vein as when Amal was in her presence saying, "Amal, I haven't forgotten you, not for a day, not for a moment. It is you who brought out what was best in me, with the essence of that I would worship you everyday."

Thus Charu dug a canal, as it were, underneath her housework and duties and in that lonely, silent darkness she built a secret temple of grief adorned with her tears. Nobody on earth, including her husband, had right of entrance there. That place was as secret as it was deep and dear. It was there that she entered with her naked self, leaving behind at its door all the disguises used in this world; when she came out she put on the mask again, joining the battlefield of this world with the usual laughter and conversation, doing whatever work was required of her.

Thus Charu, giving up all inner conflict, gained a kind of peace, becoming free to devote herself to the care of her husband with singular attention. When Bhupati fell asleep she bowed down at his feet, taking the dust to her forehead. She kept none of his wishes unfulfilled whether in domestic chores or in caring and looking after him. Knowing that Bhupati was sensitive about any neglect of his dependants Charu was careful not to create the least shortfall in her hospitality towards them. She would thus end her day with work, taking, as specially graced, a little of the food left over by Bhupati.

Bhupati became, as it were, young again through such care and attention. He felt as if newly married to his wife. He pushed all his problems aside and blossomed out in dress, laughter and jokes. As hunger is felt more keenly after recovery from illness, when one can consciously feel in oneself the capacity for enjoyment, Bhupati, after all this time, felt an unparalleled and intense emotional upsurge. He began reading poetry behind his friends' backs and even without Charu's knowledge. He began to believe that it was through the loss of his paper and much suffering that he had discovered his wife.

He asked Charu, "Why have you given up writing?" Charu replied, "My writing is not good enough."

Bhupati – "I tell you, truthfully, I find no one amongst present writers as good as you. My opinion is the same as that of *Visvabandhu*."

Charu – "Please stop."

Bhupati said, "Just see," and brought out a copy of *Sororuha* and began comparing the writing of Amal and Charu. Charu, red in the face, took away the paper from Bhupati and covered it with her sari.

Bhupati thought, "One needs a companion writer to be able to write. Wait, I am going to have to practise writing myself, then I can create enthusiasm in Charu."

So he began practising writing in secret. His unemployed days were spent in consulting the dictionary, rewriting the same line many times over, and copying. He began to gain confidence and developed an attachment to these essays written with such effort and enormous cost.

At last he had a piece of his writing copied by someone else and brought it to his wife saying, "A friend of mine has just started writing. I know nothing of such things, please read it and tell me what you think of it." Bhupati hurrying out, placed the exercise book in Charu's hands. Charu saw through this deception from simple-minded Bhupati. She read it and smiled at the style and subject matter. Alas, Charu was trying so hard to feel devotion for her husband. Why was he throwing away her offering with such childishness, trying so hard to get Charu's admiration. If he did nothing, didn't keep up such constant attempts to attract Charu's attention, it would have been easier for her to worship her husband. Charu desired merely that Bhupati should not diminish his standing with her in any way.

Charu folded up the exercise book and leaning by the pillow began thinking with a far-away look. Amal too used to bring his new writings to her.

[1] Visvabandhu?

In the evening, anxious, Bhupati kept himself busy inspecting the flower tubs on the verandah – near the bedroom. He didn't dare ask anything. Charu volunteered, "Is this your friend's first writing?"

Bhupati – "Yes."

Charu – "It is excellent, it does not feel like a first attempt."

Bhupati, mightily pleased, wondered how to claim for his own this writing supposedly by someone else. So Bhupati's exercise book began filling up at speed and it did not take long for his name to come out either.

Charu always kept track of the day when a letter was due from England. First a letter came from Aden addressed to Bhupati in which *pranam* was paid to Charu. A letter came from Suez as well, in that too, respect was paid to her. The same for the one from Malta. Charu herself received no letter. She asked for Bhupati's letters, read them over and over again, but found no mention of herself except for paying respect.

Charu, who had these days taken shelter under the cool shade of a quiet sadness, now found it shattered through this neglect by Amal. Her heart began to cut itself to pieces and an earthquake within shook the steady existence she had built up with domestic duties.

Bhupati would sometimes notice, awaking at midnight, that Charu was not in bed. Searching he would find her sitting at the window of the South room. Charu would promptly get up and explain, "It was hot in our room, so I came for some air."

Anxiously Bhupati arranged for a fan to be pulled over the bed and kept a close watch over Charu lest she fell ill. Charu smiled and said, "Why do you get so anxious? I am perfectly all right." She had to use all her efforts to assume this smile.

Amal reached England. Charu surmised that he did not have sufficient time, on the way, to write a separate letter to her but he would surely write a long letter from England. But that long-awaited letter did not come.

Every mail-day Charu became inwardly restless in her work. She could not ask Bhupati for fear that he would say there was no letter for her.

One mail-day Bhupati appeared at a slow pace and said with a gentle smile, "I have got something, would you like to see it?" Charu started and said with agitation, "Yes, show me."

Bhupati, just out of fun, started dilly-dallying, unwilling to give it to her straightaway.

Impatient, Charu tried to take hold of the desired object from inside Bhupati's shawl, thinking "My mind has been saying since the morning there will be a letter for me today, it can't be otherwise."

Bhupati's sense of fun kept growing, he went behind the bed, out of reach of Charu. Sorely annoyed Charu sat down on the bed, her eyes getting wet with suppressed tears.

This eagerness of Charu pleased Bhupati; he took out his exercise book from inside his shawl, quickly dropped it in Charu's lap and said, "Here it is, don't be angry."

Even though Amal had said that he would not be able to write for sometime owing to pressure of work, when one or two mail-days were missed the world became like a bed of thorns for Charu.

In the evening, during conversation, Charu asked her husband, with assumed indifference and in a calm voice, "Could we not send a telegram to England to know how Amal is?"

Bhupati replied, "He wrote two weeks ago. He is busy with work."

Charu – "Oh! That's all right then. I was thinking, he is in a foreign country, may be he is ill – one cannot be sure."

Bhupati – "No. We would have heard if he was ill. Sending a telegram is an expensive business."

Charu – "Is that so? I thought it would cost a rupee or two."

Bhupati – "Not at all, it would be about a hundred rupees."

Charu – "That settles it, then."

In a couple of days Charu said to Bhupati, "My sister is now in Chuchura. Why don't you go and see her there?"

Bhupati – "Why? Is she ill?"

Charu – "No, no. But they are so happy to see you."

Charu's request made Bhupati take a carriage for Howrah Station. But the carriage got bogged down by a cavalcade of bullock carts on the road. During the hold-up the telegraph boy saw Bhupati and put a telegram in his hand. A telegram from England unnerved Bhupati, he thought that perhaps Amal was ill. Opening it with trepidation he found that it said, "I am well." What did that mean? On examination he found it to be a reply to a prepaid telegram. He couldn't got to Howrah. He turned round, and back home gave the telegram to his wife. Charu's face went pale, to see the telegram in Bhupati's hand.

He said, "I cannot understand its significance." On investigation he found out that Charu had pawned one of her ornaments and sent the telegram on the proceeds.

Bhupati thought, "It was quite unnecessary, all this. If she had asked me again, I would have arranged it. To pawn an ornament, in secret through the servant, for this – it is not a proper thing to do."

The question arose again and again in Bhupati's mind – why did Charu indulge in this immoderate behaviour? An indistinct suspicion began imperceptibly to assail him. Bhupati did not want to look at it in the face; he tried to forget about it but the unease did not leave him.

Amal was well and yet he did not care to write. How could their separation become so final? She wished she could ask Amal this question face-to-face – but the ocean was between them, there was no way to cross it. A cruel separation, a helpless separation – a separation so complete that nothing could bridge it.

Charu could not keep stability any more. Her housework was left undone, she became forgetful in all things, the servants began stealing. To see her wretched appearance people began to whisper, but Charu carried on as if unconscious.

It came to such a pass that Charu flushed from time to time; she had to leave in the middle of a conversation, in order to get away to cry; the mere mention of Amal made her face lose all colour.

At last Bhupati noticed all this and was forced to think what had so far been unimaginable – and the world became for him withered, dry, decayed. He was ashamed at the memory of those few days when the hint of happiness had blinded him. Must one deceive with a fake someone who cannot tell a precious stone as the real thing?

The memory of those words and deeds of Charu, her care, which had beguiled Bhupati, now began to hurt terribly –as a mark of his utter stupidity.

When he thought of those writings he had produced by great effort and care he wanted the earth to open up and swallow him. As if beaten by an iron rod Bhupati hurried to Charu and asked, "Where are my writings?"

Charu – "I have them."

Bhupati – "Please give them back to me."

Charu was then busy frying some snack for Bhupati. She asked, "Do you want them right now?"

Bhupati – "Yes, right now."

Charu put down the frying pan and brought out his papers and exercise book from the cupboard.

Impatiently Bhupati snatched the things away from Charu's hand and threw them into the open fire.

Charu anxiously trying to retrieve them exclaimed, "What have you done!"

Bhupati got hold of her hand and pressing it tightly

shouted, "Let them burn."

Dazed, Charu stood there; the writings were reduced to ashes.

Charu understood the reason for this; she sighed and leaving her frying pan, went elsewhere.

Bhupati had made no resolve to burn those papers in the presence of Charu. But when he saw the fire burning right in front of him the blood went to his head and unable to contain himself he was impelled to thrust all his deceived, stupid efforts into the fire in the very presence of the deceiver herself.

When all was reduced to ashes Bhupati's sudden madness cooled down and the thought of Charu arose in his mind, silently going away with downcast face, carrying the weight of her guilt in deep sadness. And he noticed that Charu had been preparing something with especial care particularly because she knew he was fond of it.

Bhupati stood leaning on the railing of the verandah, thinking that there was nothing more pitiful than all these tireless efforts of Charu to please him, these deceptions carried out with supreme care. Nevertheless these deceptions were not carried out by a despicable deceiver – the unfortunate woman had had to increase the pain of her wounded heart fourfold and squeeze blood out of it every day, and night. Bhupati thought, "Alas! helpless, sorrowing woman, it was quite unnecessary to do all these things for me. All that time when I did not receive love I didn't know that I didn't possess it. I was quite happy spending my time with proofs and writings – there is no need to do all this for me."

So he created a distance between his life and that of Charu and like a doctor looking at a dangerously ill patient he looked at Charu as one quite unrelated to him. How this frail woman was under pressure from all sides! There was nobody she could talk to, since it was not a matter to be disclosed; no place where she could openly bare her heart and cry out in pain – and yet carrying this load of suffering, undisclosable, incapable of being redressed, she had to continue with her daily tasks like someone at ease, like her neighbours, who suffered no distress.

Bhupati came to the bedroom and found Charu standing, her hand on the window, looking outwards with a vacant stare in her tearless eyes. He slowly came up, stood by her side and silently placed his hand on her head.

His friends asked Bhupati – "What is the matter, why so busy?

Bhupati – "The newspaper . . ."

A friend – "Again a newspaper! Are you proposing to wrap all your property in a newspaper and throw it in the Ganges?"

Bhupati – "No, I am not starting one."

Friend – "What then?"

Bhupati – "They are bringing out a paper in Mysore. I have been offered the editorship."

Friend – "You will leave here and go far away to Mysore? Taking Charu with you?"

Bhupati – "No. My maternal uncles will come and stay here with her."

Friend – "So, you cannot give up your fascination with being an editor."

Bhupati – "One needs some fascination or other."

Charu asked at the time of farewell, "When will you be back?"

Bhupati – "If you feel lonely, write and I shall come."

When Bhupati had reached the door, after saying farewell, Charu came running and held him by the hand, "Take me with you, don't leave me here."

Stunned, Bhupati stood and looked at Charu. Gradually Charu's grip loosened and her hand dropped away. Bhupati drew away from Charu and stood by the verandah.

What Bhupati understood was that Charu wanted to run away, like a deer pursued by fire, from a place that was full of the memory of separation with Amal. But didn't she think of

Bhupati once? Where was he to escape from a wife who was constantly thinking of someone else with all her heart? Could he not get an opportunity to forget her by going away? Must he keep her company, every evening, in a lonely, far away place? How fearsome would be the evenings when he would return after working all day, with a woman there silent and sorrowing. How long would he be able to keep close to him a woman who was carrying a dead weight in her heart? How many more years would he have to live like that, every day of his life? Was he not going to be able to leave behind the shelter that had been shattered to pieces, must he carry on his shoulder the broken rubble? Turning back to Charu Bhupati said, "No, I cannot do that." In a moment all the blood drained from Charu's face and it appeared dried, white, like paper, while her hand gripped the bedstead tightly.

Bhupati at once said, "All right Charu, then come with me."

Charu said, "No, let it be."

An Auspicious Look

Kantichandra was quite young. Nevertheless, instead of seeking a second wife after the death of his first, he kept himself busy with hunting and shooting. He was tall, lean, strong and light in body, keen-eyed, unfailing in aim and dressed in the western style. Two wrestlers, Hirasingh and Chakkanlall, and Khan saheb and Mia saheb, his musicians, were members of his retinue and used to follow him as he moved about. There was no dearth of worthless followers and attendants either.

In the middle of the month of *Agrahayan*,[1] Kantichandra had gone hunting with one or two friends to the Naidighi marsh. They were living in two boats on the river; three or four more boats, full of servants and attendants, were crowding the landing-stage so that the village housewives were finding it almost impossible to fill up their pitchers or bathe there. Everywhere shook with the sound of gunshots during the day, and in the evenings, the voices of experts in classical music, elaborating *tan*[2], drove sleep away from the villagers.

One morning, Kantichandra, seated in his boat, was carefully cleaning the butt of his gun with his own hands, when he heard ducks quacking not far away. Looking up he

[1]November/December
[2]Musical improvisation.

saw that a girl had come to the landing stage, pressing two baby ducks to her breast. The river was small, almost without current, and full of a variety of moss. The girl let go of the ducks into the water and then began keeping guard over them with anxious and careful attention, so that they did not go beyond the area of her control. It was clear that at another time she would have left the ducks there, but now felt unable to do so for fear of the men hunting.

The girl was beautiful with a radiant freshness, as if *Visvakarma*[1], having just created her, had let her loose. Kantichandra was astonished, never having expected to see such a face in such a poor place; but, on reflection, the face belonged there rather than to a king's inner apartments – flowers look better on trees than in golden vases. That day the blooming *kash*[2] bush by the river bank was glittering in the morning sunlight, washed by *sarat*'s[2] dew. In the midst of this scenery, the simple, fresh-looking face drew before Kantichandra's enchanted eyes a happy picture of the approaching *puja*[3] ceremony of the mother goddess in the month of *Asvin*[4]. Young Parvati[5] must have come at times with baby ducks at her breast to the banks of the river Mandakini; Kalidas[6] had simply forgotten to mention it.

Suddenly the girl looked extremely apprehensive; she scooped up the babies to her bosom with an anxious face and left the landing-stage with an indistinct noise of distress.

Kantichandra came outside to find out why and saw one of his attendants, a practical joker, aiming an unloaded gun in jest at the ducks in order to frighten the girl. Kantichandra forced the gun up and slapped the man violently on the cheek. The unexpectedness of this blow in the midst of pleasure, felled the man with a thump. Kantichandra went back and continued cleaning his gun.

[1]God of architecture
[2]See footnote[1] p. 22
[3]See footnote[1] p. 7
[4]See footnote[2] p. 7
[5]Mother goddess in her aspect of a young woman
[6]Famous Sanskrit poet and dramatist

About three in the afternoon that day, the hunters were going towards the fields through shaded village paths. One of them fired a shot. A short distance away above the bamboo grove a bird was hit, and wounded, fell circling down beyond the grove.

Curious, Kantichandra went after it and passing through bushes and groves, came out into a clearing to find the courtyard of a well-to-do household with barns filled with rice, and a big, clean cowshed. Under a plum tree, the girl of the morning was crying her eyes out with a wounded dove on her breast. She was wetting her sari in a bowl of water and twisting it, dripping water on the bird's eyes. A pet cat, treading on her lap, was looking up with an eager glance at the dove. Now and again the girl was hitting the top of the cat's nose with her first finger, to keep the excessive interest of the tempted animal under control.

This compassionate picture amidst the peace of a domestic courtyard in a silent afternoon, instantly imprinted itself on Kantichandra's heart. Sunlight and shade had come through the thinning leaves to fall on the girl's lap; nearby, a well-fed cow was lying down, and, in a leisurely manner, was attempting to drive away the flies from its back by moving its tail. Now and again in the bamboo bush a soft, sibilant noise like that of whispering was being created by the fresh north wind. She who looked like a wood nymph by the riverside wood in the morning, in the afternoon took on the appearance of an affectionate and graceful housewife in the silent courtyard by the cowshed.

Kantichandra felt acutely embarrassed to have appeared before this sensitive girl with a gun, he felt as if he had been caught red-handed. He wanted to apologize and say that the bird had not been hit by his gun. When he was thinking how to broach the subject someone from the cottage called, "Sudha[1]", and she hurried towards the cottage with the bird. Kantichandra thought the name a befitting one!

[1]Sweetness

84

Kanti handed over the gun to a member of his group and following the main path came to the front door of the cottage. He found a middle-aged, clean-shaven, quiet-looking Brahmin sitting on the verandah reading *Haribhak-tibilas*.[1] There was a similarity between the gentle, tranquil, devotion-inspired face and the girl's compassionate expression.

Kanti put together his hands in greeting and said, "Sir, I am thirsty, could I have a glass of water?" The Brahmin at once welcomed him, offered him a seat, fetched some sweetmeats on a brass dish and water in a bell-metal container, and put these in front of Kanti with his own hands.

When Kanti had taken the water, the Brahmin inquired about his lineage and family. Kanti told him and said, "Sir, if I could be of some assistance to you I would be grateful."

Nabin Banerjee said, "My boy, I can't think of any assistance I need except that I have a daughter called "Sudha"; she is of age. If I can marry her off to a good man I would be free of all debts to this world. There is no deserving young man around here. But I can't go away and leave the image of *Gopinath*[2] that has been established here, at my home."

Kanti said, "If you would see me in my boat we could talk about a deserving candidate."

In the meanwhile, Kanti's associates made enquiries about Banerjee's daughter, Sudha. Many people said, in one voice, that such a gentle-mannered, graceful girl was rare.

When Nabin came to the boat the next day Kanti bowed down on the ground as a mark of respect and told him that he himself was ready to marry the Brahmin's daughter. This unthought-of good fortune choked the Brahmin's voice and he was unable to speak for a while. He felt that there must be a mistake somewhere and asked, "You want to marry my daughter?"

[1]Devotional book relating to Krishna under the name 'Hari'
[2]Another name for the god Krishna

Kanti replied, "I am ready, if you would agree". Nabin asked again, "You mean Sudha?" and the answer to this question was, "Yes".

Nabin steadied himself and said, "Well, in that case we must arrange for you to see ...". Kanti pretended not to have seen her already and said, "I shall, at the time of the "Auspicious Look[1]" ceremony.

Nabin said in an ecstatic voice, "My Sudha is a very good and gentle girl, an expert in cooking and domestic work. As you are ready to marry her without so much as a look, I bless you that my Sudha may bring about your well-being as a chaste and devoted wife. May she never, even for a moment, cause you repentance."

Kanti did not want to wait. The marriage was arranged for the month of *Magh*[2] and the stage was set in the old brick building of neighbours, the Mazumdars. The bridegroom arrived on an elephant, accompanied by a procession of torches and music.

During the ceremony of the "Auspicious Look" the bridegroom looked at the bride. He couldn't quite make Sudha out – her head bent downwards and adorned with a marriage crown, her face decorated with sandal paste. The excitement induced by the exultation he was going through dazzled his eyes.

When, in the bridal room, the 'grandmother' of the neighbourhood cajoled the bridegroom into taking down the bride's headcovering, Kanti started with sudden shock.

This was not the same girl! Suddenly something like black thunder surged from his heart and exploded in his head and in a moment the light in the bridal room seemed to have disappeared. A wave from that darkness covered the face of the bride with a black stain.

Kantichandra had once promised not to marry again. So fate had to play a cruel joke and break that promise with

[1]A part of the Hindu marriage ceremony when the bride and the groom look at each other, supposedly for the first time.
[2]Month in the winter season (January/February)

impunity. How many good proposals of marriage had he rejected, how many of the requests and appeals of friends and relations had he neglected! The attraction of high status gained by marriage, the temptation of money, the fascination for beauty and name, he had bypassed all this only to find himself in this terrible predicament in the house of an unknown poor man by the side of a marsh in an unknown village. How could he show his face in society?

At first he was angry with his father-in-law. "That cheat married me off to one girl by showing another". But he had to concede that the old man was not unwilling for him to see the girl before marriage; it was he who refused. That he had been so badly deceived through lack of commonsense he thought better not to disclose to anyone.

He swallowed his medicine, but it left a bad taste in his mouth. The jokes and humour proper to the ceremony of the marriage night in the bridal room appeared to him tasteless. Anger against himself and against everyone else produced a scorching sensation throughout his body.

It was then that the wife by his side suddenly screamed as a young rabbit ran by her, closely followed by the girl he had hoped to marry. She returned holding the baby rabbit to her cheek and caressing it. People remarked, "Look, the crazy girl is here" and indicated by their gestures that she should leave. She took no notice, but came and sat by the bride and groom and looked at everything with the curiosity of a child. A maid tried to take her away by the hand but the groom intervened with a concerned voice. "Why, let her sit".

He asked the girl, "What is your name?" Instead of answering she began rocking herself. The roomful of women laughed out loud. Kanti asked again, "How old are your ducks now?" The girl kept looking at him silently but without any sign of embarrassment. Bewildered, Kanti took courage and asked again, "Your dove, has it recovered?" This too produced no result. The women began laughing in a manner which suggested that the bridegroom was being badly outwitted.

In the end he was told that the girl was deaf and dumb and that her only companions were the birds and beasts of the locality. It was just supposition on his part that the girl went inside the house the other day in response to the call, 'Sudha'. Obviously there must have been some other reason for her action.

Kanti had a shock. He now considered himself fortunate to have been saved from something, which, a little while before, he had so desperately desired. He thought, "If I had gone to the father of this girl he would have sought a way out of his troubles and delivered the girl into my hands according to my prayer."

For the time that his mind was absorbed in his enchantment with this girl, now gone beyond his grasp, he was altogether oblivious of his own bride. He did not even feel any inclination to find out that there was something very consoling right there, very near him. But the moment he heard that the girl was deaf and dumb, a black screen, tearing itself down, dropped away from the face of the earth.

When the hope that had beguiled him finally disappeared, he was free to look directly at what was near him. Heaving a sigh with a deep sense of deliverance, Kanti availed himself of an opportunity to look at the face of his bashful bride. At last "the auspicious look" in the real sense of the term took place, and all the impediments were gone from his mind's eye. The light that emanated from his heart and from the lamp, all of it was reflected on one soft, tender, young face. Kanti found the face imbued with a gentle grace and a quiet charm. He knew then Nabin's blessings would come true.

The Foolishness of Ramkanai

Those who say that the wife Gurucharan married the second time round was playing cards in the inner apartments while he was dying, are scandal-mongers, they are making a mountain out of a molehill. In fact, at the time, his wife was sitting on one leg with the other knee raised up to her chin, and was eating, with concentrated attention, last night's rice steeped in water, after mixing it with green tamarind, green chillies and a hot preparation of prawns. When she was called to the outer quarters she left behind a huge pile of half-eaten vegetables and her finished plate of rice, complaining, "One doesn't even get time to taste a few morsels."

When the doctor gave up hope, Gurucharan's brother Ramkanai sat beside the patient and said in a soft voice, "*Dada*[1], if you wish to make a will, tell me." Gurucharan said in a scarcely audible voice, "You write down as I dictate." Ramkanai, having got ready with pen and papers, Gurucharan dictated, "I leave all my property, movable and immovable, to my duly wedded wife, Baradasundari." Ramkanai wrote it down, but the pen in his hand did not want to move. He had hoped that his only son, Nabadwip, would inherit all the property of his heirless uncle. Although the brothers lived separately, Nabadwip's mother,

[1]See footnote p. 31.

hoping for that particular outcome, did not let him seek a job; she had also married him off early and the marriage was fruitful, foiling the wishes of enemies. Nevertheless Ramkanai wrote Gurucheran's instructions down and put the pen in his brother's hand for signing. Gurucharan signed in his failing hand and it was difficult to decide whether the result of his effort meant his name or was simply some wavy lines drawn in a shaky hand.

When his wife finally arrived after finishing her dish of water-steeped rice, Gurucharan had lost his capacity for speech. She started to cry at this. Those who had been deprived of the property, after entertaining a lot of hopes in that direction, said that it was just crocodile tears. But that is hardly credible.

As soon as she heard about the will Nabadwip's mother rushed to the scene and started a tirade – "One loses one's wits at the time of dying. With such a deserving nephew to inherit..."

Ramkanai was full of respect for his wife – indeed so much so that, according to some, it amounted to fear, – nevertheless he could not hold back, he had to run towards her, crying, "My dear, the time for you to lose your wits is yet to arrive, then why behave like this? *Dada* is dying but I am still living. Say what you have to say at the proper time. This is not the right moment for it."

By the time Nabadwip had heard the news and arrived, his uncle was gone. He threatened the dead man, "I shall see who puts fire in your mouth at the cremation, and my name is not Nabadwip if I perform your funeral rites." But Gurucharan would not care for such rituals. He was a student of Mr. Duff[1], and had particularly enjoyed eating what, according to religious prohibitions, was forbidden food. If people called him a Christian, he would put out his tongue, as if in shame and protest[2], "By God, being a

---

[1]Famous British educationalist who spread western ideas in India.
[2]Typical Bengali gesture indicating shame.

Christian would amount to my having eaten beef." If he was
like this when alive, there was little possibility of his being
upset, when just dead, at the prospect of not having funeral
rites performed on his behalf. However there was no other
way available, just then, to take revenge. Nabadwip found
consolation in the thought that the man would remain dead
in the next world as well. As long as one was on this earth one
could manage to keep alive even without inheriting one's
uncle's property. But where his uncle had gone, even
begging would not enable one to secure funeral offerings for
oneself. Clearly it was more advantageous to be alive.

Ramkanai went to Baradasundari and said, "*Bowthak-
urani*[1], *dada* has left all his property to you. Here is the will.
Keep it in your safe with care."

The widow had been lamenting, loudly, for the deceased,
in a musical vein using lengthy phrases which were
improvised as she went along. One or two maids had joined
in, adding some new words, and the resulting song-like
elaboration of grief suggested a sleepless night for the whole
village. Its rhythm was disturbed by the arrival of the will
which also affected the continuity of the lamentation – the
link between what went before and what came after being
destroyed. The thing took on the following disjointed shape:
"My God, what a disaster has struck me, what a disaster – tell
me *thakurpo*[2], whose writing is this, yours? – stop for a
moment, don't shout, I can't hear what is being said – oh
God, why did I not die before him, why did I remain alive?"
Ramkanai inwardly sighed, saying to himself, "That is
because of our ill-luck."

As they went home, his wife turned on him. When a loaded
bullock-cart falls into a ditch the wretched buffaloes stand
still in a helpless manner for a long time, despite the
continual proddings of the driver. Likewise Ramkanai put
up silently with her accusations for a long time, then
protested in a rather aggrieved tone, "What is my fault in all

[1]Address for sister-in-law
[2]See footnote p. 44.

this? I am not my brother."

Immediately Nabadiwip's mother hissed out, "No, you are such a simple man, you understand nothing. *Dada* said 'write down' and you wrote it down. You are all the same. You are waiting to act in exactly the same way, when the time becomes ripe for you. As soon as I am dead, you will marry a wicked witch and deprive my jewel of a son, Nabadwip, of everything. But have no worry, I have no wish to die soon."

In the meanwhile Nabadwip discussed the affair with his clever friends and came to tell his mother, "Don't worry, I shall get this property yet." We must get Father away from here for a time. Everything will be spoiled if he remains here." Nabadwip's mother had not the least respect for his father and she found the proposal entirely reasonable. At last, through the urgings of the mother, this bungler, this totally superfluous and foolish father of Nabadwip, had to take refuge in Benaras, on some excuse or other.

In a few days Baradasundari and Nabadwip both went to court, accusing each other of having forged the will. The signature in the will Nabadwip had produced in his own favour clearly showed it to be the handwriting of Gurucharan. One or two selfless witnesses also appeared. Nabadwip's father was the only witness of the will in favour of Baradasundari and its signature was indecipherable. Baradasundari had a dependant cousin at home who said, "*Didi*[1], I shall be a witness for you and find some others."

When the affair was in full swing Nabadwip's mother sent for his father from Benaras. The devoted gentleman arrived forthwith, with bag and umbrella in hand, and even attempted a bit of humour by putting his hands together and saying with a smile, "The servant is here, what order of the queen can I carry out?"

The wife shook her head and said, "Enough of your antics. You spent all this time in Benaras on an excuse, never

[1]Address for an older sister or cousin

thinking of us, not for a moment..." and so on.

Thus the two sides kept bringing up complaints against each other for a time, until their accusations moved away from the individual to include the entire sex. Nabadwip's mother compared a man's love with the love of a Muslim for his chick[1] and his father said, "Women have honey in their mouth, but a knife in their heart", although it was difficult to say when he had actually tasted this verbal sweetness.

In the meanwhile Ramkanai suddenly received a sub-poena from the court to appear as a witness. Surprised, he was trying to fathom the meaning of this, when Nabadwip's mother appeared, saying, amidst a flood of tears, that a wicked demoness not only wanted to deprive poor Nabadwip of his rightful inheritance from his affectionate uncle, she was also plotting to send their jewel of a son to jail.

It took Ramkanai a little while to realise what was going on and it stunned him. Recovering he shouted at her, "What have you done? This will ruin us utterly." His wife then came out in her true colours saying, "Why, what has Nabadwip done wrong? Why shouldn't he have his uncle's property? Why should he give it up without a protest?"

She carried on – an evil being, the daughter of a sinister mother, responsible for the early demise of her husband, was an outsider who was trying to take possession of what belonged to the family. How could this be tolerated by the deserving son of a good lineage? If a bewitched uncle had lost his senses while dying, under the undue influence of this demoness's magic, it was not a sin for his golden-hearted nephew to rectify that error by his own efforts.

This dumbfounded Ramkanai. When his wife and son together began indulging in yells and screams, punctuated by profuse shedding of tears, Ramkanai struck his forehead with his hand and just sat there speechless. He took no food, nor any drink.

Two days passed in this manner with Ramkanai fasting,

[1]Insincere love, as the "chick" is later eaten.

when the time arrived for the case to be heard at court. In the meanwhile, Nabadwip had so pressurised Baradasundari's cousin, with threats and temptations, that the latter became a witness on his side without any trouble. The case was going against Baradasundari and victory seemed to be about to join the other side when Ramkanai was called as a witness.

Old Ramkanai, enfeebled through his fast, his lips and tongue dry, held tight to the witness box with his thin, shaky fingers. The clever barrister began cross-examining him, skilfully attempting to get him to come out with points in his client's favour. He began with the far-distant past, planning to proceed towards the issue carefully and in a slow, oblique fashion.

Ramkanai turned towards the judge and said, with palms together, 'My Lord, I am old and very weak, and I don't have the energy to say much. So, I shall be brief in saying what I have to say. My elder brother, late Gurucharan Chakravorty, made a will at the time of his death, in which he left all his property to his wife, Srimati Baradasundari. I wrote that will with my own hand and my brother signed it with his own hand. The will submitted by my son, Nabadwip, is forged." Then trembling, Ramkanai fainted.

Amused, the clever barrister said to the attorney by his side, "By Jove, it took little enough to push that man!"

Baradasundari's cousin ran to her and said, "*Didi*, the old man nearly sank the boat, the case survived on my evidence."

Didi replied, "Is that so? It is hard to know a man's true character. I thought he was a good man."

The wise friends of Nabadwip concluded, after a lot of reflection, that the old man had done this through failure of nerve. He was unable to maintain his wits once he got into the witness box. It would be impossible to find another man, so completely daft, in the whole town.

Back home Ramkanai developed high fever with delirium. While mentioning his son in his ravings this foolish bungler, this thoroughly unnecessary father of Nabadwip, made his exit from this world. Some of his relatives remarked, "Pity he could not have gone a bit earlier, that would have been useful."

I do not wish to say who these people were.

The In-between

It was an average household, Nibaran's, in which poetry, or imagination played no part. The need for aesthetic pleasure in life was a thought which had never occurred to him. As feet enter with assured comfort into an old pair of sandals, he occupied his accustomed place on this earth without any question, argument or elaborate dissertation on the question of truth.

Nibaran would get up early in the morning and, with utter contentment, smoke his hubble-bubble, sitting bare-bodied by the door of his house which adjoined the lane. His mind would be involved but superficially with the people going around, with the carriage on the road, with the *Vaishnava*[1] beggar singing or the hawker crying aloud collecting old bottles, and if someone came along selling green mangoes or *tapsi*[2] fish he would haggle over the price for a time before settling for a special dish for the day. Then in good time he would rub oil on his body, get his bath over, take his meal, put on his long official robe and enjoy another smoke, this time along with a dressed betel leaf (which when finished he would replace in his mouth with a fresh one). Finally he would leave for the office. On his return he would spend the evening in a contented but serious vein at the house of his

[1]A religious sect devoted to the god Krishna.
[2]A fish regarded as a delicacy.

neighbour, Ramlochan Ghosh. The evening meal over, he would meet his wife Harasundari in the bedroom.

The brief discussions and critical appraisals that would take place there concerning such matters as the marriage of the Mitras' son, and the paraphernalia of ceremonial gift-giving that took place on that occasion, the disobedience of the newly-engaged maid-servant, the importance of special spices for a particular dish and the like have never been put into rhythm by a poet. But Nibaran felt no compunction on that score.

Then Harasundari fell seriously ill in the month of *Falgun*, in springtime. The fever refused to subside. The more the physician prescribed quinine the more it raged, like a fierce current when obstructed. It dragged on for twenty, then thirty, and even forty days.

Nibaran was forced to take leave from his office and discontinue the evening meetings at his neighbour's. But at home, he hardly knew what to do. Now and again he went to the bedroom to find out how the patient was faring and sat anxiously on the verandah smoking his hubble-bubble. There was a change of physicians twice a day; whatever cure was suggested by anyone was tried.

Harasundari's condition improved after forty days – despite these love-induced uncertainties of medical care – but she had become so weak and emaciated that her body could only announce its presence in a most feeble manner that appeared to come from afar.

The southerly breeze typical of Spring had then started and the open windows of married women had given the moonlight of warm nights the right to enter their bedrooms.

Next to Harasundari's room was their neighbour's back garden. It could hardly claim to be a place of beauty or attraction. Someone had once taken some interest and planted a few crotons[2] which were subsequently abandoned

---

[1]See footnote[1] p. 39
[2]Plant cultivated for its variously coloured leaves

to their fate. On a platform of dried branches a pumpkin plant was growing. Under the old plum tree a jungle had developed. A wall by the side of the kitchen had crumbled and the bricks thrown together – to which remains of clinker and ash were being added everyday – had grown into a heap.

Lying by the window and looking at this garden Harasundari nevertheless experienced, at every moment, a deep sense of joy such as she had never known in all her insignificant life. When in Summer the tiny village rivulet – its current lost and looking thin on its sandy bed – gains a certain transparency, one can see in it the early sunlight trembling at the bottom, observe its delight when shaken by the wind, even see the stars clearly reflected, like pleasant memories, in its crystal-like mirror. In such a way joyous nature touched the frail current of life in Harasundari with its fingers, unable though she was to grasp the meaning of the music that had begun playing in her heart.

So, when her husband sat by her and asked, "How are you?" her eyes filled with tears. In her fever-thinned face, her eyes looked big and these, full of love and gratitude, she would fix on her husband's face and lie there silently holding his hand in her own thin ones. Then, from somewhere, a new current of joy would enter her husband's heart too.

Days passed in this way. One night, when a huge moon was rising through the shaking branches of a small fig tree growing on a tumbledown wall and a sudden breeze had begun to blow, breaking the humid stillness of the evening, Harasundari, playing with Nibaran's hair with her fingers suggested: "We have no children. Why don't you marry again?"

Harasundari had been thinking about it for days. When a superabundance of gladness, an exalted love, takes possession one believes onself to be capable of everything. Then a powerful desire for self-sacrifice takes hold. As the current's exuberance throws itself with force on the hard bank, the explosion of love and joy wants, as it were, to surrender itself to some noble sacrifice and immense suffering.

It was in such a state Harasundari decided, exultation in her heart, that she would do something grand for her husband. But while desire may be big, one's capabilities are small. What had she got ready at hand to offer? No wealth, no great intelligence, no expertise. There was only her life – she could offer it at once, but what would that accomplish? "If only I could offer my husband a son, white like foam on milk, soft like butter, beautiful like a little cupid." But even if she was prepared to die through wishing hard, her wish was never to be fulfilled. It was then she thought that she would make her husband marry again. She wondered why wives took such a prospect to be hard; it was really nothing very difficult. A woman who loved her husband could surely also love her co-wife. Her bosom swelled in pride at the thought.

When the proposal was first mooted, Nibaran laughed it out of court. He did not listen to it the second or third time either. His dissent and unwillingness made Harasundari's faith and pleasure in him begin to grow apace. So did her resolve to make him marry again.

On the other hand, the more Nibaran was subjected to this request the more the idea of its impossibility began to disappear from his mind. A bright picture of a happy household with children formed itself before his eyes as he sat smoking by the door.

Soon he broached the subject himself one day. "I cannot be expected to take charge of a young girl at this advanced age."

Harasundari replied, "You don't have to worry about it. I shall take charge." The image of an adolescent girl-bride, gentle, shy, recently separated from her mother, rose in her mind as she said this, and her heart surged with affection.

Nibaran responded, "I have got my office, my job and you. I shan't have time to listen to the demands of a young girl."

Harasundari assured him, repeatedly, that he would not have to spend much time on the matter and then remarked, jokingly: "Once it has actually happened I've no doubt we'll hear another tune." Nibaran did not think it necessary to answer; he just struck Harasundari's cheek with his first finger, as if in punishment. So far for introduction.

Nibaran got married to a girl called Sailabala, young enough to have an ornament hanging from her nose. He thought her name was sweet and her face very appealing. He wanted to keep looking at her bearing, her body and her movements, but that was difficult. He had to pretend on the contrary that she was rather a problem, this young girl; one would prefer somehow to bypass all this and feel safe in one's own accustomed field of responsibility, befitting one's age.

Harasundari was rather amused by this "threatened" posture of Nibaran's. Sometimes she would take hold of him by the arm and say, "Why are you running away? She is only young; she won't devour you."

Nibaran would then pretend to be doubly in haste and say, "Please, I am rather busy," as if eager to run away. Harasundari would whisper to him, "A girl has come to you from another household, you should not neglect her so." She would make Sailabala sit by Nibaran, make her let go of the sari-covering on her head and holding her chin up would say, "See what a beautiful face, like the moon."

Sometimes she would herself disappear on the pretext of work and close the door from outside. Nibaran knew for certain that two curious eyes were fixed on him, gazing through a chink in the door. So he would turn round and pretend to go to sleep while Sailabala would huddle up in a corner, her sari drawn across her head, her face turned the other way.

In the end Harasundari gave up (though it did not make her particularly unhappy). But where Harasundari left off, Nibaran took up. When one finds a diamond one wants to turn it about and look at it from many angles – and this was a human mind belonging to someone young and good-looking – something of incomparable value. He had to touch her with caresses, look at her from behind, front and sideways – give a playful shake to her earrings, pull down her head-covering and discover fresh limits to her beauty, sometimes suddenly like lightning, sometimes from staring for a long time, with a star-like gaze. Nothing like this had ever happened before in the experience of the Head Clerk of the Macmoran Company, Shri Nibaranchandra. When he had got married for the first time he was a mere boy; when he attained his youth his wife was someone he was already used to and married life had become a matter of habit. He certainly loved Harasundari – but never before had he known this gradual awakening of passion in this conscious fashion. An insect born within a ripe mango, that never had to seek out juice or learn to taste it gradually, when let loose in a flowering garden in Spring, flies around the half-open face of the rose with tremendous interest. A little scent, a little taste of sweetness intoxicates it.

Nibaran started by secretly giving presents to Sailabala – sometimes a porcelain doll in a gown, sometimes a bottle of perfume or sweets; thus was intimacy begun. Then one day Harasundari, her housework finished, discovered through her spy-hole in the door that Nibaran and Sailabala were playing a game of cowry shells.

A game indeed for his age! Nibaran had taken his meal, intending to go to his office, but had gone instead into his room. Where was the need for such deception? It was as if somebody had opened her eyes with a burning stick and in its heat her tears dried up and evaporated like gas.

She thought to herself: "It was I who brought her into this household, I who was the cause of their union. Then why this kind of behaviour towards me, as if I were a hindrance to their happiness."

Harasundari took it upon herself to give Sailabala lessons in household chores. One day Nibaran interfered, "She is only young and not very strong. You are making her work hard."

A curt reply sprung to Harasundari's lips, but she stopped

herself in time and said nothing. From that day on the new wife no longer did any house-work. She herself did everything, cooking and supervising. As a result Sailabala began to behave as if she was incapable of movement. Harasundari had to serve her like a maid, and her husband kept her entertained like a clown. So Sailabala never learnt to appreciate that there was such a thing as housework, or that one has to consider the others in one's life.

Harasundari worked hard, like a slave, but with pride; there was nothing of the humble and downtrodden about her. She conceded, "You two children can be together and play. I will take on myself the whole responsibility of this household."

Alas, where is that strength today which made Harasundari think that she could for ever give up, for the sake of her husband, half share of her claim to love. When the tide comes on a full moon night and banks burst one is apt to believe that one can break through all limits. But to keep the promise that one makes at that moment, through the long-drawn-out period of life's ebbtime makes heavy demands on life itself. If you give away all you own, in the days of riches, with one scratch of a pen, you have to pay back that action in the days of poverty, little by little and for a long time. You then understand how wretched is man, how frail his heart, how insufficient his powers.

That day, Harasundari was like the moon on the second day of the white fortnight[1] – just a thin line and nothing more – she was weak, anaemic and pale at the end of her long illness, floating lightly on this earth. But she felt that day that she wanted nothing from this world for herself. But as the body gained strength and the flow of blood in her gathered force, a host of claimants appeared in Harasundari's mind, shouting, "You have signed a deed of sacrifice,

[1]See footnote 3 p. 16

but we do not wish to give up our rights.''

When Harasundari first realised what she had done to herself, she gave up her own bedroom to Nibaran and Sailabala and slept alone in another room. She left the bed she had first slept in at the age of eight on her marriage night, after twenty seven years. The night this married woman put out the lamp and delivered herself with unbearable pain in her heart to her new "widow's" bed, it happened that, at the other end of the lane, a dandy young man was singing the song of Malini in *Behag* ragini[1], accompanied by a tabla and the audience was raising a chorus of appreciation at suitable places.

In the next room the song sounded enjoyable in that silent moonlit night. Sailabala, a mere girl, was very sleepy, but Nibaran was softly saying, close to her ears, "My beloved!" He had in the meanwhile read Bankimbatu's *Chandra-sekhar*[2] to Sailabala and had even recited some modern poetry.

At some lower layers of Nibaran's soul lay a source of youth so far suppressed. Suddenly called upon, it rushed out into the light of day at an untimely hour. No-one was prepared for it – and as a result his commonsense went awry and all the arrangements of his household were turned upside down. The poor man was unaware that such troublesome elements existed in man, such potent, turbulent forces that can put to naught all calculations, all balance and discipline.

Not only Nibaran; Harasundari too came to know a new kind of agony. What sort of desire was this, what unbearable torment! What the mind wanted now it neither desired before, nor received. When Nibaran used to go to the office regularly in his orderly way, when he talked for a while before sleep about the account for the milkman, the high price of things, or social proprieties, there had never been

[1]Name of musical mode – a female raga.
[2]Novel by Bankimchandra – see footnote p. 70

any inkling of today's inner turmoil. They used to love, but there was no brightness in it, nor any heat. That love was like unlit fuel.

Today she felt that someone had deprived her of the fruition of her life. As if her heart had been on a fast for ever. Her woman's life had been spent in utter poverty. She was busy with marketing, spices, vegetables and such tiresome details and twenty seven years of her life had been spent in this slavery. Today, in midstream, she found that right next to her bedroom a mere girl had unlocked a treasure chest and was sitting there occupying the position of a queen. A woman can be a slave but she can also be a queen. But the division that made one woman a slave and the other a queen meant that the slave lost her pride – but the queen did not get the happiness due her either.

For Sailabala did not taste the real joy of a woman's life. She was constantly pampered, and it left no scope for her to love. The river finds its fulfilment in running towards the sea and then losing itself in it. But if instead the sea leans towards the river, attracted by the tide, the river flows back within itself. The world with all its endearments moved constantly towards Sailabala, making her pride in herself sky-high, but it failed to help make her love her family. She came to believe that everybody and everything existed for her – but that she existed for herself, not for anything else. This no doubt is very gratifying for one's ego, but it does not bring real fulfilment.

The day was full of dense cloud and the darkness inside was so thick that it was difficult to do anything. The rain could be heard splashing outside. The jungle of creepers and bushes under the plum tree was nearly under water and through the ditch by the wall muddy water was babbling on. Harasundari was sitting by the window in the lonely darkness of her bedroom.

Nibaran stealthily entered like a thief through the door,

undecided whether to turn back. Harasundari noticed him but said nothing. Suddenly Nibaran shot up to her like an arrow and put in breathlessly, "I need a few ornaments. You know, I am heavily in debt and the creditors are getting insulting. I have to mortgage these, but I shall be able to release them quite soon."

Harasundari made no comment. Nibaran kept standing there, looking like someone found guilty. In the end he asked again. "You will not give me the ornaments today?"

Harasundari simply said, "No."

To get out of the room was as difficult as it had been to enter it. Nibaran cast a glance around and said in a vacillating tone, "Let me try elsewhere then." He departed.

Harasundari understood quite well what the debt was about and why the ornaments had to be mortgaged. Last night the newly-wed had shouted at her tame and befuddled man, *"Didi*[1] has a chestful of ornaments. Why can't I have some?"

When Nibaran was gone she unlocked the chest and took out all her ornaments. She called to Sailabala, first made her wear her marriage sari, a Benarasi, and then decorated her body with her own ornaments, one by one. She dressed her hair carefully and in the light of the lamp saw that the girl's face was very sweet, and full of appeal, like the flavour of a freshly ripened fruit with its natural smell. Sailabala went away with a jingling sound that kept ringing in Harasundari's blood for a long time. She said to herself, "Today there is no comparison between you and me. But one day I too was your age, I too was filled to the brim with youth. But why did nobody tell me about it, why wasn't I informed when it came or went? But look at Sailabala, she moves with such pride, with such a wave of glory round her!"

While Harasundari had not been aware of anything beyond household matters, these ornaments had been of tremendous value to her. She could not have then foolishly

[1]See footnote p. 92

let go of all these in one moment, as now. Now she knew of something priceless, ranging far above her housewifely duties, in comparison with which the value of these ornaments, or thoughts about the future, meant nothing.

And Sailabala, glorying in gold and jewels, went back to her own room. It did not occur to her even once what a sacrifice Harasundari made for her sake. What she knew was that service, wealth, good fortune from everywhere would by their own natural inclination find their way to her, because she was Sailabala, "the beloved."

Some people, sleep-walking, tread through hazardous paths without a thought. Some people who are awake may be permanently in a trance, when they lose their bearing and proceed through the narrow alley-ways of danger without a trace of anxiety, until they finally wake up, facing absolute disaster.

This is what happened to our Head Clerk of Macmoran Company. Sailabala was like a whirlwind in his life which sucked up many a valuable thing, leaving nothing behind. It was not just Nibaran's humanity and monthly pay or the happiness of Harasundari and her belongings – the cash in the treasury of the Macmoran Company got entangled too, in secret. A few bundles of notes began to disappear now and again. Nibaran conjectured that he would return the money he was "borrowing" out of next month's salary. But as soon as next month's pay was received it got pulled into that whirlwind and very quickly evaporated down to the last penny.

In the end, he got caught. His was a hereditary service and the Sahib loved him, so two days were granted for repayment. Nibaran hardly knew how he had managed to embezzle two and a half thousand rupees. So he went to Harasundari, like one mad, and said, "I am ruined."

The story made Harasundari turn white. Nibaran appealed, "Please bring out the ornaments, now."

Harasundari replied, "I have given them all to the young wife."

Nibaran's adult world dissolved itself, and becoming an agitated child again, he kept questioning her: "Why did you have to do that, tell me why? Who asked you to?"

Harasundari gave no straight answer to this but said, "What does it matter? The ornaments haven't disappeared."

Nibaran said in dismay, "Then you go, and get them out of her on some pretext. But promise that you won't tell her that I want them or why."

Harasundari felt angry and said with utter contempt, "This is no time for excuses or worry about endearments. Come with me."

She entered Sailabala's room with her husband. The young wife was not interested to hear anything about it at all. To everything, her only reply was "It does not concern me."

There had never been any contract that she would have to worry about family affairs. Everyone would look after themselves, and pulling their resources together would worry about Sailabala's comfort. This was the rule – and any exception was utterly unjust.

Then Nibaran took hold of Sailabala's feet and pleaded. But she was adamant, "I know nothing about all this. I shall not give what is mine." Nibaran at last realised that this seemingly weak, tender, small and beautiful girl was in fact harder than an iron chest. Her husband's weakness at this moment of crisis only increased Harasundari's scorn and she tried to take the keys from Sailabala by force. Sailabala at once scaled the wall and threw the bunch of keys into the pond. Harasundari said to her bewildered husband, "Why don't you break the lock?" Sailabala rejoined in a calm manner, "I shall then commit suicide." Nibaran, dishevelled and distraught, went away saying, "I shall try elsewhere."

Within two hours Nibaran sold his ancestral home for two and a half thousand rupees. He was not sent to jail, but his job went. All the movable and immovable property that remained were his two wives. Of these two his girl-wife was pregnant and she was well-nigh immobile with distress. This small family had to take shelter in a tiny, damp house in the lane.

There was no end to the discontent and ill health of the young wife. She was incapable of accepting the fact that her husband had no means – if so, why did he marry?

There were only two rooms upstairs, one for Sailabala and Nibaran, the other for Harasundari. Sailabala complained, "I cannot spend all my time in the bedroom."

Nibaran gave her false assurances: "I am looking for a better house. We shall soon move." Sailabala said to this, "Why, there is another room next to us."

Sailabala never had any time for neighbours. When they came to visit Nibaran one day, sorry at his misfortune, she closed her door and refused to open it. After they left she created a scene, hysterically abusing him, crying and refusing to eat. Such scenes began to take place regularly.

In the end in her dangerous condition Sailabala became seriously ill and the risk of miscarriage became real.

Nibaran appealed to Harasundari, "Please, save Saila." Harasundari began nursing Sailabala, day and night, who called her names at the slightest lapse. Harasundari made no reply.

Sailabala didn't fancy eating sago. She would throw away the bowl when offered it and demand instead to eat rice with green mango despite her fever. Harasundari used endearing words, such as "My dear, good sister" and the like to pacify her. But Sailabala did not live. She took with her all the endearments and caresses heaped on her, but the girl's small, incomplete life ended on a note of discomfort and discontent.

Nibaran was badly hit at first, but then he discovered that a knot that had tied him up had been loosened, and even in his grief he felt some joy of freedom. Suddenly it appeared to him that he had been heavily laden with a bad dream for a long time and the moment he woke up life became very light. Was his dear Sailabala like the sweet *madhabi*[1] creeper which had been torn apart? He felt, taking a deep breath, that she was rather the rope to hang himself with.

And Harasundari, his life's companion? He found her within the temple of his memory, full of both happiness and misery, sitting and taking responsibility for his household all by herself. Nevertheless, there was a distance between them, as if a small, sharp, beautiful but cruel knife had drawn a painful dividing line between the right and left side of a heart.

The once at dead of night when the whole world was asleep Nibaran, with creeping steps, entered the privacy of Harasundari's bedroom. Silently he took his place, according to old custom, on the right side of the bed and lay there. But this time he had to take what was once his rightful place like a thief.

Harasundari said nothing, nor did Nibaran. They lay side by side, as before, but between them a dead girl took her place, whom neither of them could overcome.

[1]Creeper with scented flowers which blooms in the Summer and rainy seasons.

The Royal Mark

The god *Prajapati*[1] smiled a little from amidst the smoke of the sacrificial fire as the marriage ceremony of Nabendusekhar and Arunlekha was taking place. Unfortunately, what is just a game for Prajapati is not always particularly amusing for us.

Nabendusekhar's father, Purnendusekhar, was quite well-known in English Government circles, and he managed to arrive at the lofty height of the title "Raibahadur"[2] - a task normally as hard as crossing a desert - purely by making frequent obsequious *salaams*, which he used to cross the sea of this world. Indeed, he had the wherewithal for even more difficult-of-access honours. But all of a sudden, at the age of fifty-five, this Government-favoured person departed for a place that is beyond all titles - fixing his pathetic, greedy gaze on the not-far-away mountain height of a Government title. So at last the muscles of his jaw, made loose by many a *salaam*, found their rest in a bed in the cremation ground.

But science says that energy can only be transferred or transformed, not destroyed. So the energy of *salaam*, a steady friend of the fickle goddess Lakshmi, came down from the shoulders of the father to plonk itself on those of the son, and Nabendusekhar's young head began untiringly rising and

[1]God who arranges marriages between mortals.
[2]Title bestowed by British Government on Indians who rendered them some service.

falling at many an English door like a pumpkin moved by waves.

The history of the family from which he took a wife for the second time, after his first wife died leaving no children, was altogether of a different kind. Pramathanath was the oldest son of that family. His acquaintances were fond of him and regarded him highly, his relations looked up to him with affectionate esteem; everyone, family and neighbours, thought of him as an example to be followed.

Pramathanath was a B.A. and he was intelligent and wise. However he did not care for a fat pay cheque or for wielding a sharp pen. Nor did he have patrons to back him. If the English kept him at bay, he did the same with them. So, although Pramathanath shone brightly at home and amongst his acquaintances in his own environment, he did not become influential enough to attract the attention of people far and wide.

It had not always been so. Pramathanath had once gone to England for three years. The politeness of the English in their own land captivated him and he returned home dressed in western clothes, forgetting the dishonour and suffering of India. His brothers and sisters were a little put out by this at first, but soon they began to say that western clothes suited their brother better than anyone. The family managed, in time, to take pride in the glory of donning western dress.

Pramathanath had returned thinking, "I shall be a shining example of how to mix with the English on equal terms. If one says that it is not possible to meet the English and not bow down, one only shows the lowly state of one's own mind, not to speak of the unjust accusation that this makes." He brought back with him letters of introduction from some important people in England, and these helped him to find an entrance to the society of the English in India. He and his wife even began going to teas and dinners with the English, sharing in their games and their humour. The nerves of his body became quite taut, intoxicated by this success.

While he was enjoying this favour, a new railway line was being opened and the Railway Company invited the Governor, and along with him a few respected natives favoured by the Government, for the inaugural train ride. Those invited, Pramathanath among them, filled up a few carriages. But despite this invitation, an English Inspector of Police insulted some of the respected Indians, and on their return journey began turning them out of one of the carriages. Pramathanath, dressed in western clothes, was about to get off when the Inspector said, "Why are you getting off? You can stay."

This honour of being particularly singled out turned Pramathanath's head a little, but as the train started and evening sunlight spread itself everywhere from the west, it looked to him like sad, red shame. Pramathanath was sitting alone and looking out of the window with a fixed gaze at the unremarkable land of Bengal. He began thinking and his heart burst with the shame of it all; tears flowed from his eyes like fiery liquid.

He was reminded of a story: a donkey was drawing the chariot containing a god's image through the main street, and people on the road were showing respect to it by bowing down to the ground; the foolish donkey thought that what they were all honouring was itself.

Pramathanath said to himself, "I have only this difference with the donkey, that I have at last understood that the 'honour' was shown not to me but to the load I carry on my shoulders." As he came home he called the children and built up a sacrificial fire on which he dropped one by one all his western clothes, delighting the children who became more and more excited with joy as the flames rose. Pramathanath gave up sipping tea and breaking bread with the English after this, and once again he sat tight in the castle of his home. But the 'favoured' people who were dishonoured on the train still kept up bowing their turbans from one English door to another.

It must have been a matter of ill-luck that Nabendusekhar

somehow got married to Pramathanath's second daughter, Arunlekha. The girls of this family were educated and good looking; Nabendu thought himself a winner. But he lost no time in trying to prove that it was his in-laws who were fortunate in getting him. He began handing over to his sisters-in-law some letters he carried in his pockets – as if by mistake and purely by chance – and these were letters his father once got from some Englishman or other. The responses he got were sharp, mocking smiles that appeared between their soft lips, like shining swords in bright velvet sheaths, and the poor man became aware that these people were made of a different stuff. He understood that a mistake had been made.

The oldest of his sisters-in-law, Labanyalekha, was the most beautiful and accomplished of all. One auspicious day she placed a pair of boots, made in England, in an alcove in Nabendu's bedroom and decorated them with vermillion paste. She also put flowers, sandalwood paste, two lighted candles and burning incense in front of them. As soon as Nabendu entered the room two of his sisters-in-law took him by the ear and said, "Now, bow down to your favourite god, let its blessings help your promotion."

The third sister-in-law, Kironlekha, took a lot of trouble by stitching with red thread, a hundred current English names, such as Charles, Smith, Brown and Thomson on a piece of cloth and presented it to Nabendu with great ceremony. It was meant to be used as a covering for the upper part of his body, as one does a *chaddar*[1] with one hundred names of God written on it.

The fourth sister-in-law, Sasankalekha – not really to be counted yet because of her tender age – said, "Listen, I shall make a telling-bead for you to tell the names of sahibs". Her elder sisters reprimanded her, "Go away, you don't have to act so mature".

Nabendu would feel angry but, at the same time, ashamed. Nevertheless, he could not keep himself away from his

[1]See footnote[3] p. 7

sisters-in-law, particularly the oldest one, she was so beautiful. But she was as full of thorns as of honey, and Nabendu was gripped both by the fascination and the irritation she caused. He was like an insect with wounded wings, which makes a buzzing noise in anger, but although blind and senseless, still flutters around.

The intense fascination for the company of his sisters-in-law meant that in the end Nabendu had to disclaim all desire for the favour of English sahibs. On the day that he went to render his *salaam* to his sahib chief he told his sisters-in-law that he was going to listen to the lecture of Surendra Banerjee. When going to pay his respects to the sahib second-in-command who was returning from Darjeeling he told his sisters-in-law, "I am going to see my second uncle." With a foot in each boat – Englishmen and sisters-in-law – the poor man was in great trouble when the sisters-in-law resolved to sink one of them.

The rumour currently abroad was that Nabendu would step on to the first rung of the ladder to the title-heaven, Raibahadur, on the coming birthday of the Empress of India. But the poor coward couldn't disclose the ecstatic news of this possible honour to his sisters-in-law. However one evening of the bright fortnight[1] in the season of *sarat*[2], a malevolent moonlight filled him with passion, and driven by that force, he came out with the possibility of promotion to his wife. The next day she went to her elder sister, in a palanquin, and began lamenting about her husband in a tearful voice. Labanya consoled her, "What of it? Your husband is not going to acquire a tail if he becomes a Raibahadur." Arunlekha kept on repeating, "No *didi*[3], whatever else I have to be, I do not wish to become the wife of a Raibahadur". The reason why there was such a vigorous dislike of the title was that Bhutnathabu, an acquaintance of Arun, was a Raibahadur.

[1]See footnote[3] p. 16
[2]See footnote[1] p. 22
[3]See footnote p. 92

Labanya assured her, "Don't worry about it". Her husband, Nilratan, was working at Boxer and Nabendu received an invitation from Labanya to visit there at the end of the season. He at once started for Boxer with a delighted heart. His left limbs did not quiver at the time of boarding the train; this only proves that the idea that approaching danger is signalled by the quivering of one's left limbs is a baseless superstition.

Labanya, in the full bloom of her youth, was glittering with laughter and happiness, like the *kash* bush that grows on the lonely bank of a river in the unblemished season of *sarat*, and she appeared full of that light golden glow of health and beauty which the near approach of winter in the west of India brings with it.

A *madhabi*[1] creeper in full bloom began, as it were, showering in sprays the fresh dew that the touch of winter had brought about before the enchanted eyes of Nabendu.

Nabendu lost his indigestion in the pleasure that Labanya brought him and in the fresh air of the western provinces. He began to feel that he was walking on the sky rather than on the earth, such was his feeling of well-being provided by good health, by the enchantment of the beauty around him and by the delightful care that his sister-in-law took of him. And when the Ganges, brimming over, ran passionately in front of their garden with its rushing current, it seemed to reflect his own unruly and crazy feelings. He felt totally fulfilled as he returned from an early morning walk on the river bank in the soft sunlight of the winter morning, warm like a meeting with one's beloved. Labanya liked to do some fancy cooking and Nabendu volunteered to assist in this when back from his walk. He was quite green in such matters, but the inexpert fool showed no eagerness to pay attention and learn through practice. Rather, he could not have his fill of the mock censure and rebuke he received everyday because of his shortcomings. In matters like measuring difference spices, picking up a utensil from or

[1]See footnote p. 109.

115

putting one on to an open fire, taking care that the curry did not get burned, he was as helpless as a new-born babe; at least this was what he tried to prove with calculated design, enormously enjoying in the process the pitying and laughing censure that this provoked in his sister-in-law.

When it came to eating however, he found it hard to keep to any limit – such was the combined pressure of hunger, the cajoling and the eagerness of his sister-in-law in feeding him, and his own interest because of the excellence of the food and its graceful serving. Playing cards after lunch was another matter however, and Nabendu was no good at it. He would steal cards, have a peep at other hands, create noisy arguments, but he still could not win; nor did he admit it when he lost the game. He came in for a lot of criticism for all this but the sinner remained totally indifferent to correcting himself.

His transformation was complete only in one matter, he totally forgot for the moment that currying favour with a sahib was the highest aim of his life. He was savouring instead, with all his heart, the pleasure and pride that the affection and respect of his relations brought him.

In any case, he found himself in a different environment. Labanya's husband, Nilratanbabu, even though an important lawyer in the Court, never paid visits to any Englishman. If asked why, his answer was, "What is the good of it, tell me? If they do not show me courtesy in return, I cannot take back what I have already given. Is there any pleasure sowing seeds in the desert sand just because it is bright and white. If you wish for returns, seed is better sown in the black earth."

Nabendu was drawn into this group and was apparently no longer worried about what the result of it would be. The cultivation that he and his father had already achieved was thought to be enough towards his Raibahadur title and he felt there was no need for the moment to renew his efforts. The latest one had been the building of a race course, at enormous expense, in some town favoured by the English.

In the meanwhile, it was time for a meeting of the Congress party, and Nilratan was requested to collect donations. One day when Nabendu was playing cards with Labanya, in total peace of mind, Nilratan suddenly appeared with a pledge form in his hand and said, "You have to sign here." Nabendu's latent ambitions came to the surface and instantly his face went pale. Labanya said in a great hurry, "Careful, don't you do it, your race-course will then come to nothing." Nabendu was unable to do anything but brag, "Yes, I can't sleep for fear of it."

Nilratan assured him that his name would not appear in any paper. Labanya looking wise and apprehensive said, "Still, why do it? Who knows – someone may spill the beans." Nabendu rejoined rather sharply, "If that happens, I don't think that my name will go to waste." Then he forced the paper from Nilratan's hands and signed for a thousand rupees, hoping in his heart of hearts that his name would not come out in the papers. Labanya, her head in her hands, said with apparent despair, "What have you done?" Nabendu replied with a show of pride, "Why, what's wrong with it?"

Labanya observed, "The guard at the Sealdah station, the assistant at the shop, White Ab, the coachman at Hart Bros., suppose these people get annoyed, suppose it hurts their sensitive souls and they stop drinking champagne with you during the Pujas or no longer slap you cordially on the back!" Nabendu replied with some vehemence, "If that happens I shall have to go home and die in shame."

A few days later Nabendu was reading the newspaper at breakfast when it suddenly came to his notice that a letter writer, signed X, had thanked him profusely for his donation to the Congress, expressing inability to measure the strength that was added to the Congress through having someone like him join the party.

Adding to the strength of the Congress! Alas for the departed father Purnendusekhar, was this your purpose, adding strength to the Congress, in bringing this wretched man into being, in this land of India?

But there was some consolation too. Nabendu was not a negligible person. The British community on the one hand and the Congress on the other were spreading their nets and sitting with a fixed gaze to catch him for their own. This was not information to be kept secret, so Nabendu laughingly showed the paper to Labanya. She pretended not to know who had written the letter and said, "Oh, dear, this has disclosed all; dear, dear, who do you have for an enemy? May his pen be destroyed by white ants, his ink fill up with sand, his paper get eaten by worms..." Nabendu said smilingly, "Don't curse any more. I forgive my enemy and bless him; may he get a golden inkstand and pen."

A paper, edited by an Englishman, which belonged to a group opposed to the Congress, came into the hands of Nabendu through the post in course of the next two days. He found there a protest by someone, under the signature, "One who knows", against the news about Nabendu. The writer said that those who knew Nabendu could never believe this scandalous news about him. It was as impossible for Nabendu to add to the strength of the Congress as it was for the leopard to change its spots. Babu Nabendukumar was a person of means, he was not an unemployed supplicant, or a briefless lawyer. He was not one of those who had gone to England for a short while, copied the dress, the manners and customs of the English, tried with impudence to enter their society and having failed, returned disappointed. Why then should he be..." etc. etc.

We call on you, his late father Purnendusekhar, you did not die until you made a name amongst the English and got their trust in ample measure!

This letter was also worthy of being displayed like a peacock's tail before his sister-in-law. There was some valuable suggestion here, that Nabendu was not unknown, unworthy and poverty-stricken; he was a man of substance.

Labanya again showed absolute surprise and asked, "Which one of your great friends has written this, which ticket collector or dealer in hide or musician in a band?"

118

Nilratan said, "You ought to protest against this letter."

Nabendu assumed a superior pose, saying, "Well, one does not have to protest against everything that is said." Labanya's response to this was loud laughter which spread like the current of a stream in springtime. Embarrassed, Nabendu asked, "What makes you laugh so much?" But she continued laughing with an irrepressible force, rocking her beautiful body back and forth.

Nabendu was put out of countenance, by this laughter which was springing at him, as it were, from all directions. Defensively, he asked, "Do you think that I am afraid to protest?"

Labanya replied, "No, no, I was only thinking that you haven't yet given up trying to save the race-course you once pinned your hopes on; and of course, one hopes as long as one breathes." Nabendu protested, "That's not why I did not wish to write." Angered, he sat down with pen and paper; but his writing did not show much sign of passion.

So Labanya and Nilratan took upon themselves the responsibility of redressing this, and the resultant affair looked like the sharing-out of the task of cooking *nan*[1]. As if Nabendu mixed the dough in water and clarified butter, made it cool and soft, and then rolled out the pastry, as flat as possible, which was in turn, fried by his two associates and turned into something hot, crisp and puffed. The writing asserted: when one's own people becomes one's enemy, they turn out to be much more dangerous than an outside foe. The Pathan or the Russian is not as much an enemy of the Government of India as the conceited Anglo-Indian community. They constitute an impenetrable barrier to the creation of a secure and friendly relationship between the Government and the people. The Anglo-Indian papers are obstructing the broad highway now opened to effect a good and lasting relationship between Congress, Government and the ordinary masses.

[1]Puffed bread

119

Nabendu felt full of misgivings, but now and again also a little pleased that the writing had turned out so full of spice. It was beyond his capability to have produced anything like that.

For days afterwards, debates, questions and counter questions appeared in various papers, declaring, as if with a drum, the topic of Nabendu's donation and the likelihood of his joining the Congress. Nabendu, desperate by now, turned himself into a fearless nationalist when in the company of his sister-in-law. Labanya smiled to herself, and said "You haven't yet gone through the test of fire."

One morning, Nabendu, in preparation for his bath, had massaged oil in his breast and was trying out a tactic to rub it on an inaccessible part of his back, when the bearer brought him a card on which was printed the name of the Magistrate. Labanya was watching the fun, in secret, with a curious smile.

One couldn't see the Magistrate with a body drenched in oil, and Nabendu became harassed and fretful – like a spiced *kai* fish before being fried. He took his bath in a great hurry, put on his clothes anyhow and controlling his breathlessness, appeared as fast as he could in the outside lounge. The bearer told him, "The sahib left after waiting a long time." It would be a subtle problem in mathematics to work out how much of the blame attached to this out-and-out lie belonged to the bearer, and how much to Labanya.

Like a common lizard without its tail, Nabendu's distressed mind began blindly shifting and throwing itself about with force inside him. He found no ease all day in whatever he did. Labanya erased all traces of amusement from her face, and assuming an anxious attitude, asked him from time to time, "What's the matter with you today, you are not feeling unwell?" Nabendu smiled with some effort and somehow managed to find a suitable reply, "How can I be ill within your domain, you are my master physician."

But soon his smile faded and he began wondering, "I have contributed to the Congress, to start with, then written a strong letter to the paper, and to cap it all, kept the Magistrate himself waiting when he came to see me; what mightn't he be thinking? Oh! my dear father, Purnendu-sekhar, I have proved myself to be other than I am through a sheer muddle of fate."

Nabendu was going out the next day; he had dressed with care, his watch chain hanging from his pocket and a big turban on his head. Labanya asked him, "Where are you going?" Nabendu replied, "Oh, I have some business to see to." She pressed no more.

As soon as he showed his card at the door of the Magistrate's house, the orderly said, "You can't see him now." Nabendu brought out two rupees from his pocket. The orderly said, "There are five of us". Instantly Nabendu produced a ten rupee note. The sahib called him. He was busy doing his paper-work in his dressing gown and slippers. Nabendu did his *salaam*, the Magistrate gave him permission to sit down with a gesture of his fingers, and without raising his head from the papers said, "Say what you have to say, Babu."

Twirling his pocket chain Nabendu said in a shaky and submissive voice, "Sir, you were so kind as to come yourself to my place yesterday to see me, but . . ."

The sahib frowned, and lifting one of his eyes from the papers barked, "To see you? You are talking nonsense." Perspiring, Nabendu somehow managed to make an exit saying, "I beg your pardon, Sir, my mistake." In bed that night a sentence kept coming back to him like some incantation heard in a far distant dream, "Babu, you are a howling idiot."

Nabendu had surmised, as he came away from the Magistrate's place, that the Magistrate was angry, and that was why he had declined to admit that he had visited him. This thought made him wish that the earth would open up and swallow him. But the earth paid no heed to him and he reached home safely.

The excuse he gave Labanya was that he had gone to buy

rose-water to send home. Before he had finished talking, six flunkeys in the uniform of the Collector's office appeared, offered their *salaams* and stood smiling in silence. Labanya said with a smile, "I hope that they haven't come to arrest you for contributing to the Congress fund."

The six flunkeys showed twelve rows of teeth and said, "Bakshis, Babusaheb". Annoyed, Nilratan came out of the next room and asked, "Bakshis for what?"

The bearers still showing their teeth said, "Bakshis for the visit Babu paid to the Magistrate." Labanya laughed, "Has the Magistrate started selling rose-water? He was never one for such a refreshing business before."

Nobody could understand what nonsense the wretched Nabendu uttered, trying to produce a coherent relation between rose water and a visit to the Magistrate. Nilratan rebuffed the flunkeys, "Nothing has been achieved that deserves bakshis, you won't get any." Diffidently Nabendu brought out a note from his pocket and said, "They are poor, no harm in giving them something." Nilratan took the note from Nabendu's hands and said, "There are poorer human beings in this world. I shall give it to them."

Nabendu found himself in the position of not being able to appease even in some measure, the attendants of the enraged god Siva. When the flunkeys were about to leave, casting thunderous eyes on Nabendu, he looked at them dolefully as if silently pleading, "Please, chaps, do not hold it against me, you know how it is."

The Congress session was being held in Calcutta and Nilratan arrived at the Capital with his wife to attend it. Nabendu too returned with them. The moment he arrived the members of the Congress party surrounded him, giving him a frenzied reception. There was no limit to the honour, felicitation and praise heaped on him. Everyone said, "Our country cannot be saved unless leaders like you join the task of freeing it." Nabendu could not but agree with the fittingness of the remark and somehow in the midst of the tumult he found himself to have become a leader. When he arrived where the meeting was being held, everyone stood up in a body and welcomed him, furiously chanting the foreign, indeed English, words – hip, hip, hoorah! The ears of the Motherland became red to their tips in shame.

The birthday of the Empress of India arrived in due time and Nabendu's Raibahadur title, that had seemed almost within reach, vanished like a mirage.

The same evening, Labanyalekha beckoned Nabendu with great ceremony, dressed him in new clothes and put a mark of red sandal paste on his forehead with her own finger, while each one of the sisters-in-law placed a garland, made with their own hands, on his neck. Arunlekha sparkled behind the scene with a shy mile in a red sari, adorned with her ornaments. Her sisters tried to pull her in, placing a garland in her cold and bashful hands, but she did not yield to the pressure. That most important of all garlands waited in privacy, encircling Nabendu's neck at night when there would be no crowd around.

The sisters-in-law said to Nabendu, "We have made you a king today. There is no one else in India who is enjoying this honour."

Only Nabendu's own heart and his indwelling deity knew whether this provided sufficient solace for him. We, on our part, remain doubtful on this matter. We believe that he is still firmly set on becoming a Raibahadur before he dies, and that his death will not fail to be mourned in one voice by both the *Englishman* and the *Pioneer*. So, in the meanwhile, three cheers for babu Purnendusekhar. Hip, hip, hoorah! Hip, hip, hoorah!

My Neighbour

My neighbour was a girl-widow, like a dew-washed *saphali*[1] flower fallen from its stalk on a morning of the season of *sarat.*[2] She was not made for a flower-bedecked bridal suite, she had been consecrated solely for use in the adoration of God.

I used to worship her in my mind. What my feeling towards her was I do not wish to express by any other clearly understood term but "worship" – certainly not to others – and not even to myself. I revealed none of this even to my most intimate and dear friend Nabinmadhab.

I used to feel a measure of pride in being able to keep the deepest passion of my heart so secret and pure. But like a mountain spring, passionate feelings do not want to remain confined within their birthplace; they seek to break out by some means or other, and if unsuccessful, create agony in one's heart. That's why I was considering letting my feelings out through poetry. But my unsure pen did not get very far.

An exceedingly surprising thing was that, at the very same time, the inclination to write poetry possessed my friend Nanimadhab with great force, like a sudden earthquake.

The poor man's fate hadn't played him up like this before. So he was not the least prepared for this novel agitation

[1]See footnote[3] p. 48
[2]See footnote[1] p. 22

within. He didn't have any skill in the matter of rhythm or rhyme but this didn't put him off, I was surprised to see. Poetry got hold of him like a young second wife of an old man. So Nabinmadhab had recourse to me for help and correction of his lines.

The subject matter of his poems was not new, but it wasn't old either. That is, one could say it was ever old or ever new – love poems for the beloved. I gave him a push and asked with a smile, "Tell me, who is she?"

Nabin smiled in response saying, "I haven't found her yet."

I felt comfortable in being able to help such a novice writer. I used my own suppressed passion for Nabin's imaginery beloved. As a hen deprived of a chick will sit incubating a duck egg, ill-starred I sat pressing on Nabinmadhab's feelings with all the warmth of my heart. I began correcting his immature writings with such enthusiasm that nearly ninety per cent of these turned out as my contribution, in actual fact.

Surprised Nabin asked, "How do you do it? This is exactly what I want to say but am unable to do."

I replied like a poet, "By imagination. You see truth is silent, imagination is highly vocal. Facts sit on feelings like the deadweight of stones, but imagination frees them."

Nabin considered this for a while with a solemn face, and said, "That's what I find, it is true." He thought a bit more and reiterated, "You are right."

I have already said that there was a melancholy diffidence in my loving, so I could not write as myself. I had to put Nabin as a screen in-between, then only could my pen be released. It acquired flavour and heat, and was boiling over. Nabin said, "This is really your writing; let me publish it in your name."

I said, "No, no, it is your writing, all I have done is to change it a little."

In time Nabin came to think so too.

As an astronomer keeps looking at the sky in the hope of a

rising star I looked at the window next door from time to time – I cannot deny this. Now and again that anxious gaze of a worshipper was successful. From the dignified face of that *sannyasini*[1], practising the yoga of work, reflected a benign, serene light and all my agony was appeased, instantly.

But suddenly, I was alerted. Did volcanic eruptions still occur in the land of the moon? Was it that all the burning in that meditative lonely mountain cave had not yet been extinguished?

The *Vaishakh*[2] afternoon cloud gathered in the north-east. In that cloud-dispersed stern light of the approaching storm my neighbour was standing alone by the window and I noticed in her deep, black eyes a far-reaching depth of torment.

Yes, there was still heat in my land of the moon. Warm breathing took place there even now. She was not for God, she was for man.

The immense anguish of her two eyes that day had taken to its wings like an eager bird in that stormy light, moving not towards heaven but a nest in some human heart.

It became very hard for me to keep my perturbed heart under control after I had seen her eager eyes lit by desire. It was no longer satisfying just to correct someone else's green writings – I felt an urge to do something.

I resolved to engage all my powers in the work of making remarriage for widows an acceptable custom in Bengal. Not just lecturing and writing, I went forward with financial help.

Nabin started arguing with me. He said, "There is a sacred peace in lifelong widowhood, an immense charm like a place of contemplation lit by the feeble light of the moon on the eleventh day of its fortnight. Doesn't this disappear as one opens up the possibility of remarriage?"

[1]Woman who has renounced all wordly goods
[2]Month in Summer (April/May)

I used to get angry to hear such poetic nonsense. How does it feel if, to a worn out man dying of famine, one preaches hatred for the grossness of food, advocating filling up his belly with scent of flowers and song of birds?

I said with annoyance, "You see Nabin, aesthetes say that there is a certain beauty in the sight of a ruined house. But a house is not a picture, one has to live in it. So, whatever an artist says, repair is necessary. You want to wax poetic from a distance on the subject of widowhood, but you ought to remember that inside that a desiring human heart lives with its very particular kind of misery."

I thought that I would never be able to get Nabin on my side, the reason why I talked with some extra heat that day. But when I had finished I found him accepting all I said with a deep sigh; he did not even give me scope to say a few more worthy words I had assembled.

In a week Nabin came and said, "If you help, I am willing to marry a widow."

I was so pleased I hugged him to my bosom and said, "I shall give you all the money you require." Nabin told me his history then. I saw that his beloved was not imaginary. He had fallen in love with a widow from a distance, but hadn't told anyone about it. The monthly journals in which Nabin's – in other words my – poems appeared reached her and the poems did not go in vain. My friend had found this means of attracting a heart without so much as a meeting. According to Nabin he had not planned these tactics. He even believed, so he said, that the widow was illiterate. He used to send those journals, free, to her brother, without mentioning names. This was merely a crazy way of getting some satisfaction; he felt that he was simply giving offerings of flowers to a deity; no matter whether she knew or accepted them or not.

According to Nabin again, the fact that he had managed to get acquainted with her brother was not in any way motivated. But if you loved someone the company of her near relations was agreeable.

It is a long story how a meeting with the sister took place and the agency through which this was accomplished was a severe illness of the brother. A first-hand knowledge of the theme of those poems and the presence of the poet himself had produced a lot of discussion; discussion was not confined to those few printed poems either.

When Nabin lost in argument with me, he had gone to the widow and proposed marriage. At first she did not agree. Nabin then used all my arguments and mixing these with a few tears had quite conquered her. Now, the guardian, the widow's uncle, wanted some money. I said, "Take it now."

Nabin said, "Apart from this, my father is sure to stop my allowance for a few months after I marry. You must arrange for our expenses in those days."

I signed a cheque then and there, without question. Then I asked him, "Now tell me her name. There is no fear as I am not in competition with you. I promise, on your body, that I shall not write a poem in her name and if I do I shall send it to you rather than to the brother."

Nabin said, "Of course, I have no such fear. She is very touchy about remarrying as a widow; that's why she forbade my discussing her with you or any one else. But it is not necessary to be secretive any more. She is your neighbour, lives at number sixteen."

If my heart was an iron boiler it would have burst, instantly, with a bang. I asked him, "She is not against widow remarriage?"

Nabin laughed, "Not any more."

I asked, "So enchanted just by reading those poems?"

Nabin replied, "Why, those poems of mine were quite good."

I said in my mind "Shame!"

Shame to whom? Her, me or fate?

But shame, all the same.

Number One

I do not even smoke. I have a gigantic addiction that killed off all other addictions at their root. That is my addiction for books. My guiding light lay in this *mantra*:

As long as you are alive, it does not matter how you do,
Make sure you read books;
When no money for it, borrow.

As some people who fancy travelling but have no wherewithal to do so, read timetables instead, I used to read catalogues of books in my days of penury. An uncle-in-law of my elder brother used to buy all Bengali books (without consideration of cost or quality) as soon as they were published, and was enormously proud of the fact that he hadn't lost even one of them, ever. Perhaps nobody else in Bengal is blessed with such good fortune. It happens to be the case that of all the things in this world – money, age, the umbrella of an absentminded person – that are influenced by momentum, a Bengali book is the most susceptible in that direction. One can easily understand from this that the uncle-in-law's book-case was not easy of access – even to the aunt-in-law. When I used to go with my brother to his in-laws I would spend a great deal of time gazing devoutly at these locked book-cases, rather like a humble man paying his visit to royalty. Greed would shine from my eyes. Enough to say that from childhood, I read so many books that I failed my examinations. I had no time to do the kind of selective reading needed to pass them.

A great advantage to one like me – an examination failure – was that I did not have to confine myself to the measured doses of information doled out by university text books; I could let go and swim in the sea of learning itself. These days some M.As and B.As pay me visits, but however much they may belong to the modern age, their perspective is confined within the limits of the Victoria era. Like Ptolemy's out-moded explanation of the Earth, their world of learning is limited to the eighteenth/nineteenth century; as if the students of Bengal, and after them, their grand children, would revolve for ever around that time. The carriage in which they take their mental ride has with difficulty gone past Mill and Bentham, and is now tilting on one side with Carlyle and Ruskin. They cannot venture out for a walk beyond the fence erected by their masters' utterances.

But the literature of the country which we are using as a stake to which to tie our minds down and ruminate, is not something static; it is moving with life itself. I may not enjoy that life but at least I am trying to follow that movement. I taught myself French, German, Italian and have now been learning Russian for some time. You can see that I have bought a ticket for the express train of the modern age, running at sixty miles an hour. This is the reason why I haven't got stuck with Huxley and Darwin, am not afraid to criticise Tennyson, or why I abhor the established custom of seeking easy fame by riding on the back of Ibsen and Metterlink in our monthly journal.

It was beyond my dreams that people would one day seek me out and recognize my worth, but I find, contrary to expectation (or lack of it), that there are one or two young men in Bengal who, while continuing with their college education, also respond to the call of the goddess *Saraswati*'s[1] music that plays outside their college precinct. A few of

[1]Goddess of learning and fine arts

these, by and by, began gathering together in my room as a group.

So I developed my second addiction – lecturing. You could call it 'discussion' if you wanted to be polite. I find our literature, modern and not so modern, on the one hand quite green and on the other so hackneyed that I feel like dispelling its stifling and sweaty stuffiness by letting the fresh air of free thinking blow over it. However, I was too lazy to write, and was therefore naturally relieved to meet up with people who listen to a talk with attention.

The size of the group was growing. My name is Advaitacharan (*advaita* meaning non-duality) and our group somehow got named the *dvaitadvaitya* (duality in non-duality) society. No-one in our society had any sense of time. One of them would appear in the morning with a newly published English book in hand, using a punched tram ticket as a book mark, arguments with him would continue till one o'clock without reaching any conclusion. Someone else would arrive in the afternoon with an exercise book containing his college notes, and he would not consider leaving, even at two in the morning. Often I asked them to dine with me, as I have found that those who delve in litrature possess the power to relish the flavour of things not only through their brains but also through their palates. It was too inconsequential a matter for me to consider how the person who had to arrange it all fared, when I asked these hungry men to dinner whenever I liked. How could I have any eye for domestic affairs, or the kitchen fire, when I was so busy with the huge potter's wheel of learning and feeling, which was constantly creating some of human civilisation on the one hand – and then through firing making it strong and durable – and on the other, demolishing something else before it had a chance to harden.

I have read in literature that only the God Siva knows the meaning of the Goddess' frown. But then he had three yes; I had but two and even these had lost a lot of their power through constant use. So the signs of disturbance that appeared between the eyebrows of my wife when I asked her to provide dinner at an untimely hour were not something I noticed. Gradually she came to understand that in my household the untimely was timely and irregularity the regular thing. Not only that, time was out of step in my family and the whole set-up suffered from neglect. Whatever means I possessed went through one open drain, that of book-buying. How the other necessities of life were met – they were like a greedy native dog maintaining itself on the left-overs of my foreign pet, this addiction of mine – was something that was known more by my wife than by me.

Someone like me has a particular need to indulge in talking about many different things in the field of learning. Not to show off one's knowledge, but to help others. This is just a way of thinking through talking – an exercise through which to digest knowledge. If I were an author or a professor this kind of exercise would have been unnecessary. Those who do regular physical labour do not have to look for ways to digest their food – those who are of a sedentary nature must at least take a brisk walk on the roof. I am of the latter kind. When my "duality" group had not yet been formed the only duality was provided by my wife. She had borne, silently and over a long time, this noisy process of my mental digestion. Although she could afford only cheap mill-made saries and her ornaments were not of genuine solid gold, whatever "discussions" she heard from me – be they eugenics, Mendelian law or mathematical logic – had nothing cheap or adulterated in them. After my group increased in size she was deprived of all these discussions; but I never heard her complain.

My wife is called 'Anila'. What this word means I do not know and I do not believe that my father-in-law knew either. It sounds pleasant and one somehow feels at first hearing that it must mean something. Whatever the dictionary says, the real meaning of the name is that my wife was her father's favourite daughter. When my mother-in-law died, leaving a two-and-a-half year old son, my father-in-law married again, considering that to be a suitable way of providing care for the young child. You can guess how successful this was if I let it be known that two days before his death, he took hold of Anila's hands and said, "My dear, I am leaving, there is nobody left to think about Saroj other than you." I do not really know what provision he made for his second wife or her children, but he placed his savings of seven and half thousand rupees, in cash, in Anila's hands and said, "You should not use this for earning interest; spend this to arrange for Saroj's education."

I was rather amazed at this. My father-in-law was not only intelligent, he was wise. That is, he generally acted not on impulse but calculation; so it was on me rather than anyone else he should have placed the responsibility of having his son educated – I feel no doubt on this score. But I cannot tell how he figured that his daughter was a more suitable person than his son-in-law. Yet, had he not known me to be absolutely honest in money matters he couldn't have placed so much money in cash in my wife's hands. In fact, he was a philistine of the Victorian age and did not quite manage to recognize the worth of someone like me.

At first I was very annoyed and resolved not to say anything at all on the subject. I kept silent and believed that Anila would have to broach the subject with me since she had no alternative but to seek my help. But when she did not come asking for my advice I thought to myself that this might be timidity on her part. So one day during conversation I asked, "What are you doing about Saroj's education?" She replied, "I have engaged a tutor; he is going to school as well." I hinted that I was quite prepared to take on myself the burden of tutoring Saroj. I even tried to instruct her in some of the new teaching methods recently in vogue. Anila said neither 'yes' nor 'no' and for the first time I suspected that she had no respect for me. Perhaps it was the fact that I hadn't passed a college examination that made her think I had no expertise or any rights in the matter. I was now sure that she had not understood anything of evolutionary eugenics or radio waves I had talked to her about for so long. She probably believed that even a boy in second grade knew more than that. The reason? Their learning (unlike mine) gets fixed in their minds through the repeated twisting of their ears by their teacher. Vexed, I said to myself that those who have only intelligence and knowledge, but no degree, must give up all hope of proving their worth to women.

In real life, most dramas are revealed when the scenery is suddenly drawn back at the end of the fifth act. When I was busy discussing Bergsonian theory and Ibsenian psychology with my "dualities" I had assumed that no fire at all had been lit at the altar of Anila's life. But when, today, I look back to those past days, I can see quite clearly that the creator, who through firing and hammering creates the real images of life, was very much alive and alert at the centre of Anila's life. A play was constantly in progress, with strokes and counter-strokes, involving an elder sister, a brother and a step-mother. The earth which is said to be held up by the snake Vasuki in the *Puranas*[1] is steady; but for the woman, who has to carry a world of turmoil within, her world is constantly created anew through continual upheavals. Who but the indwelling spirit would know what goes on inside someone who has to move through the daily necessities of domestic life, nursing injuries in motion? At least I understood nothing of it, I never got to know the agony, the humiliating exertions, the inner worries of distressed affection taking place right next to me behind a screen of silence. I used to think that the day when my "duality" group had to be fed, with its many preparations, was the most eventful one in Anila's life. Today I knew for certain that it was through the experience of great pain that her younger brother had become the most intimate person in her life. I had not bothered to look at this aspect of her life because she had totally ignored the need for my advice and

[1]Religious myths and legends

help in bringing Saroj up. Nor had I ever asked how things were shaping in this respect.

In the meanwhile the first house along in our lane acquired a tenant – we lived in the second house. The first house had been built in an earlier age, in the days of the famous and rich trader Uddhab Boral. Within two generations the wealth of the family was exhausted, and its members were depleted too, leaving only one or two surviving widows. They didn't live there, so the house took on an air of abandonment. From time to time people rented it for a few days on the occasion of a marriage or for similar ceremonies, otherwise a house of that size had little hope of finding a tenant. The person who rented it this time – say his name is Sitangshumouli and let us assume that he is the landlord of Norottampur[1]. I would probably have known nothing about the arrival of such an important person next door to me – for like Karna, born with armour on him, I too possessed a god-given defence – my habitual absent-mindedness. This armour of mine is very thick and durable; so I had a way of saving myself from all those pushings and pullings, and from the noise and abuse that goes around all over the place in this world of ours.

Rich people of this age constitute something more than a natural disturbance; the disturbance they create is unnatural. Those who have two hands, two legs and one head are human beings. But those who suddenly acquire extra hands, legs and heads are demons. They constantly and noisily break out of the limits of their domain, and with their excesses, unsettle both heaven and earth. It is impossible not to let one's attention wander to them. Those to whom nobody really needs pay any attention – and yet nobody can escape doing it when they are around – constitute the ill-health of the world. Even Indra[2] goes in fear of them.

I realised that Sitangshumouli was a man of this kind. I

[1]Village in Bengal.
[2]The King of gods

135

never knew before that just one man by himself could constitute such an excess. With his carriage, horses, servants and retinue, he had started to play a part, as it were, of someone with ten heads and twenty hands. So with the various vexations created by him the barricade I had built around my heaven-like world of knowledge began crumbling bit by bit.

My first acquaintance with him was at the turn of our lane. The great virtue of this lane hitherto was that someone unmindful like me, could saunter around here without a look forwards or backwards and without the least attention to one's right or left. While walking here one could even carry on internal debates on Meredith's stories, Browning's poetry or on some writing by one of our Bengali poets, and still escape death by accident. But the other day I suddenly heard a loud noise, 'heio' and turning, found a pair of red horses drawing an open Brougham nearly on top of me. The owner of the carriage was driving – his coachman alongside – and was pulling the reins forcefully with both hands. I somehow saved myself, clutching on to a corner of a tobacco shop by the side of the road. I noticed his annoyance with me. Those who drive carelessly cannot by any means forgive a careless pedestrian, for this reason – the pedestrian has got only two legs, he is an ordinary man; but the man who drives a carriage has eight feet, he is a demon. By this unnatural excess he creates mischief. The god of the two-legged man was not prepared for this unexpected eight-leggedness.

By the healthy law of nature I would have forgotten, in time, both the chariot and its driver, for in our wonderful world they are not particularly memorable things. But the natural allowance each man has to make trouble is forcefully exceeded by these demon people. So although I could manage to remain unaware of my number three neighbour for days and months, it became difficult to forget my number one neighbour even for a moment. The non-musical beats his eight horses' hooves made on the wooden floor of the stable at night dispersed my sleep all over the place. On top of that, when his numerous grooms noisily massaged his numerous horses in the morning, it became difficult to remain civil, and then neither his servants from Orissa and Bihar, nor his doorkeepers from Uttar Pradesh, cared to restrain their voices or practise economy in speech. And that is why I said that there was only one man, but one who possessed many avenues for creating disturbances – the sign of a demon. All these factors may not have created any hindrance to his own peace; perhaps Ravan's sleep never used to be disturbed when he snored with his twenty nostrils, but think of his poor neighbours. The most important feature of heaven is its graceful balance, but what marked the demons who destroyed its garden was excess and lack of measure. Now an unbalanced demon, riding on its bag of money, had invaded human habitation. Even if I wished to pass it by, it breathed on my neck with its four horses, and not content with that, delivered a dire warning.

My "dualities" had not yet arrived that afternoon. I was sitting, reading a book on the theory of ebb and tide, when over the wall of our house and through its gate arrived evidence of the presence of my neighbour, falling on my window-pane with a clatter. It was a tennis ball. For all the gravitational force of the moon, the waves of the earth, the eternal rhythm of the poem that is the universe, I was reminded of the fact that I had a neighbour. He was too much there, and although he was quite unnecessary to my existence he was still there – inevitably. The next moment my old bearer, Adodhya, arrived, running and gasping. I have only this one servant. He is often missing when I call him and he remains unperturbed when I shout. If I should ask why he is so elusive his answer would be that he is only one man with a lot of work to do. But that day, without being urged, he picked up the ball and ran towards next door. I came to know that each time he picked up a run-away ball he was rewarded for his labours by four pennies.

So it was not just my window pane or my peace that was

being shattered, the minds of my followers and my servants were being affected too. It was not particularly surprising that my bearer, Ayodhya, was getting more and more snooty about my meagre means – but most importantly the mind of the leader of my "duality" group, Kanailal, was getting increasingly drawn towards next door. I was hitherto convinced that his devotion to me was a matter of heart and that he was immune to the lure of mundane values; but then I noticed that he had overtaken Ayodhya and was running towards next door with the retrieved tennis ball. I realised that it was an excuse for striking up an acquaintance with my neighbour. I had a suspicion that his mental disposition was far from that of Maitreyi, the seeker after Brahma knowledge; he could not be fed just on immortality.

I used to banter in a most penetrating manner against the luxuries of Number One, saying, "To try to conceal the emptiness of one's mind with dresses and embellishments is like the futile attempt to cover up the whole sky with coloured clouds. A little wind removes the cloud and the sky is seen through the gap." Once Kanailal protested, "The man is not that empty, he has passed his B.A." Kanailal himself was a B.A., so I could hardly say anything against that degree.

The main virtues of Number One were sound-based. He could play three instruments, cornet, *esraj*[1] and cello, and I am reminded of that every now and then. I have no pretensions about being an expert on music or melodies, but I do not find it an art of the superior variety. When man was dumb and without language, singing evolved – man shouted because he could not talk; even today primitive man loves to make noise – for no reason at all. But I couldn't fail to notice that there were at least four young men amongst my "duality" group who couldn't concentrate even on the latest findings of mathematical logic when the cello played next

[1]Stringed instrument played with a bow.

door. When quite a few of my group were leaning in this direction, Anila said to me one day, "A troublesome element has arrived next door to us. Let's leave this house and find something else."

I was extremely pleased. I told my group, "You see how women have an easy, intuitive facility. Although they cannot comprehend things that have to be established by proof, their understanding can easily get hold of things that do not need it." Kanailal laughed, "Like ghosts, the high potency of the dust from a Brahmin's feet, the merit acquired by worshipping one's husband and the like." I countered, "No, no, you see we are quite taken in by the ostentatious pomp of Number One; not so Anila."

Anila urged me about changing our residence two or three times. I wanted to, but lacked the perseverence needed to look for a house in the lanes and by-lanes of Calcutta. In the end I found that Kanai and Satish were playing tennis next door. There was hear-say evidence that between Jati and Haren, one played the harmonium and the other the tabla[1] in the musical soirées at Number One and that Arun had made a name for himself by singing comic songs there. I had known these people for the last five or six years and had never suspected that they possessed these virtues. I believed, in particular, that Arun's main interest lay in comparative religion. How could I guess that he was an expert in comic songs!

Truth to tell, however much I openly despised Number One I was jealous of him. I can think, judge, extract the inner essence of all things, can solve big problems – so it was impossible to consider Sitangshumouli my equal in mental riches. In spite of all this I was jealous of the man. If I disclose why it will make people laugh. In the morning Sitangshu went riding on a powerful horse which he controlled with fantastic skill. I used to see this every day and think, "I wish I could ride like that, with such ease, in control." These skills

[1]A drum

were something that were totally lacking in me, and the reason why I was secretly greedy about them. I do not know much about music but often, in secret, saw Sitangshu playing his *esraj* – and his command of the instrument, unhindered, graceful, appeared to me of uncommon attraction. I used to think that the instrument was in love with him, like a beloved woman, and had voluntarily surrendered all its melody to him. Sitangshu's effortless possession of things, buildings, animals, human beings created around him a scene that was full of charm – it was really something indefinable, and I could not but believe it to be rather rare. I used to think, "It is unnecessary for this man to ask for anything in the world, all things will come to him of their own accord; wherever he wishes to sit down he will find a seat already set for him."

So when, one by one, quite a few of my "dualities" began playing tennis or music in Number One, I could find no means of recovering these tempted men other than a change of residence. An estate agent brought the information that a likeable house was available near Baranagar-Kashipore. I agreed. It was then half past nine in the morning and I went looking for my wife to ask her to get ready. She was not in the store room, nor in the kitchen. I found her sitting silently with her head resting on the bar of a window. She got up as soon as she saw me. I said, "We could move to a new house the day after tomorrow." She said, "Wait for a fortnight."

"Why?", I asked. Anila replied, "The result of Saroj's examination will soon be out. I am very anxious about it, and don't feel like moving for these few days."

Among the other matters this was one thing which I never discussed with my wife. So moving house was postponed for a while. In the meanwhile I heard that Sitangshu was going on a tour of south India, so the huge shadow over Number Two would be removed.

The end of the fifth act of an unseen drama suddenly became visible. My wife went to her father's place yesterday. When she came back today she entered her room and closed the door behind her. She knew that the moonlight feast of our "duality" group was going to be held tonight. I knocked at her door to discuss the menu with her. There was no response for a while. I called to her, "Anu". She opened the door after a time. I asked her, "Do you have everything ready for cooking tonight?"

She moved her head to indicate that she had, but did not speak. I said, "Don't forget they particularly relish your fish-kachuri and hog-plum chutney."

When I came to the outer quarters I found Kanailal waiting. I said, "Kanai, you should all come a bit early today". Surprised he asked, "Why, are we going to have a meeting today?" I said, "Certainly. Everything is ready, the new stories from Maxim Gorky, Russell's criticism of Bergson, even fish-kachuri and hog-plum chutney."

Stunned Kanai kept looking at me. Finally he said, "Advaitababu I suggest leaving it for today."

At last I discovered by questioning him that my brother-in-law committed suicide yesterday afternoon. He failed his examination and the resulting upbraiding from his step-mother was so severe that, unable to bear it, he died by hanging himself with his own *chaddar*.[1]

I asked, "Where did you hear all this?"

He said, "From Number One".

Number One! This is how it all happened. When towards the evening information reached Anila, instead of waiting at home for a carriage, she went out with Ayodhya and, hiring one from the road, went to her father's place. When Sitargshumouli heard this from Ayodhya he went there immediately, managed to deal with the police and arranged for the burning of the body. He was even present at the cremation ground himself.

I went to the inner quarters with anxious steps. I thought that Anila must have taken to her own room, to be behind

[1]See footnote[3] p. 7

closed doors. But instead I found her sitting in the verandah in front of the store room, making preparations for hog-plum chutney. I realised from one look at her face that in this one night, her whole life had turned upside down. I said in an accusing tone, "Why didn't you tell me anything?" She just stared at me with her big eyes but said nothing. I felt very small and full of shame. If Anila had said, "What good would that have done?" I could have found nothing to say in reply. All these upsets of life – sorrows and happiness – I know nothing about how to deal with them. I persisted, "Anil, leave all this, we won't have a meeting today."

Keeping her attention riveted on the work of peeling hog-plums Anila replied, "Why, it must be held, I have arranged all this, I can't let it all go to waste."

I said, "No, it is impossible to hold a meeting today."

She replied, "Well, if you can't hold a meeting you can't; but I am inviting you all tonight."

I took comfort in thinking that her grief could not be that overwhelming and that her mind had become somewhat dispassionate as a result of all those ideals I once preached to her. True, she did not have the education or the ability to truly comprehend the topics I raised but there is something in me called 'personal magnetism', which helped.

In the evening some members of our "duality" group kept away. Kanai did not turn up. Those who joined the tennis club at Number One stayed away too; I heard that Sitangshumouli was leaving tomorrow morning, so they had gone there for a farewell dinner. But the elaborate arrangements Anila made for that night's feast were unprecedented and even I, never one to count my pennies, thought the fare was excessive.

It was one o'clock or one-thirty in the morning before the night's festivities were over. Tired, I went to bed at once. I asked Anil, "What about going to bed?"

She said, "I have dishes to clear."

When I got up next morning it was nearly eight o'clock. One the bedside table in my room, where I deposit my glasses before going to sleep, I found a slip of paper which said in Anil's handwriting, "I am leaving. Do not try to look for me. You won't succeed even if you do."

I couldn't quite take it in. On the table there was also a tin box. I opened it and found all Anila's ornaments down to her bangles, except for conch and iron ones. In one compartment there was a key ring; in another some loose change in a paper packet. In other words, whatever was saved out of the monthly allowance for expenses had been left to the last penny. In an exercise book she had left a list of things like dishes, utensils etc., and details of clothes that had gone to the dhobi. Alone with these there was an account of money owing to the milkman and the grocer – everything except her address.

All I could understand was that Anila had left. I searched everywhere, sent word to the in-laws, she was nowhere to be found. I can never, ever, rise to the occasion whenever anything extraordinary like this takes place, and deal with things as required. I felt absolutely empty inside. Then I looked at Number One. The doors and windows of the house were closed. The doorkeeper was smoking his hubble-bubble, near the gate. The master had left early that morning. I felt my heart pounding, realising all of a sudden that while I had been discussing the latest logic with single-hearted attention, a net was being spread in my house for the oldest vice in society. When I read of an event like this in the writings of Flaubert, Tolstoy, Turgenev and other great novelists I take great pleasure in analysing its significance in the minutest detail. I never imagined even in my dreams that it could happen, with such certainty, in my own home.

After digesting the initial shock I tried to make light of the whole affair like a wise philosopher. I smiled a wry smile, thinking of the day when I got married. It occurred to me that a lot of man's desires, efforts and passions are just an enormous waste. How many days, nights, years I had spent amidst a sense of security with my eyes closed, knowing that something alive, called a wife, was undoubtedly there. Then

143

my eyes were suddenly opened, and I found that the bubble had burst. Well, what of it, not everything in this world is a bubble. Have I not known things which survive aeons, transcend life and death?

Even so, I found that this unexpected blow knocked down the "civilized" and the "wise" in me and some primeval animal woke up, crying with hunger. I walked the roof, the verandah, the empty house, then finally went to the bedroom where I had often found my wife sitting quietly by the window – and began searching among her things like one possessed. When I pulled open the drawer of the dressing table, where Anil kept her hair-dressing things, a bunch of letters tied up with a ribbon of red silk came into my hands. The letters had come from Number One. I felt a searing sensation in my heart. I though of burning the lot. But that which hurts the most attracts the most as well. I had no way out but to read them.

I have read these letters at least fifty times. The first letter had been torn in several bits; it appeared that the reader tore it up after reading and then put them together with adhesive on a piece of paper.

The letter says; "If you tear up this letter without reading I shall not complain. But I must say what I have to say. I have seen you, I had my eyes open all this time but for the first time in my thirty-two years they have found something really worth seeing. A screen was drawn over my eyes and I was sleeping. You have touched them with a golden rod – I saw with the eyes of someone just awakened – incomparable, you are worthy of being wondered at even by the Creator himself. I have received what is mine, and want nothing else but to sing a hymn to you. If I were a poet there would have been no need to write this letter; my rhythm, taking on the voice of the whole world, would have declared what I want to say. I know that you will not reply to this letter – but please do not misunderstand me. All I want is that you should accept my homage in silence without the least suspicion that I mean harm to you in any way. If you would respect the respect I am paying you, you could only gain. No need to tell you who I am, but I know that this will not remain a secret to your heart."

There were twenty-five letters like this, but no evidence among them that a reply ever went from Anil. It would have gone out of tune then, or the magic of the golden rod would have been lost and the hymn silenced.

But what a stunning revelation! For the first time, after eight years of intimacy, I saw, through letters written by another, someone whom Sitangshu had discovered through the help only of fleeting glimpses. The screen over my sleeping eyes must be very thick indeed. I received Anil through the hands of a priest but did not pay the price to receive her from the hands of her Creator. My "duality" group and the new logic had meant so much more to me than Anil. So, as she was the person whom I have never seen, who never was mine even for a moment, how could I complain if someone else offered her his whole life?

The last letter said: "I do not know much about you, looking in from the outside, but I have known the bruises you bear inside you. This is a great trial for me. These two arms of mine do not find it easy to remain inactive. I want to rescue you from the utter futility that constitutes your life now, breaking down all the rules that govern heaven and hearth. But then I think, your suffering is for you the seat of your God. I have no right to rob you of that. I have given myself time till tomorrow morning. If in the meanwhile some divine dispensation solves my dilemma something drastic will have to happen. The lamp to light our way is often extinguished by a gust of wind blowing from our desire. So I must keep my mind still and concentrate on a *mantra* for your well-being."

It seemed clear that, all hesitation finally over, the paths of these two had met. Strangely, these letters from Sitangshu became mine. Today they represent the hymns and chants that I sing.

Days passed. I lost my taste for reading and became

possessed by such a powerful and anguished desire to see Anil that it was impossible to remain still. I found out that Sitangshu was then in the hill station of Mussourie.

I went there. I often saw Sitangshu out taking a walk but Anil was never with him; I feared that he might have abandoned her. I could hold myself in no longer. I had to approach him. It is not necessary to say in detail what transpired. Sitangshu said, "I have received only one letter from her in all my days – have a look."

He brought out from his pocket a golden card-case worked with enamel and took from it a piece of paper. It read, "I am leaving . Do not try to find me. You will not succeed even if you do."

The same letter, the same writing – and the blue paper on which it was written was the other half of the blue paper that I possess.

The Rescue

Gouri was the beautiful daughter of an ancient and rich family, brought up with a lot of doting affection. Her husband, Paresh, had managed to improve his circumstances somewhat, beginning from a rather mean state. For as long as he was poor his in-laws did not send Gouri to him for fear that she would suffer. So Gouri came to her husband's household at rather an advanced age (for an Indian woman of that time).

Perhaps it was for all these reasons that Paresh did not think of his young, beautiful wife as fully within his control. Or it may be that suspicion was a disease with him. Paresh was a lawyer in a small town in the west of India with no relatives to speak of, and he was in a state of great anxiety over his wife, left all by herself at home. Now and again he would leave court early and come home. To begin with, Gouri failed to guess the reason for the sudden appearance of her husband.

From time to time Paresh would get rid of an old servant for no reason; and no servant managed to give him continued satisfaction beyond a certain time. He became particularly displeased with servants whom Gouri was eager to keep. The more the spirited Gouri felt hurt at this treatment, the more her husband was incited to behave in a most odd manner.

147

When at last, unable to control himself, Paresh began privately asking the maid various questions of a suspicious nature, Gouri became aware of the matter. Her vanity hurt, this woman of few words felt insulted. She raged inside like a wounded lioness. And this crazy suspicion fell between the couple like a sword of destruction, totally separating them in their affections.

When the sordidness of his suspicion was thus openly revealed to Gouri – and Paresh's sense of shame was overcome as a result – he began quarrelling with his wife, questioning her every step. The more that Gouri, through her wordless contempt and her sharp oblique look like a whiplash, made him feel wounded and battered, the more vigorous his obsessive suspicions became.

Thus deprived of happiness from her husband the childless young woman involved herself with religion. A new missionary of Harisabha, Brahmachari Paramananda Swami, initiated her and she began listening to his elaborations of the Bhagavat.[1] All her futile affection and love congealed as devotion, and was offered at the feet of the Guru. No-one had any doubt about the purity of Paramananda's character; everybody worshipped him. Paresh was thus unable to cast doubts on his character openly, and like a concealed wound his suspicions gradually began to dig a tunnel through his soul.

One day it happened that the poison poured itself out on the flimsiest pretext. Referring to Paramananda he accused him of being a lecherous fraud to his wife and demanded of her, "Can you touch your *salgram stone*[2] and promise that you do not love that hypocrite?"

Like a she-snake just trodden on Gouri instantly looked up with hauteur and piercing her husband with a daring falsehood said in an anger-choked voice, "Yes, I love him. What are you going to do?" Paresh at once locked her up in a room and went away to Court. In unbearable anger Gouri

[1]Devotional literature depicting life of god Krishna
[2]Black stone symbolically representing Krishna

somehow managed to get the door unlocked and left the house.

Paramananda was reading scriptures in his lonely room on a deserted afternoon. Suddenly Gouri broke in on his scripture-reading like cloudless lightning.

The Guru asked, "What is this?"

The disciple said, 'Gurudev, please rescue me from this dishonourable domestic life and take me away somewhere. I shall dedicate my life in your service." Paramananda rebuked her sternly and sent her back home. But unfortunately for the Guru the disjointed thread of studying could not be reassembled as before.

Back home Paresh saw the door open and asked, "Who came here?"

She replied, "Nobody. I went to Gurudev's place".

Paresh went pale just for a moment and then reddening he demanded, "Why did you?"

Gouri answered, "Just because I wanted to."

From that day Paresh set up a guard over Gouri and locked her up in her room, oppressing her so much that a scandal was created throughout the town.

The news of this sordid insult and torture made it impossible for Paramanda to concentrate on thoughts of Hari. He felt it imperative to leave the town immediately but could hardly go away leaving the oppressed woman. The history of those few days and nights for Paramananda was known only to God.

At last Gouri, while still incarcerated, got a letter. "My child, on reconsideration I find that many a chaste female spiritual aspirant has left the world for love of Krishna. If the oppression of this world has diverted your mind from the feet of Hari, let me know and I shall try to rescue God's devotee with his help and consecrate her to the Lord's feet. On Wednesday, 26th of *Falgun*[1], you could meet me, if you wish, at two o'clock, by the side of your pond."

[1] See footnote 1 p. 39.

Gouri tied up the letter in her hair and covered it with a bun. When she let down her hair just before taking a bath on the 26th of *Falgun* she found it was missing and wondered whether it had fallen onto the bed while she slept and found its way into her husband's hands. She felt a kind of scorching pleasure to think that her husband must be burning with jealousy reading it. But at the same time the thought of her esteemed letter being disgraced at the hands of a godless sinner made her impatient and at once she went to her husband's room.

She found him on the floor groaning, foam oozing out of his mouth, his pupils fixed upwards. Gouri forced the letter from his right hand and sent for the doctor. The doctor diagnosed apoplexy – but by then the patient was dead.

That day Paresh had had an urgent case in a subdivisional town. The sannyasi Paramananda had fallen so low that he had managed to find that out and had fixed the date of meeting with Gouri accordingly.

When Gouri, made a widow that very day, saw from her window her Gurudev arriving at the pond like a thief she cast down her eyes, as if awakened by lightning. At that moment the position the Guru had descended to, from his once exalted state, flashed suddenly in her heart in the illumination of that lightning.

The Guru called, "Gouri".

Gouri replied, "I am coming, Gurudev".

When the news of Paresh's death reached his friends, and they appeared for the cremation, they found Gouri's dead body lying by the side of her husband's. She had committed suicide by taking poison. This example of a woman dying with her husband in these modern times rendered everyone speechless at the sublimity of spirit that characterizes a chaste woman.

The Halder Family

There was no good reason for the trouble brewing in the Halder family. Its members were not bad, as people go, and their circumstances were easy. Yet, it happened.

If, where human beings were concerned, everything happened according to reason, human affairs would resemble an exercise in mathematics, and with a little care one could avoid errors in life's accounts. And in case a mistake did occur all one would have to do is to use an eraser and correct it.

But the God of man's fate is inclined to take aesthetic pleasure in life's drama. I do not know if he is an expert in mathematics, but he is certainly not very keen on it and his attention is not particularly engaged in getting his sums right. That is why he has inserted something into his arrangements called 'randomness' which appears suddenly to upset the natural course of events. Then the plot thickens, and the storm of laughter and tears rages, making the current of life overflow its banks.

That is what occurred in this case, like the entry of a mad elephant in the lotus pond – when the mud and the lotus got mixed together; otherwise, there would have been no story to tell.

There is no doubt that Banowarilal was the most worthy member of the family I am talking about. He was aware of it himself and this knowledge made him restless. His inner worth, like a steam engine, pushed him ever forward: all was well if there was a clear track on which to move; if not, there would be a clash with whatever lay ahead.

His father, Monoharlal, lived in the old-fashioned style of a wealthy man of those days. His desire was to reside at the top of the society he belonged to and flourish there without any connection with its lower limbs. Ordinary human beings work and move about. Monoharlal lived in the centre of a huge structure that called for no work or movement such as ordinary mortals have to undertake.

It is often the case that people like this draw towards them, like a magnet, one or two human beings who are strong and honest. There is no other reason for this other than that some people are born in this world with an inner urge to serve others. It is to fulfil their own natures that they seek a human being who is incapable of looking after himself and so willing to leave it all in their able hands. These natural servers take no pleasure in their own affairs. But to give another person confidence, to keep him in comfort, save him from all untoward happenings and to increase his status in society; these arouse their greatest enthusiasm. They are like a male mother, not however towards their own issue, but to someone else's.

The only aim of Monoharlal's servant, Ramcharan, was to nurture the body of his master, for which purpose he lived and could die. He was willing to puff and blow, day and night, like a smith's bellows, if this extra work could do away with the necessity for his master to breathe. From the outside, people could think that Manoharlal was oppressing his servant by making him work unnecessarily hard. When, at times, the tube attached to his hubble-bubble dropped on the ground, it was not difficult for Manoharlal to pick it up himself, and it looked very odd indeed to call Ramcharan and make him run from another room. But Ramcharan took great pleasure in making himself indispensible for such countless unnecessary matters.

He had another follower like Ramcharan, called Nilkantha, and the responsibility for looking after the estate was vested in him. Ramcharan, basking in his master's grace, was rounded in form, but there was hardly any flesh on the bones of Nilkantha's body. He guarded the storehouse of his master's wealth, himself looking like an embodiment of famine. The property belonged to Manoharlal but possessive attachment to it was solely Nilkantha's.

Conflicts between Banowari and Nilkantha were a matter of longstanding. Suppose Banowarilal, by appealing to his father, had obtained permission to buy a new ornament for his wife. It was his wish to get hold of the money and have the article made after his own choice. But in no way could this be accomplished, as all spending had to be done through Nilkantha. The result was that the ornament was made, but not one that pleased Banowari. He was convinced that Nilkantha was in cahoots with the jeweller. A strong man does not lack enemies and Banowari heard from all and sundry that what Nilkantha made by depriving others was added to his own possessions, which were increasing proportionately.

All these concerned small sums. Nilkantha was no fool, and it was not difficult for him to understand that unless he kept in step with Banowarilal there might be trouble in future. But Nilkantha was obsessively miserly when it came to his master's wealth. He could not make himself spend it in matters that looked to him quite unnecessary – even when permission came from the master himself.

But Banowari often had need for 'unnecessary' expenses. The reason was the same as for many an unnecessary thing in a man's life. It would be useless to discuss the beauty of Banowarilal's wife, Kironlekha, on which there could be different opinions. In the present context, what is useful to consider is the opinion of Banowari himself. The attachment he felt for his wife appeared exaggerated to the womenfolk of the family, that is, it was as much as they would like to have had from their own husbands but failed to get.

Whatever the age of Kironlekha she looked very young. She was not at all what the oldest daughter-in-law of the family was supposed to be – with the gravity proper to a housewife both in nature and appearance. Altogether she appeared slight. Banowari fondly called her 'Anu' (a particle) and at times even this description was not enough and Banowari used the term 'Paramanu' (the smallest possible particle). Those who are experts in physics know that particles possess not a little power in the universe.

Kiron had never asked anything of her husband. She had a dispassionate nature, as if she had no need of anything. There was quite a few sisters-in-law in the household and Kiron was fully occupied with them. She did not feel much need for a private pursuit of the newly-awakened love that blossoms in fresh youth. So she showed not a great deal of interest in her affairs with Banowari; what she got from him she accepted calmly but never volunteered to ask for anything. As a result Banowari had to think out for himself how to please his wife. If a wife demanded something one could try and reduce its size, but one could not haggle with oneself. So unasked-for presents cost him more than things demanded would have done.

It was not at all easy to fathom how pleased Kironlekha was to get endearing gifts from her husband. When asked, she would merely say, "It is all right, quite nice," which did not remove Banowari's misgivings, and often he surmised that the gift was not to her liking. Kiron would then rebuke him, "It is your nature to be so pernickety, it is quite pleasing."

Banowari had read in text books that contentment is a great virtue. But the presence of this virtue in his wife troubled him. His wife had not only satisfied him, she had overwhelmed him, and he wanted to overwhelm her in turn. His wife did not have to make much effort – the grace of youth in a woman shows itself spontaneously, so does a woman's expertise in serving her family, which she naturally undertakes. But a man has no such easy opportunity, he has to do something special to prove his manliness. If he cannot prove that he has some special power he becomes insignificant. If nothing else is available there is at least wealth, as evidence of power. If he could have spread the glow of that power, like a peacock, before his wife there would have been some consolation. But Nilkantha had repeatedly put a spanner in the works of this particular design of Banowari's love-game. He, the oldest son of the family, was master over nothing: Nilkantha, a mere servant, was lording it over him through the indulgence of his master. The disadvantage and insult this involved was felt in nothing so much as in the matter of Banowari's inability to supply suitable arrows for the god of love's bow.

One day he would inherit it all, but youth would not last for ever. A day would come when there would no longer be this natural filling-up of the cup of Spring with honey-sweet love. One would then be possession-conscious, and collect money in a pile like a snow cap on the mountain top – there would be no occasion for wasting it on this or that excuse. The need for money was now, when one's power to throw it about out of the sheer joy of spending was still intact.

Benowari had three hobbies – wrestling, hunting and the Sanskrit language. His exercise book was full of quaint Sanskrit poems. They came in useful on a rainy day or on a moonlit night when the south wind was blowing. A good thing about them was that Nilkantha had no power to cut down the excessive ornamentation of their language, nor did one have to answer for them to any paid official, whatever their exaggeration. There was a shortage of gold for Kiron's earrings, but the *mandakranta*[1] rhythm whispered in her ears never lacked a beat; the emotion they carried never had to be restricted within any limit.

Banowari had a tall and strong physique, like a wrestler, and people took to flight on seeing him angry. But this strong, hard body contained a soft mind within. When his

[1] A slow rhythmic metre in Sanskrit poetry

brother Banshi was young he had looked after him with a mother-like affection. It was as if there was in his heart a hunger for giving succour. His love for his wife had an element of this – this desire to foster and care. Kironlekha was slight, looking like a lost ray amidst shadows cast by trees – it was this that aroused a great deal of care and concern in her husband, as well as a great interest in adorning her with various dresses and ornaments. His interest was not so much in the enjoyment, as in the creation – the joy of creating many Kironlekhas out of one, through seeing her in different colours, dresses and ornaments.

But this fancy of Banowari could not be satisfied just by quoting Sanskrit poetry. It gave no scope to express the manly power within him, nor did it fulfil his wish to enrich the object of his love with many accessories. So this rich man's son, possessing such coveted good things of life as prestige, a beautiful wife and full youth, became a troublesome element in his father's environment.

Sukhada was the wife of Madhu, the fisherman, a tenant of Manoharlal. One day she suddenly appeared and started crying at Kironlekha's feet. What was involved was this: a few years ago some fishermen, as was their wont, borrowed a few thousand rupees from Manoharlal's treasury – against a written document – so as to be able to arrange extensive fishing in the river. When the enterprise was successful, there was no problem about returning the capital with interest, which was the reason why they did not worry about the high rate charged. One year the catch was not sufficient and for three years running there had been so little fish that the men had had to suffer loss, on top of being embroiled in the net of debt. The fishermen who belonged to other areas disappeared, but Madhu was a resident there and because he had nowhere to go the whole load of that debt devolved on to him. Hence this approach to Kironlekha to save himself from utter ruin. Everyone knew that it was useless to appeal to her mother-in-law, as she was unable to comprehend that the arrangements made by Nilkantha could in any way be set aside. Madhu sent his wife to Kironlekha because he knew that Banowari was dead against Nilkantha.

However ill-disposed Banowari was towards Nilkantha and whatever his braggings against him, Kiron knew for certain that he had no jurisdiction over any of Nilkantha's doings. So she tried hard to make Sukhada understand – "My dear, we can do nothing, we have no power in this matter: the master is there, let Madhu go to him."

That attempt had already been made. Whenever a petition was made to the master he forthwith, and without fail, transferred the responsibility for settling it to Nilkantha. This made things doubly difficult for the petitioner. If ever a second attempt was made at redress, the master became furious – if he had to be confronted with all these irritations, where was the pleasure in having property?

When Sukhada was thus begging Kiron for mercy, Banowari was busy greasing the butt of his gun in the next room. He heard it all. The pathetic voice of Kiron and the repeated submission that they were totally powerless to do anything about it hit him hard, like a bullet.

It was the beginning of the month of *Falgun*[1] and the day of the full moon. After a stuffy day suddenly a wild wind broke out in the evening. The cuckoo was sending out anxious calls, repeatedly, as if trying to break down someone's indifference with its song. The atmosphere was thick with the scent of flowers, jostling one another as in a crowd. From the inner garden next to the window of their room came the smell of the *muchukundu*[2] flower to create enchantment in the Spring sky. Kiron was dressed in a sari of reddish colour with a garland of *bel*[3] flowers round her hair made up in a bun. According to an established custom, the couple's own, there was a garment of the same colour and a garland too, ready for Banowari, in celebration of Spring. The first quarter of the night was over but Banowari did not appear; he felt no taste today for youthful dalliance. How

[1]See footnote 1 p. 39
[2]Flower belonging to the magnolia family
[3]Small white scented flower that blooms in Spring and Summer

could he enter the domain of love with a crippling feeling of
impotence? He had no power to solve the problem of the
fisherman, Madhu; it was Nilkantha who held this power.
Who would thread a garland to put round the neck of a
coward?

First he had Nilkantha called to his sitting room,
forbidding him to destroy Madhu on the score of his debt.
Nilkantha replied that if Madhu was pampered like this a lot
of rent would go by default, particularly now when it was
time to count lapsed time and settle accounts. Everyone
would make excuses. When argument was of no avail
Banowari took to abuse, calling him a lowly, mean person.
Nilkantha agreed that he was lowly, why otherwise should
he be there, serving a rich man? Banowari accused him of
being a thief. Nilkantha replied, "Quite so, a man to whom
God has given no wealth of his own must live by what
belongs to another." He thus agreed with whatever names
Banowari called him and in the end remarked, "I must go,
the lawyer is waiting, I have business with him. If you
consider it necessary, call me again later and I shall come."
Banowari decided to get his younger brother Banshi on his
side and together approach their father. He knew that his
going by himself would produce no result, as there already
had been differences with his father on the subject of
Nilkantha, causing annoyance to the former. There was a
time when people thought that Monoharlal loved his oldest
son most. But it seemed now that he was partial to Banshi,
which was why Banowari wished to make Banshi a party to
his complaint.

Banshi was what is commonly known as a 'good boy'. It
was only he in the family who had passed two examinations
and was now preparing for the law. God only knows
whether there had been some profit inside him as a result of
all this day and night studying; but as far as his body was
concerned it showed only expenditure. The window of his
room on this Spring evening was tightly shut, as he was
fearful of changes of season. As for air, he felt no respect for

it. There was a kerosene lamp on his table, some books were
lying on the floor by the bed, some were on the table. In the
recess there was a series of medicine bottles.

He just did not agree with Banowari's proposal. Angry,
Banowari shouted, "So, you are afraid of Nilkantha."
Banshi kept silent. In fact, he was ever careful about keeping
on the right side of Nilkantha. He spent most of his time in
Calcutta where money was more often required than granted
in his allowance. So he had got into the habit of keeping
Nilkantha happy. Banowari, in a hot temper, called him
chicken-hearted, a coward, and Nilkantha's sycophant to
boot, then angrily went to his father alone.

Manoharlal, bare-bodied, was enjoying the air, sitting by
the pond in the garden. His courtiers, seated nearby, were
relating to him the pleasant story of how the land-owner,
Akhil Mazumdar, of a neighbouring estate, was humbled the
other day at the District Court through the questionings of a
Calcutta barrister. That tale, mingled with the scented air of
the Spring evening, was indeed very enjoyable.

The sudden appearance of Banowarilal in the midst of this
put an end to the enjoyment being relished. Banowari was in
no state to broach the subject with proper introduction or do
it in stages. Raising his voice, he started with the statement
that Nilkantha was ruining them. He was a thief, and was
feathering his own nest – with the master's money. There
was of course no proof of this, and it was not true either.
Nilkantha had added to the property, and not taken any of it.
Banowari's understanding was that it was because
Manoharlal had such absolute faith in Nilkantha that he
depended on him in such a blind way. This was a mistake.
Manoharlal was sure that if an opportunity occurred
Nilkantha would not be above misappropriation. But he did
not lack respect for him on that account. The reason – such
was the way of the world for always; the rich were
maintained by the left-overs after the attendants had their
pickings; a man who was not clever enough to steal would
not be cunning enough to maintain his master's property

either; the job of looking after an estate could not be done by someone like the righteous Judhisthira[1] of the *Mahabharata*.[2] Monohar felt extremely irritated and he snarled, "Well, you don't have to worry about Nilkantha's doings." Then added, "You can see, Banshi makes no trouble, he is busy with his studies, a much worthier boy."

After this the story of Akhil Mazumdar's discomfiture lost its beauty. The result – the wind that Spring evening blew to no effect, and moonlight on the black water of the pond was of not much use either. Only for Banshi and Nilkantha the evening was not spoiled. Banshi closed his window and burnt midnight oil over his studies and Nilkantha spent half the night conferring with his lawyer.

Kiron had extinguished the lamp and was seated by the window. The dinner had not yet been taken, but she was waiting for Banowari. She had completely forgotten about Madhu. It did not grieve her in the least that Banowari was unable to help him. She was not eager for evidence of any special competence on the part of her husband. Her husband's glory lay in the glory of the family. He was the eldest boy of her father-in-law and it never occurred to her that he had to be more than that. Enough that they were the famous Halder family of Gosaigunge.

Banowari kept walking and rewalking the veranda till late at night and then entered their room. He had forgotten about dinner. The fact that Kiron was waiting for him made him feel very guilty. This forbearance of Kiron did not fit his sense of total lack of power. The food felt like sticking to his gullet. Extremely agitated, Banowari said to his wife, 'I shall save Madhu in whatever way I can'. Kiron, surprised at this unnecessary heat, exclaimed, "Listen to this! How can you save him?"

Banowari had promised himself to pay up Madhu's debt, but he had no savings. He decided to sell one of his three guns and a costly diamond ring to secure the money. But

[1]Eldest of 5 Pandava brothers, who found it difficult to lie
[2]Indian epic relating the Pandaras' war with the Kuros.

there was hardly any buyer in the village for such commodities. Moreover an attempt to sell would cause a lot of whispers. So Banowari went to Calcutta on some excuse, assuring Madhu that he had nothing to fear.

Nilkantha was furious, realising that Madhu was taking shelter behind Banowari. He made it difficult for the neighbourhood of the fishermen to maintain its standing, through high-handed behaviour by his bailiff.

The day that Banowari returned from Calcutta, Madhu's son came running and gasping; crying aloud he took hold of Banowari's feet. "What is it, what is the matter?" Swarup said that Nilkantha had kept his father incarcerated since last night in the landlord's office. Shaking in rage and fuming Banowari said, "Go at once to the police station and report it to them."

A disastrous path! The police! Against Nilkantha! Swarup was extremely reluctant to do any such thing, but he had to go in the end at Banowari's insistence. The police suddenly appeared, released Madhu, then taking Nilkantha and a few employees sent them to the Magistrate's court.

Monohar was extremely perturbed. His advisors in law began bleeding him on the excuse that money was needed for bribes. That money was shared with the police. A newly qualified inexperienced barrister from Calcutta was engaged, the advantage of this being that what was credited in the books as his fee did not all have to go to his pocket. An experienced lawyer from the District Court represented Madhu and it was not immediately clear who appointed him. Nilkantha was jailed for six months. An appeal to the High Court made no difference.

The price fetched by the gun and the ring was thus put to good use. For the time being Madhu was free and Nilkantha in jail. But how could Madhu continue to remain on the estate after this? Banowari assured him, "You stay, there is nothing to be afraid of." One wondered what this assurance was based on – maybe just male vanity.

Banowari did not make much effort to conceal his part in

the affair and it became public knowledge. Eventually it got to Monohar's ears. He ordered Banowari, through his servant, never to appear before him. Banowari did not disregard the order.

Kiron was astounded at her husband's behaviour. What sort of going-on was this? The eldest son of the family – not on speaking terms with the father! Disgraceful to dishonour one's family before the whole world by sending one's employee to the jail – and that too for the insignificant Madhu!

This was strange indeed. In this branch of the family there had been many an eldest son, and the Nilkanthas too had always been there. It is they who had taken on the responsibility of running the estate while the eldest sons had been entirely unenterprising and inactive, solely engaged in maintaining the honour of the lineage. A contrary affair like this had never happened before.

The degradation of the status of the eldest son of the family struck at the honour of the eldest daughter-in-law too. And this gave real cause for the disrespect Kiron felt for her husband. Her Spring adornments, reddish-coloured sari, the garland of bel flower, everything became pale and dull in the shame of it all.

Kiron was getting older but she failed to produce a child. Nilkantha had once, and with the master's consent, nearly managed to get Banowari married again through fixing a prospective bride for him – for one must above all remember that Banowari was the eldest son of the family and it was unthinkable that he should remain childless. The move made Kiron's heart pound in anxiety but she had to admit to herself that it was a just proposal. She felt no complaint against Nilkantha and bemoaned only her own fate. If her husband had kept quiet and not attempted to thrash Nilkantha in anger or quarrelled with his parents to break up the marriage arrangements, she would not have blamed him either. Indeed, the fact that Banowari was not interested in continuing the line made her secretly lose some respect for him. The demands of a family of high status were not to be treated as insignificant. Before a matter of such momentous importance the sorrows of a young wife or those of a fisherman were as nothing.

Banowari did not comprehend that people were unable to forgive any lapse in an established convention. He ought to have been a typical 'eldest son of the family' – It was clear to everyone but him that to worry about right and wrong over irrelevant matters of no concern to himself meant a grave failure of duty on his part, breaking the continuity that had hitherto obtained.

Kiron had often expressed her misgivings over this to her brother-in-law, Banshi. Banshi was clever. His digestion was bad and even a mild wind gave him a cough and cold, but he was steady, patient and wise. He placed the law-book he was reading open and face-down on the table saying, "This is nothing but madness." Kiron shook her head in extreme anxiety and said "You know *thakurpo*[1], when your brother is in his senses he is all right but nobody can cope with him when madness starts. What am I to do?"

What wounded Banowari most was that Kiron's 'sensible' opinion in no way differed from that of the rest of the people in the family – a woman so slight in appearance, soft like the newly-blossomed *champa*[2] flower, yet all his manly powers failed to draw her heart close to his pain. If Kiron could at this point be one in her feelings with Banowari, the wound in his heart would not have grown to such proportions, with such rapidity.

He had to save Madhu. This matter of natural duty became something of an obsession with Banowari, as a result of pressure put on him from all sides. Everything else became as of no significance. Then Nilkantha came back from jail with such aplomb as if he had merely gone to keep an invitation with his in-laws. He continued with his work, as before, with a clear conscience.

[1]See footnote p. 44
[2]Yellow flower belonging to the magnolia family

Nilkantha could not maintain his prestige with the tenants if he were unable to dispossess Madhu of his residence. His prestige, by itself, was of no great moment, but he had to do his work and for him to get on with his job it was essential that the tenants must acknowledge his power. So he began sharpening his weapons to uproot Madhu. Banowari did not take recourse to secrecy, this time. He told Nilkantha quite openly that he was not going to allow Madhu to be driven out of his house. He cleared up Madhu's debt himself and, finding no other way to stop Nilkantha, went to the Magistrate's court and lodged a complaint to the effect that Nilkantha was trying to endanger Madhu.

His well-wishers advised Banowari that Manohar would dispossess him, if he carried on like this. Manohar would have turned Banowari out by now, if it were not for the fact that such a step would have created a lot of disturbance in the family. Banowari's mother was there and other members of the family would not have agreed to it. Manohar forced himself to keep quiet because of his unwillingness to stir up a hornet's nest.

Such was the state of affairs when one day Madhu's residence was found to be under lock and key. He had gone away somewhere under cover of night, nobody knew where. The whole affair with Madhu was getting so unbecoming that Nilkantha had given Madhu money, taken from the estate's treasury, and sent him off to Benaras along with his family. The police knew about this, so no trouble was stirred up. But Nilkantha skilfully let it be generally known that Madhu and his family had been sacrificed to the Goddess Kali[1] on the night of the new moon and their dead bodies, in sacks, had been thrown into the Ganges. People shuddered in fear and their respect for Nilkantha increased in proportion.

So the problem engaging Banowari's urgent attention was temporarily solved. But things did not get back to their

[1]See footnote 5 p. 48

former state.

There was a time when Banowari loved Banshi very much. Now he found out that Banshi was not his – he belonged to the Halder family. And Kiron, whose image had totally captured his heart since early youth, was not his either; she too belonged to the Halder family. Previously Banowari had grumbled about the ornaments made according to Nilkantha's orders as not becoming enough for his beloved Kiron. Now he discovered that all the love poetry – from Kalidas[1] to Amaru and Chaura – he had offered at the feet of his beloved was not at all becoming for the eldest daughter-in-law of the Halder family.

Alas! The wind still blew at Springtime and the downpour of the rainy season arrived just the same. The anguish of his unfulfilled love kept pace with these and roamed around the pathways of his heart.

Not everybody has a need to feel love in all its intensity. Most people can happily make do with fixed allowances in which it is made available. And that limited measure is also compatible with the arrangements of life in a big joint family. But a few need more. They cannot live, like unborn young in the egg, on a meagre supply. Having come out of the shell they need a wide field in which to secure their own food by their own effort. Banowari was born with that hunger and eager to fulfil it by his own manly capabilities. But the solid structure of the Halder family barred all doors to this, and every time he moved, it caused a bruise.

Days passed as before. Banowari got himself involved in hunting more energetically, otherwise no visible change was there to notice. He continued to go to the inner quarters for his meals, when some conversation took place with his wife. Kiron had not yet forgiven Madhu as he was the root cause for her husband's loss of place in the family. So now and again she raised the topic of Madhu with acid in her tongue – Madhu was wicked to the bone, foremost in devilry

[1] See footnote 6 p. 83.

and only a man thoroughly deceived would take pity on him. All this she said again and again, without exhausting the topic. An attempt at protest, made once or twice by Banowari, only incensed Kiron the more, so he learned to keep quiet. Thus did he carry on with the regularity of his family life. Kiron was perfectly happy with this, seeing nothing wanting or incomplete, but the inner man in Banowari felt colourless, dried-up and ever-hungry.

It then transpired that the younger daughter-in-law of the family, Banshi's wife, was pregnant, and the whole family went wild with excitement. The duty in which Kiron failed was being fulfilled by another – at long last. The only anxiety was now whether the goddess *Sasthi*[1] would help further by producing a son rather than a daughter.

Happily a male child was born. The younger son of the family not only had passed his College examinations, he came first in the matter of continuing the family line as well. He who for some time had been increasingly held in favour, now enjoyed it more than ever.

Everybody in the family made much of the baby boy, particularly Kiron, who did not want to let go of him for a moment. Her involvement with the baby was so total that she almost forgot about the wickedness of Madhu.

Banowari, by nature, was fond of children. Whatever was small, helpless and soft he felt great affection and compassion for. God allows something contrary in every nature, otherwise it would be hard to understand how Banowari could enjoy shooting birds.

He had long felt an unsatisfied desire for a child by Kiron. The birth of Banshi's child made him a little jealous at first, but it did not take him long to be rid of that feeling. Banowari could love this boy very much indeed. What interfered with that process was Kiron's excessive involvement with him. So gaps began to appear in the relation between Kiron and Banowari. He realized quite clearly that

[1]See footnote p. 2

Kiron now had something truly capable of filling up her heart. It was as if Banowari was just a tenant of her heart; as long as the owner was absent he could enjoy the whole house without much trouble – with the presence of the owner he could now take up no more space than a corner room. How engrossed Kiron could be with affection, how great was her power of self-sacrifice – when Banowari noticed these he said to himself in self-assessment, "I was incapable of causing a stir in this heart, for all that I acted to the best of my ability."

Not only this, Banshi's family became dearer to Kiron than her own because of the boy. All the conferences and discussions were now with Banshi. That dried-up, feeble, timid man, with an emaciated body but keen intelligence, was increasingly becoming contemptible to Banowari. He could tolerate the fact that people should consider Banshi a worthier member of the family than himself, but when he discovered that even as a human being Banshi was valued over himself by his own wife, he could hardly be pleased with his fate or the world around him.

The time was close to one of Banshi's examinations when information reached the family from Calcutta that he was ill and that the physician feared the worst. Banowari went to Calcutta and nursed Banshi day and night but to no avail. Death took away all the unpleasant details from Banowari's memory – that Banshi was his younger brother and had, as a child, a secure place of affection with him, remained shining bright in his tear-soaked heart.

When he came back he decided to bring up his brother's child with all the care he was capable of. But Kiron had lost faith in her husband over the boy, having noticed what she thought was her husband's lack of affection for him from the start. Her idea was that her husband's nature was contrary to what was natural for everyone else. This boy was the only light in their family line, something clearly understood by everyone. That is precisely the reason why it must be the case that Banowari would fail to find it so. Kiron remained ever afraid lest Banowari's ill-will caused the boy some harm. Her brother-in-law was dead, and there was no question of she herself bearing a child; so this boy must be saved from all possible dangers by whatever means available. So Banowari failed to find a natural way to express his care for the boy.

The boy was named Haridas and he grew enveloped in care from all sides. Under the shade of such excessive concern his physique took on a thin and brittle appearance. His body was covered with talismans and he had around him a band of people keeping guard.

From time to time gaps occurred in this vigilance, when he would meet Banowari. He loved to play about with the whip his uncle used for riding, and whenever they met he would utter its half-formed name. It made him very happy when Banowari brought the whip out and made a swishing noise with it by turning it around. Occasionally Banowari would make him sit on his horse and this would cause the whole household to rush in anxiety to stop it. If Kiron ever found the boy playing with his uncle and his gun, she would hurry and take the boy away. But Haridas was most attracted by these forbidden pleasures, so hurdles notwithstanding, he got rather attached to his uncle.

Then, after a respite, death again struck the household. First to die was Monoharlal's wife. When Nilkantha was busy discussing his remarriage and finding a prospective bride, Monoharlal too died. Haridas was then eight years old. Before Manohar died, he placed the sole responsibility for bringing up this little descendant of his in the hands of Nilkantha and Kiron; nothing was said of Banowari. It was found that Manohar had left the whole of his estate to Haridas in his will. Banowari would get only a lifelong allowance of two hundred rupees per month. Nilkantha was appointed the executor of the will and on him rested the duty, as long as he was alive, of looking after the family estate as well as other family affairs.

Banowari found that nobody trusted him either with the boy or with the estate. There were no two opinions on this – that he did not have much capability and was quite likely to ruin the estate if it came into his hands. In effect all that was ordained for him was that he should eat – an allowance having been made for this – and sleep in his corner of the room.

He said to Kiron, "I do not wish to live on a pension doled out by Nilkantha. Let us leave this house and go to Calcutta!" What he got in reply was, "What a strange thing to say! The estate belonged to your father, and Haridas is like your own son. Why should you mind that the estate has been willed to him?"

How hardhearted was her husband, capable of being jealous even of this young boy! Kiron in her own mind fully supported her father-in-law's action and was convinced that if the estate came into the hands of Banowari, all the lower castes, every Jadu, Madhu, fisherman and labourer, would cheat him right and left – altogether ruining the prospect of the future hope of the family. A descendant to continue her father-in-law's line had at last arrived and the fit person to look after his future was Nilkantha, nobody else.

Banowari found Nilkantha in the inner quarters, making a list of all the belongings in different rooms and locking up all the boxes and chests. Eventually he came into Kiron's bedroom to add its contents – things being used by Banowari – to the list. Nilkantha was allowed in the bedroom, so Kiron was not shy in his presence. She was shedding tears, now and again, in grief for her dead father-in-law and in a choked voice helping the sorting-out.

Banowari roared at Nilkantha, "Get out of my room, now!"

Nilkantha said in mock humility, "Sir, I am not at fault. According to the will of the master, I must take care of everything. All this furniture belongs to Haridas."

Kiron said to herself, "What a to-do! Is Haridas not like our own? Where is the shame in enjoying what belongs to him, virtually our own son! In any case one cannot take property with one. It is the younger generation who will enjoy it eventually, tomorrow if not today."

The house began to oppress Banowari, pricking and burning him at every step. There was no one in the huge household to understand the anguish he was going through. Banowari's disturbed mind wanted to go away at once, leaving it all. But inflamed by anger he could not accept either that he should have to go, leaving Nilkantha to lord it over all. He could not find peace – wanting to do some damage and thinking "Let us see how Nilkantha can save the estate."

He went to his father's room and found that there was nobody there. Everybody was busy taking account of the furniture, ornaments and so on in the inner quarters. Even the most careful person makes the occasional slip and Nilkantha did not know tha the master's box he had opened to take out the will had not been put back under padlock. In that box were valuable deeds tied up together in a bundle. On those deeds rested the Halder family's claim to the estate.

Banowari did not know anything about deeds. But he well understood that these papers were important, without which one could not win law suits. He secreted them in his handkerchief and went outside, to the garden, to sit on a cemented terrace under the cluster of champa trees, and think.

The next day Nilkantha came to Banowari to discuss the funeral rites. His demeanor was outwardly meek; nevertheless some lurking expression in his face put Banowari in a state of extreme rage.

Nilkantha started, "About the funeral rites of the late master..."

Banowari stopped him, "What do I have to do with that?"

Nilkantha – "How do you mean? You are the person entitled to perform the rites."

"A great entitlement indeed! To perform funeral rites! That is all in this world that I am supposed to be good for, nothing else." He then began shouting, "Get out, don't disturb me!"

Nilkantha went away, and looking at his receding back Banowari felt that he went suppressing laughter. He guessed that the staff were having fun among themselves at his expense, making him – dishonoured, abandoned – an object of jest. There was no one more ridiculed by fate than a person who, ostensibly a member of the family, nevertheless did not belong there; not even a begger from the street.

Banowari went out with that bundle of deeds. The Barujje family of Pratappur were the neighbouring landowners; and competitors. Banowari decided to hand over the deeds to them, with a view to ruining the estate.

As he was going out, Haridas called from upstairs, saying in his sweet young voice, "Uncle, you are going out? Take me with you."

Banowari thought, "The evil star of this boy has made him say this. I am out in the street myself, and I am going to get him out there too. Let everything be destroyed."

He had gone only as far as the garden outside when a hue and cry was heard. A nearby cottage of a widow, adjoining the market place, was on fire. As was Banowari's wont, he could not remain unmoved, and leaving the bundle of deeds behind on the terrace underneath the champa trees, he rushed to the fire.

On return the bundle was missing. In a moment he was struck as if by a bullet in his heart, thinking that it meant another defeat by Nilkantha; he should not have bothered even if the widow's cottage had been reduced to ashes. He was left with no doubt that the cunning Nilkantha had got hold of the deeds.

He appeared at the office like a storm. Nilkantha quietly closed his box and saluted him respectfully, standing up. Banowari thought that he was hiding the papers in the box. Without a word he opened the box and began searching amongst the papers. It contained only account books and related documents. The box was emptied, turned upside down, but the deeds were not found. Banowari said in an almost choked voice, "Did you go to the champa grove?"

171

Nilkantha replied, "Yes sir, I did go. I saw you running in a hurry, so went out to see what was happening."

Banowari – "You have taken my papers, tied up with a handkerchief."

Nilkantha said, quite innocently, "No, Sir."

Banowari – "You are telling a lie. Give them back to me. Otherwise you will have to suffer."

In vain Banowari shouted and roared. He could not say what he had lost and knowing that he himself had no right over that stolen property began to call himself a careless fool, tearing himself apart in the process.

After this demonstration of madness in the office he went back to the champa grove to look again. He vowed, taking an oath on his mother, that he would recover the papers, by whatever means possible. He was not in a state to think out how; all he could do was to stamp his feet repeatedly on the ground and say, "I must recover the papers, I must." Then, tired, he sat down under the trees. He felt he had nobody and nothing to call his own. Resourceless, he would have to fight, from now on, alone, with his fate and the world. There was no question of there being for him prestige, respect, love or affection, and nothing meant anything at all. The only prospect he was left with was death, and the capacity to cause trouble.

Restless with thought he became exhausted and fell asleep on the cemented ground. When he came to, he did not at first know where he was. In a while, fully awake, he found Haridas sitting at his head. He asked Banowari, "Uncle do you know what you have lost?" Banowari, surprised, did not answer him. Haridas said again, "What would you give me if I return it to you?"

Banowari did not connect it with the deeds, and thinking that it must be something else replied in jest, "All I have." He knew he had nothing.

Then Haridas brought out from under his clothes that bundle of deeds wrapped up in the handkerchief. There was a picture of a tiger on the handkerchief, something that his

uncle had shown him many times before, making Haridas
rather keen on its possession. That is why he recognised it
from a distance, lying under the trees, as he came out in the
garden, along with the servants who had rushed out at the
cry of fire. Banowari drew Haridas to his bosom and sat
silently for a moment, with him there. After a while tears
began to flow. He remembered that long ago he had had to
whip a newly-obtained dog in order to discipline it. Then his
whip got lost and he could not find it anywhere. When he
had given up all hope, he found the dog sitting near him,
wagging its tail in pleasure with the whip between its teeth.
He could never whip it again.

Banowari quickly dried his eyes and asked, "Haridas, tell
me, what would you like?" Haridas answered, "Your
handkerchief please, uncle." Banowari said, "Come I will
give you a piggy back." He then went to the inner quarters
with Haridas on his shoulders. He found Kiron in the
bedroom, smoothing out the carpet on the floor after it had
been in the sun all day. She got into a state of anxiety to see
Haridas on Banowari's shoulders and said, "Please put him
down, right now. You could drop him."

Banowari fixed a steady gaze at her and said, "No need to
be afraid of me any more. I shant't drop him." He brought
Haridas down and led him towards Kiron, then placing the
papers in her hands said, "These are the deeds for Haridas'
property. Keep them with care." Puzzled Kiron asked, "How
come you have got them?" Banowari replied, "I stole them."
Then he drew Haridas close to him, placed the handkerchief
in his hands and said, "Take this, son, your uncle's treasure
you so desire."

When he looked at Kiron, he found her no longer slim, as
unnoticed, she had grown plump. Now she had the
appearance suitable to the eldest daughter-in-law of the
family. The poems of Amaru were of no use any more and it
was best to abandon them along with the rest of his
belongings.

That night he went missing, leaving a note behind that he

was going in search of a job.

He could not bear to wait even till the funeral ceremony of his father. Everyone cried shame at this inconsiderate behaviour.

The Way to Deliverance

Fakirchand displayed a solemn demeanour from a young age; even then he could quite easily fit into the company of the elderly. He could not bear to have anything to do with cold water, icy weather or amusing jokes.

His seriousness, added to the black woollen muffler that was to be found round his neck for most of the year, made him look like a person of high calibre. To add to this his upper lip was covered with a substantial moustache and his face with a beard, neither of which left much scope for laughter to show.

His wife, Haimabati, was young and her mind totally engrossed with worldly things. She craved reading *Bankim-chandra's*[1] novels and the idea of worshipping her husband held no particular appeal for her. She loved laughter and fun and as a flower yearns for breeze and early sunlight she too, at her time of blossoming youth, ardently longed for caresses and joviality in adequate measure from her husband. But he preferred to read the *Bhagavat*[2] to her at every opportunity, made her listen to the *Gita* every morning and even went to the extent of dealing her occasional physical punishment for the sake of her spiritual upliftment. The day *Krishnakanter Will*[3] was discovered under her pillow Fakir was not content

[1]See footnote p. 70
[2]See footnote 1 p. 148
[3]Famous Bengali novel by Bankimchandra.

till he had made the light-hearted young woman shed tears all night. This was not just novel reading, it was deception carried out against her husband! Anyway, through persistent commands, advice, requests, talks on morality and chastisement Fakir finally succeeded in leaving Haimabati barren of laughter, happiness and youthful passion.

But there are many things in this world that get in the way of detachment for a man. Fakir's ties with the world increased as a son and a daughter were born to him in quick succession. The pressures that his father put on him then made even solemn Fakir go out to look for a job at various offices – but there did not appear to be much hope for him.

He thought then, "I shall leave the world, like Buddha". And not long after this, late at night, he left.

Now it is necessary to tell another story.

Sasticharan of Nabagram had a son named Makhanlal. As no issue appeared for a time after his marriage he married a second time, urged on by his father but also because of his own temptation for a new face. After this marriage his two wives began producing children in earnest – seven daughters and one son in all. Makhan was fickle minded and given to amusement and totally disinclined to be bogged down by responsibilities. Now he had all these children and his two wives as a constant source of irritation – unable to put up with all this he too left home late one night.

He was gone a long time. Rumour had it that in order to taste the happy state of monogamy he had gone to Benares and married again. It was also said that the wretched man had at last found some peace – except that from time to time he felt an earnest longing to visit places near his home, a pleasure of which he had to deprive himself for fear of getting caught.

After wandering about for a time Fakirchand arrived at Nabagram in a state of detachment. He sat down under a banyan tree by the roadside, breathed a sigh and said to himself, "Relief from fear comes only out of renunciation. Wives, children, they are nothing to one. Who is your wife, who your son?" He started singing, with words to the effect that one's turbulent mind should listen to the sayings of wise men about what brings happiness and, breaking out of one's shell, should seek the pearl of renunciation.

Suddenly he stopped singing – "Who is that? My father? So, he has found out about me; this is disastrous! Now I shall be dragged into the dark well of this world again, I must fly."

Fakir entered a nearby house in great haste. The old householder was sitting quietly, smoking his hubble-bubble. Seeing Fakir enter he asked, "Who are you?"

Fakir: "Sir, I am a *sannyasi*[1]".

Old man: "*Sannyasi?* Come close, let me have a look at you in the light". He dragged Fakir to the light and bending over his face, as one does over a book, inspected him closely, while muttering to himself, "This indeed is Makhanlal, the same nose and eyes, only the forehead looks different, and that fine face is now overshadowed by all this moustache and beard". The old man stroked Fakir's face once or twice and then said aloud; "My dear Makhan". Needless to say that old man was Sasticharan.

Fakir (surprised): "Makhan! I am not called, 'Makhan'. Whatever was my name before I left the world, I am now Chidananda Swami, or you may call me Paramananda, if you like."

Sasti: "You may now call yourself 'flattened rice' or 'consecrated food', as you fancy. But I cannot forget that you are my Makhan. My son, what made you leave home? What did you not have here? Two wives – if you cannot love the older one the younger one is there, for you. And no dearth of children, seven girls, one boy – defying all evil-wishers! And I am now old, I shan't live for ever, your family remains yours".

[1]See footnote p. 4.

Fakir shuddered – how ruinous; even to hear such things was a frightening prospect! Then he understood what the matter was and thought, "This is not bad, let me hide here for a day or two, then when my father fails to find me and leaves I shall run away".

Fakir's silence convinced the old man beyond any doubt that this was indeed Makhan. He called his servant, Kesta, and asked him to tell everyone that Makhan had come back.

In a moment a crowd had gathered. Most of the neighbours said that it was Makhan all right, but a few had doubts. But people were so zealous to believe that they were sorely annoyed with the doubters, as if they were wilfully spoiling the pleasure of this homecoming. Their behaviour was comparable to making the metrical order called *"Payar"*[1] contain seventeen letters instead of the usual fourteen – but the neighbours were not going to be comfortable until the thing was reduced to size. These doubters did not believe either in ghosts or exorcists and when everybody was so wonder-struck at the fascinating tale, they dared to raise questions – they were surely a band of atheists. It was not so bad not to believe in ghosts, but it was most heartless to disbelieve when the only son of an old man was concerned. Anyway the doubters were pressurised by others into silence.

The neighbours took not the least notice of Fakir's gravity and sitting around him they began, "This is great! Our old Makhan had turned into a wise man, a renouncer! All his previous life was spent in frivolity, today he has all of a sudden become the great sage, *"Jamadagni"*.[2]

High-minded Fakir was greatly troubled by such unbecoming words but, helpless, he had to put up with it. One of the curious leaned over his body and asked, "Tell me Makhan, you used to be black as coal, how did you manage to become fair?"

[1]A metrical system in Bengali poetry
[2]Sage of ancient times renowned for his spiritual prowess

Fakir replied, "By practising yoga."

Someone present added, "This is nothing surprising. It is said in the *Ramayana*[1] that when the great warrior, Bhim, tried to pick up the tail of the monkey, *Hunuman*, he failed. How was that possible? By sheer force of yoga".

This had to be admitted by all.

Then Sasticharan told Fakir, "My son, we must go to the inner apartments."

Fakir hadn't reckoned with this possibility – it suddenly struck him like thunder. He kept quiet a long time, digesting the undignified jokes and jibes of the neighbours and then replied, "Father, I am now a renouncer, I cannot go to the inner quarters." So, Sasticharan addressed his neighbours, "I shall have to ask you to retire for a while, I must bring his two wives here; they are getting extremely agitated."

Everyone left. Fakir thought of taking this opportunity to run away. But he knew that the moment he appeared on the road the neighbours would be after him like dogs – this consideration kept him sitting, motionless.

As soon as Makhan's two wives entered where he was sitting Fakir bowed down to them saying, "Mothers, I am your son."

Instantly a bangled arm flashed before him like a sword while a metallic voice rang, "You wretched, miserable man, whom are you calling your mother?"

Another voice, raised a few tones higher, said aggressively, "Are you blind? Why doesn't death claim you for its own?"

Fakir was not used to such colloquial communications from his own wife. Much flustered he pressed his palms together at them saying, "You are making a great mistake. Let me stand up in the light and you two have a good look at me."

The two wives said one after the other, "We have seen enough, our eyes are over-worked through looking at you. You are not an infant, nor a newborn babe; you have lost

[1]One of two famous Sanskrit epics in which good triumphs over evil.

your first set of teeth a long time ago and your years have gone beyond count. We haven't forgotten you, just because the king of death has."

One cannot say how long these one-sided conjugal felicitations would have continued – Fakir was standing there, dumb, with his head down – but Sasticharan then entered the scene, attracted by the exchanges in the room and by the assembled crowd in front, on the road. He remarked, "My home was silent all this time with no sound to be heard anywhere. Today I can indeed feel that my Makhan has returned."

Fakir appealed with palms pressed together, "Please, sir, rescue me from your daughters-in-law."

Sasti: "My son, you have just returned after a long time, the commotion is bound to make you feel impatient at first. Well, my daughters, you'd better go inside now. Makhan is going to be here from now on, he will not be allowed to go away again."

When the two women retired Fakir said to the old man, "Sir, I can quite understand why your son left it all and fled. My respects to you, but I am going."

The old man began lamenting so loudly that the neighbours thought that Makhan was beating his father up. Greatly concerned they came running and reprimanded Fakir, warning him that they were not going to allow him to practise his pseudo-renunciation here, he must behave himself. He was then subjected to further jeering.

Fakir's gravity, beard and muffler had hitherto saved him from having to hear such unseemly and abrasive words. From now on the neighbours remained alert lest he tried to run away again. The landlord himself took the side of Sasti in this battle, and Fakir found himself under such strict surveillance that there was no way he could manage to go outside except through the door of death. Alone in a room he started singing the words of a sage on what brought freedom to man. Needless to say, the spiritual import of these words now only provided a backcloth for his thoughts.

However unwholesome the situation, he could manage to carry on a bit. But the news of Makhan's return brought in a swarm of brothers and sisters-in-law from his two wives. The first thing they did on arrival was to pull Fakir's beard, voicing a suspicion that it could not be real, just stuck there by glue as a disguise.

A pull at the moustache under his nose made it difficult to maintain gravity even for someone as high-minded as Fakir. Then his ears were subjected to a proper treatment. First they were twisted, then language of a kind was used that did not need a twist to make them go red.

Fakir was then ordered to sing songs which even distinguished pundits would not be able to attribute a spiritual meaning to. They blackened his face while he slept, and arranged all sorts of inedible things to be offered him in place of the usual delicacies. He was then made to slip over when a whole betel nut was placed under his seat; a monkey's tail was attached to him and a thousand and one other conventional ways of pulling a brother-in-law's leg put his momentous gravity to a severe test.

However much Fakir showed his fury and his pique, however much he screamed and threatened, his "oppressors" could not be scared off. On the contrary, as he persisted, Fakir became more and more of a laughing stock to everyone. When his ears picked out a sweet voice from inside the house which appeared familiar to him he became doubly impatient with all this tom-foolery being practised on him.

The reader is not unacquainted with this familiar voice. Enough to know that Sasticharan was related to Haimabati as a sort of uncle. Oppressed by her mother-in-law after her marriage, Haimabati, an orphan, used to take shelter from time to time with one relation or another. After a long time she had come to her uncle's house and was watching the drama going on from the inner quarters with great amusement. Experts in psychology will have to decide whether the instinct for revenge was added to Haimabati's natural sense of fun – we are unable to say.

Relatives whose tie with the son-in-law of the house was predominantly one of fun and jest would sometimes rest, not so those whose bond was one of love and affection. The seven daughters and a son did not leave him alone even for a moment, for their respective mothers were urging them constantly to claim their share of the "father's" love. The two mothers were in competition, each trying to get more for her own issue; so each kept inspiring her own children and the two lots were around their "father's" neck all the time, kissing him or engaging in some such act of affection in competition with one another.

Needless to say that Fakir was by temperament a dispassionate man, otherwise he could not so easily have left his own children. Children were devoid of devotion and unlearned in being impressed by the virtues of renunciation – so Fakir felt not the least attachment to them. On the contrary what he desired was to be able to keep them at an arm's length, like worms and insects. Now he was surrounded by a swarm of children, rather like a historical article adorned top to bottom by notes, long and short, in italics. There was a huge difference of age between the children and they did not all behave with him in a civilised, adult way. So tears would at times flood into Fakir's eyes and these were not tears of joy. He felt like trying his brutal animal strength when addressed as "father" by someone else's children but fear kept that impulse at bay. All he could do was to sit there, contorting his eyes and face.

In the end Fakir was impelled to shout, "I am going to leave, let me see how you can stop me."

The villagers then brought along a lawyer who questioned him, "You know you have two wives?"

Fakir: "I learnt that for the first time here, sir."

Lawyer: "You have a son and seven daughters of whom two are of a marriageable age?"

Fakir: "You seem to know about it more than I do."

Lawyer: "If you do not accept responsibility for this huge household of yours, your two wives will go to court. You'd better know that."

Fakir was mortally afraid of lawsuits. It was his view that lawyers had no respect for men of distinction – their honour, status or gravity. They were quite openly insulting and they thought nothing of sending their reports to the newspapers. Fakir, with tear-drenched eyes, tried to furnish detailed information about his real self, as a result of which the lawyer began appreciating, more and more, Fakir's cunning, his presence of mind, his uncommon ability to concoct false stories and so on. Fakir felt like biting his own hands and feet. Finding him inclined to run away again his "father" was overcome with grief, and neighbours, surrounding him on all sides, poured down abuse in ample measure while the lawyer threatened him with such dire consequences that Fakir was rendered speechless.

The icing on the cake was when the eight children, hugging him all over, nearly choked him, and Haimabati watching from inside the house did not know whether to laugh or cry.

Fakir, finding no way out, wrote to his real father, revealing all. As a result Haricharanbabu appeared. But the neighbours, the landlord and the lawyer were totally disinclined to let go of their claim. They brought in a thousand and one "fool-proof" bits of evidence that this man was Makhan and not Fakir. They even managed to produce the old wet-nurse who brought Makhan up. She held up his chin with her two shaking hands and looking at Fakir began shedding streams of tears on his beard.

When Fakir refused to own up even after this, his two "wives" appeared, their saris covering their heads and faces. With appropriate gestures of their hands they demanded of him, "Which funeral pyre, which door of the king of death are you going to choose for your exit?"

As Fakir couldn't tell for certain he kept quiet. But the way he looked did not suggest preference for any particular door of the king of death; any door would do for now, to let him out of the trap.

At that moment another woman entered the room and bowed down to Fakir. He was at first non-plussed; then over-joyed he cried out, "Thank God, here is Haimabati." Never in his life had his eyes displayed such love for any wife, his own or anyone else's. He felt that deliverance herself had appeared in embodiment to save him.

Another person was watching all this from a hiding place with a cloth covering his face: his name, Makhanlal. He was mightily pleased to see an unknown innocent being forced into his own place. At last with the appearance of Haimabati he understood that the innocent man was in fact a close relative. Overtaken by pity he entered the room and said: "It is a great sin to involve a relative in such trouble." Then pointing his finger to his two wives, he admitted, "These two happen to be my rope and my pitcher."

The neighbours were stunned at the nobility and courage of Makhanlal.

The Judge

When the man who had eventually given shelter to the no-
longer-young Kshiroda, after she had gone through many
vicissitudes, also cast her aside like a worn-out piece of cloth,
in her shame she no longer felt any inclination to look for
another source of security that was necessary for her survival.

The age that comes to the end of youth is – like the white
seasons of *Sarat*[1] – full of depth, tranquil, profound and
graceful, the time for fruit and corn to ripen. The Springtime
restlessness of exuberant youth is then no longer appropriate, and by then our nest-building in the world is nearly
over. The inner self has matured through digesting a lot of
good and bad, joys and sorrows. We have withdrawn our
wild desires from the imaginary world of delusory and vain
hopes beyond our reach and established them firmly within
the four walls of our limited capabilities. One can then no
longer attract the bewitching look of a new love, but one
becomes dearer to old acquaintances. The grace of youth no
doubt gradually withers but the ageless inner nature
becomes, through long association, printed in a most
distinct manner in one's eyes and face – one's smile, look,
voice become saturated with its spirit. We give up hope for
the unobtained, give up grieving for those who left us,

[1]See footnote 1 p. 22

forgive those who deceived us, take those to our bosom who have come near us and loved – the few remaining through stormy weather, suffering and separation – while we build a secure, well-tested nest amidst long-familiar, affectionate ties. There we reach the end of our striving and the fulfilment of our remaining desires. There is none as wretched as one who even at this time of pleasant evening at the end of youth, this time for peace, must strive for new accumulation, new acquaintance, for the futile hope of a new tie – one who does not yet have a bed ready for rest or a lamp lit awaiting one's return.

When Kshiroda woke up one morning at the extreme end of her youth to find that during the night her lover had fled with all her ornaments and money without even leaving enough for her rent – or for milk for her three year old son – it occurred to her that she had not succeeded in making even one man her own, in getting the right to even the corner of a room in which to live or die. And when she remembered that she had again to dry her tears and put collyrium on her eyes, red colour on her lips and cheek, cover up her departed youth by deceptions and with a smiling face and great patience try to spread a fresh net of attraction for capturing yet another heart, she closed her door and lying on the floor began striking her head again and again on its hard surface – remaining there all day, as if dead, without food. Darkness gathered in the unlit room. Fortunately or unfortunately a former lover came just then and began striking at the door with 'Kshiro! Kshiro!' All of a sudden Kshiroda opened up the door and with a broom in hand came chasing him – roaring, like a lioness in action. The pleasure-seeking young man instantly fled.

The hungry child had cried for a long while and had at last fallen asleep under the bedspread. The noise woke him up and he began crying and calling his mother in a feeble anxious voice from amidst the darkness.

Then Kshiroda pressed the crying child to her bosom and like lightning ran to a nearby well and jumped.

Attracted by the sound the neighbours came there with a lamp. It did not take them long to pick them both up. She was unconscious and the child dead.

Kshiroda recovered in hospital. The magistrate committed her to sessions, on a charge of murder.

The judge Mohitmohum Dutta was a statutory civilian[1] By his severe judgement she was sentenced to be hanged. The lawyers tried their best to save the wretched woman in consideration of her circumstances, but failed. The judge would not in any way consider her to be deserving of pity.

He had his reasons to justify this. On the one hand he referred to Hindu women as *devi*[2], on the other hand he was full of mistrust of the female sex. According to him, women were ever anxious to rescind family ties; if restrictions were eased even a little bit, there would not be even one woman remaining in the cage of society.

There were reasons lying behind Mohit's belief, to be found in the history of his youth.

When Mohit was a second-year student at college he was altogether a different person in conduct and appearance. Nowadays Mohit had a bald patch in front and a tuft of never-cut hair (to indicate holiness) at the back of his head; his clean-shaven face felt the use of razors every day, to demolish the least appearance of moustache and beard. But as a young man, he with his gold-framed glasses, moustache, beard and western style haircut was like a new edition of the god *Kartick*[3] in the nineteenth century. He was particularly careful about dress, had no distaste for meat or drink and there were one or two associated vices as well.

Not far away lived a householder. He had a widowed daughter called Hemsashi. She was quite young, not more than fourteen or fifteen years old.

[1]Civilian permitted to act as judge by Government statute.
[2]Goddesses in human form.
[3]A handsome god – the general of the Gods' army.

The wooded shore of a sea does not look as attractive, dreamlike and picturesque from the shore itself as it does from a distance. The distance that was created through the widowhood that encircled her between Hemsashi and family life made her look upon that life as a highly mysterious pleasure-house way out on the horizon. She did not know that the world is a machine with very complicated parts and that it is hard like iron - a mixture of happiness and sorrow, weal and woe, doubt and danger, hopelessness and repentance. She thought that life in that world was easy, like the transparent water of a bubbling spring, the paths in front of that enticing world all wide and straight. Happiness was just outside her window and frustration only inside the palpitating, warm and soft heart between the ribs of her breast - particularly when from far and away through the sky of her heart blew the wind of youth, adorning the world with the enchanting colour of Spring, when her heart-beats filled the whole sky and the world bloomed, layer over layer, like soft petals of a red lotus around the scented cells of her inner being.

At home there were only her parents and two younger brothers. The brothers went to school early after their meal and back from school they went again, after food, to night school in the evening, to prepare their lessons. Their father earned very little and couldn't afford a private tutor.

In between work Hem used to sit in her lonely room and watch people coming and going on the road in front or listen to hawkers noisily pleading their wares. She used to think that the people walking were happy, that the beggers were free, and it did not occur to her that the hawkers were engaged in a hard struggle for their livelihood - to her they were all just actors in a happy theatre where people kept coming and going.

And she could see well-dressed Mohitlal, morning, afternoon and evening, his breast swelling with pride. He appeared to be like *Indra*[1] - enjoying all possible good

[1]See footnote 2 p. 135

fortune – the best of men. She felt that the well-dressed good-looking young man, his head held high, possessed everything and deserved to be offered everything. As a girl plays with a doll pretending that it is a live human being, the widow used to play with the idea of Mohit, endowing him with every glory and placing him in the position of a god.

Now and again she found Mohit's room well lit, resounding with dance bells and the sound of music from a female voice. She would then spend all night sitting, staring with sleepless, thirsty eyes at the fleeting images on the wall. Her troubled, tormented heart, like a caged bird, would be pounding in her ribs with unnatural force.

Did she mentally upbraid or censure her pseudo-god for such indulgence in amorous dallying? No. As fire attracts an insect, tempting it with the illusion of the kingdom of stars, that room of Mohit, well-lit, full of music and of the heady wine of pleasure, used to attract Hemsashi like a mirage of heaven. She would sit, awake, alone, at the depth of night and mix the light, shade and music of the nearby window with her own desires and imagination to create a land of magic, and, placing her mental idol in the midst of that land, watch him with wonder-struck, captivated eyes. She would offer him adoration with her life and youth, joys and sorrows, this world and the next – all these burned like incense in the fire of her desire – in that lonely silent temple. She did not know that inside the building in front of her and amidst that flow of pleasure rippling by, there was much weariness and exhaustion, sordidness, monstrous hunger and life-wasting affliction.

Hem could have spent all her life in a dream-like trance with her magical heaven and imaginary deity. But unfortunately the deity decided to favour her and heaven came near. When that heaven touched the earth it disintegrated and the person who all by herself had built that heaven for so long was shattered; ruined she fell to the ground.

Mohit's greedy eye sometime fell on the girl in the

window. He sent her one letter after another with a false signature, *'Vinodchandra'*, and in the end received a reply full of apprehension, anxiety, spelling mistakes and boundless emotion. After that a storm began to rage for a while with strokes and counter-strokes, delight and diffidence, doubt and respect, hope and apprehension, making the world whirl round the widow as she was seized with a destructive but pleasurable excitement. How, as all these things were happening, the world vanished like an unreal shadow, and how in the end, one day the woman was flung off to a great distance by the speed of that whirling movement, suddenly cut off from that world which still continued to revolve – these things do not have to be told in great detail.

At dead of night Hem left her parents, her brothers and her home, and boarded a train with Mohit, passing himself off as *'Vinodchandra'*. When the image of the deity made of clay, straw and tinsel ornaments, became a reality at her side, shame and repentance made her want to sink through the ground. As the train started she fell at Mohit's feet, crying, "Please, oh please, take me back home!" Mohit hurriedly pressed his hands over her mouth.

As one's whole life-story appears before one in an instant while drowning, Hemsashi began recollecting in the darkness of the closed carriages – how her father would not sit down to a meal without her being present there, how her younger brother loved to be fed by her when he came back from school, how she used to sit down with her mother and dress betel leaves, how her mother cared for her hair in the afternoon. Every insignificant corner of the house and the meanest of housework took on an appearance of splendour before her mind's eye. Then her lonely life and her little world began to feel like heaven to her – that betel leaf preparation, dressing of hair, fanning at her father's meal, picking out his grey hairs during siesta on holidays, putting up with the demands of her brothers – all these appeared to her as a serene and highly prized happiness. She no longer thought that with all this within one's grasp any other happiness was needed.

She thought of all the protected daughters with their families, now enjoying deep sleep. Why hadn't she realized before how full of contentment was that secure sleep on one's own bed in a silent night. Family girls would wake up tomorrow morning in their own room and would be engaged in their daily chores without a thought. But in what sort of a morning would this sleepless night of Hemsashi end? In that cheerless morning when the familiar, peaceful and smiling sunlight would fall on their very ordinary domestic life by the lane, what shame would be revealed there – what degradation and grief would be awaiting!

Hem cried and cried. Broken-hearted and with pitiful appeal she begged, "It is still night, my mother and my two brothers are not awake yet. Please take me back now." But her deity paid no heed and instead took her towards her long-awaited heaven in a chariot of a second class carriage full of the noise of revolving wheels.

Soon afterwards the deity with his heaven boarded another seedy second class chariot and left for another place – the woman remained sunk in mud upto her neck.

I have just mentioned this one incident from Mohitlal's previous history. I shan't bring in others for fear that this narrative would become boring.

Anyway, it is not necessary to talk about that old story any more. It is doubtful whether there was anyone alive who remembered the name, 'Vinodchandra'. Mohit had now become a strict observer of religious rules. He offered homage to a deity morning and evening and was frequently engaged in discussing sacred books. Even his young children were made to practice yoga and his women were kept secure under strict control in inner apartments inaccessible even to the sun, the moon and the wind-borne deities. But because he had once done wrong to more than one woman, he now passed the most severe judgement against any social transgression by them.

A day or two after he had passed Kshiroda's death sentence, gourmand Mohitlal went to the jail garden to get his vegetables. He was also curious to know if Kshiroda was sufficiently repentant for her disreputable life. He entered the cell.

From a distance he had heard the noise of a quarrel going on there. As he entered he found Kshiroda engaged in a serious altercation with the guard. Mohit laughed to himself. He thought, 'Such is the nature of women. Death is near but she can't give up quarrelling. Perhaps they fight even with the king of death in his own abode."

He considered it his duty to create repentance in her heart with due reprimand and good counsel. As he approached her with that noble intention, Kshiroda with her palms together pleaded in a most solicitous tone, "I beg of you, Mr Judge, please ask him to give me my ring back."

Questioning, he found out that there was a ring hidden in Kshiroda's hair which by chance the guard had discovered and taken away by force.

Mohit laughed to himself again, "She is going to the gallows in a day or two and yet is unable to give up her attachment to a piece of jewellery. Ornaments are the be-all and end-all to women." He asked the guard, "Where is the ring? let me have a look."

Suddenly it was like a live coal in his hand, it startled him so. On one side there was a tiny oil painting on ivory of a young man with a moustache and beard and on the gold on the other side was inscribed, 'Vinodchandra'.

He raised his head away from the ring, and looked at Kshiroda. Instantly he was reminded of another face of twenty years ago, tear-soaked, full of the gentleness of love and bashful apprehension – That face had similarities with this one before him.

Mohit looked at the ring again and when he raised his face the next time, that unchaste and fallen woman had taken on

192

the radiant appearance of a goddess in the bright illumination of the golden ring.

Punishment

When the two day-labourer brothers, Dukhiram and Chidam Rui, went out to work in the morning with their cleavers in hand, their two wives were busy bickering and shouting at each other. But the neighbourhood had by now got used to this noisy quarrelling, as to various other kinds of regular sounds of mother nature. As soon as shrill voices were heard, people observed amongst themselves, "Ah, so it has started at last." That is, it was happening exactly as expected, no exception had occurred in the regularity of 'nature'. As people do not ask 'why' when the sun rises in the east of a morning, it no longer aroused anyone's curiosity to find out the reason when an uproar was created between the two sisters-in-law in the household of the Ruis.

No doubt the waves of these querulous exchanges touched the husbands more than others in the neighbourhood, but they did not consider it particularly inconvenient. It was as if the two brothers were travelling on the lengthy pathway of this world on a one-horse-drawn cart, accepting as a natural and lawful part of this journey of their life's chariot the continuous squeaking and scratching noise of the springless wheels on two sides. Not only did they take it as natural, but, the day when there was no noise in the house and it was dreadfully still and full of an eerie sensation, apprehension arose of some unnatural trouble and nobody could foretell what would happen and when.

The day our story begins, the two brothers, tired after labouring the whole day, returned home to find that their house was resounding, as it were, with total silence.

It was very stuffy outside. A heavy shower or two had occurred in the middle of the day and cloud was still hovering around with no trace of wind. The rains had contributed to a heavy undergrowth of wild creepers and weeds around the house; from there and from the jute fields under water a gaseous smell of wet vegetation had solidified everywhere like a motionless wall. From the pit full of water beyond the cowshed came the call of frogs and the silent sky of the evening was filled with the chirrup of crickets.

Not far away, the river Padma in the rainy season had assumed, under the shadow of new clouds, a still but fearful appearance. It had washed away most of the cultivated land near it and had edged nearer to human habitation. Even the roots of a few mango and jack-fruit trees had become visible by the side of the crumbling bank, as if their fingers, spreading out of their helpless fists, were trying to hang on to some ultimate support in emptiness.

Dukhi and Chidam had gone that day to work on the landlord's estate. On the strip of the sandy land by the river Padma seasonal paddy had ripened. Before the rains managed to wash this land away, all the poor people got busy reaping grain from the paddy fields, either their own or other peoples', on which they were employed. But over-seers from the administrative quarters of the landlord forced these two brothers to go with them, and there they were engaged in mending the office roof through which rainwater was coming in in various places. They had worked hard all day at it, making some wicker doors as well. They were not able to come home for their midday meal, having to be content with light refreshment at work. They were soaked with rain at times while working, were not given their proper due as wages, and to top it all were subjected to unjust abuse.

The brothers came home in the evening splashing through mud and water to find the younger wife, Chandana, lying still on a part of her sari spread on the ground. Like the cloudy day itself she too had shed copious tears all day before stopping towards evening and putting on a sultry look instead. The older wife, Radha, sat on the verandah with a sour face. Her year-and-a-half-old son had been crying nearby for a long time, but when the brothers entered the house they found him lying naked on his back in a corner of the courtyard – now fallen asleep.

Hungry, Dukhi said without any delay whatever, "Give us our food." The older wife, her shrill voice reaching up to the sky, exploded like fire on a gunpowder bag, "Where is rice, to serve? Did you give me any? Am I supposed to earn to get it?"

After day-long toil and abuse – hunger raging through him in that cheerless dark room without food – the hidden and ugly implication of the last few mocking words suddenly became unbearable to Dukhi. Like a lion's deep roar he shouted, "What did you say?" and without a thought brought down the cleaver on his wife's head in the flash of a moment. Radha dropped down, almost brushing her younger sister-in-law, dead on the instant.

Chandana, her clothes wet with blood, cried out, "What have you done?" Chidam pressed his fingers on her lips. Dukhi dropped the cleaver, put his hand to his mouth and sat down, totally bewildered. The young boy woke up and frightened began to cry.

It was very peaceful outside. Cowherds were returning to the village with their cows. Those who had gone to the sandy strip to cut newly ripened paddy, grouped in fives or sevens, hired small boats, and arriving this side of the river had, most of them, reached home with a few bundles of paddy on their heads as reward for their labours.

"Uncle" Ramlochan was smoking his hubble-bubble, quiet and contented, having returned from the village post office where he had gone to post a letter. Suddenly he remembered that a lot of rent was owing him from his sub-tenant Dukhi, who had promised to pay some of it back today. Deciding that they would have returned from work by now he placed his *chaddar*[1] on his shoulders and went out with his umbrella.

It felt uncanny when he entered their house. The lamp was not lit, one or two indecipherable figures were seen, indistinctly, on the dark verandah. Now and again a muffled sob rose up from one corner and the more the child tried to break out crying 'Mother' the more Chidam was using pressure to stop him.

Ramlochan, somewhat frightened, asked, "Are you there, Dukhi?"

The moment his name was called, Dukhi, who had sat so long like a figure of stone, broke out into unrestrained crying, like a senseless young boy. Chidam came down into the courtyard in a hurry and came near Ramlochan who asked, "So, the women have quarrelled good and proper today? They've been heard shouting all day."

Not knowing what to do, Chidam was busy, all this time, with impossible plots going through his mind. He had decided as a temporary measure that the dead body would have to be removed somewhere when the night had advanced a little. He hadn't reckoned with the possibility of Ramlochan arriving in the meantime . . . Not finding a ready answer he blurted out, "Yes, there was a terrific quarrel today." Ramlochan, attempting to advance towards the verandah asked, "But why should Dukhi be crying for that?"

Chidam, realizing that the situation had gone beyond saving, abruptly came out with, "The younger wife used the cleaver on the older wife's head during the quarrel."

One forgets, in the heat of the moment, that there could be other dangers awaiting besides the one now being faced. Chidam was worrying about how to save themselves from the dreadful truth. He failed to understand that falsehood may turn out to be even more dreadful than the truth. He instantly came out with the first thing that came into his

[1]See footnote 3 p. 7

head the moment Ramlochan started questioning him.

Startled, Ramlochan asked, "What! Is that so? She is not dead?"

Chidam replied, "She is," and immediately took hold of Ramlochan's feet. Ramlochan wanted to leave there as fast as he could, thinking, "By God, what an awkward predicament I am in, at this time of the evening. I shall be nearly dead with all the witnessing I have to do at court." But Chidam did not let go of his feet; he said, "Sir, tell me how I can save my wife."

Ramlochan was foremost in the village in counselling in matters of law. He thought for a while and said, "You see, there is a way out. Run to the police station now and tell them that your elder brother, Dukhi, wanted food when he returned in the evening and not finding it ready, used the cleaver on his wife's head. I tell you, I have no doubt about it; if you say that your wife will be saved."

Chidam's mouth began drying up. Getting up he said, "Sir, I can get another wife if I lose this one, but not another brother if he is hanged." Not that he had thought of this when first depositing the guilt on his wife. Rather, unconsciously his mind was looking for justification and consolation too for what he had said in a hurry and without thought.

Ramlochan too thought it reasonable. He observed, "Well then, report it as it happened. It is impossible to save everything."

Forthwith Ramlochan departed and it was soon all over the village that in the Rui's house Chandana had, in a state of fury during a quarrel, used the cleaver on her sister-in-law's head.

Like water flooding through a damaged embankment the police noisily entered the scene and everyone, guilty and not guilty alike, became extremely agitated.

Chidam considered that he had to continue on the path he

had already carved out. He had given a certain version of the happening to Ramlochan which had spread everywhere in the village. He did not know what the consequences would be if another version now got into circulation. He figured that the story had perforce to be retained and the only way left to him to save his wife was to add a few more incidents to it.

When Chidam asked his wife to take the crime on to her own shoulders she was stunned. He assured her, "Do what we are asking you to, but there is no need to be afraid, we can save you."

He gave her this assurance, no doubt, but his tongue dried up and his face went pale. Chandana was no more than seventeen or eighteen years of age. Her face was cheerful, full and round, she was of medium height, firm and well-built. She had a certain grace and could carry herself about with ease. Like a new-built boat, she was trim, well-shaped, moving easily with no slackness anywhere in her body. She also had a natural sense of humour and curiosity about everything in the world, loved visiting her neighbours for a tête-à-tête and while going to the pond with a pitcher at her waist she would push her head-cover a little with her fingers to create a gap so as to be able to see whatever was worth seeing on the way with her glinting, roving and deep-black eyes.

The older wife was the exact opposite of this, rather haphazard, sluggish and disorderly. Her head-cover; the child on her lap; domestic work; she could not cope well with any of these. Even when there was no pressure of work she could not make any time for leisure. Her younger sister-in-law didn't have to say much to her, just a few sharp, biting remarks in a soft voice, and she would scream, flame up in a rage and bandy words in volumes, disturbing the peace of the whole neighbourhood.

There was a surprising similarity of nature between husband and wife of these two couples. Dukhiram was a person of ample proportions – his bones large, nose snubbed and eyes moving over the visible world without much comprehension, but not questioning anything. Such a man, strong but helpless, peaceable in nature but fearsome in looks, is rare.

And Chidam? As if someone had carved him with care out of shining black stone; totally devoid of any excess anywhere in his body but no hollow depression either, his every limb, mixed with strength and skill, had reached a certain completeness. Whether in diving from a high bank, punting with a pole, climbing and cutting young pieces of bamboo, in all he did there was a certain measured orderliness, an effortless expertise. His long hair down to his shoulder was dressed with oil and carefully combed, his outfit and toilet showed a lot of attention.

Even though he was not indifferent to the beauty of other young wives of the village – he was quite mindful of making himself attractive in their eyes – he particularly loved his young wife. They quarrelled, then got together again, but in this game neither could subdue the other. And there was another reason why the tie that bound the two together was strong. Chidam used to think that one couldn't altogether trust a woman as restless and swift-moving as Chandana, and Chandana felt that Chidam was much too interested in his surroundings and that if one did not keep a tight grip on him he could, one day, cut himself loose.

Before the incident we are talking about happened there was quite a tussle going on between the husband and wife. Chandana had found that her husband was going away from time to time for two or three days on the excuse of work and yet he brought nothing back in wages. Considering that a bad sign she too started indulging in immoderate behaviour – began going to the pond at the wrong times and praising the second son of Kasi Mazumdar after coming back from her visits to the neighbourhood.

This poisoned Chidam's days. He was restless when out on work on which he couldn't concentrate. He upbraided his sister-in-law one day for not controlling Chandana's movements. Enraged, she invoked her father's name and, with appropriate gestures with her hands, flared up, "She runs before the storm, how can I be expected to control her? I am afraid one day she will cause a scandal." Chandana came out of the next room and asked, quietly, "Why *didi*[1], what makes you so fearful?" This started a squabble between the sisters-in-law. Chidam said with fury in his eyes, "If I hear again that you have gone to the pond on your own I shall break every bone in your body." Chandana calmly observed, "My bones will then find peace." And at once she made a move to go out. With one leap Chidam pulled her by her hair, pushed her into a room and bolted the door from outside.

Back home from work in the evening he found the door open with nobody inside. Chandana had crossed three villages and gone to her uncle's place. After a lot of cajoling and a great deal of effort Chidam managed to bring her back from there, but this time he had to admit defeat. He found it as impossible to take a tight hold of this chit of a wife as to hold tight a fistful of quicksilver – she slipped between his fingers.

He did not put any more pressure on her but his life became one of agitated misgivings. His love, ever full of apprehension, began troubling him like a sharp pain. He even thought that if she died he could feel secure and rest in peace. Man is never as jealous of the king of death as of another human being.

It was then that the mishap took place. Chandana stared in stunned disbelief when her husband asked her to take the blame on to herself. Her two eyes, like black fire, began burning her husband with their look. Her whole body and mind shrunk, as if wanting to release themselves from this monster of a husband while her inner being felt totally averse to him.

Chidam assured her, "You have nothing to fear." And

[1]See footnote p. 92.

201

then taught her again and again what she had to tell the police and the Magistrate. Chandana heard nothing of this rigmarole and sat there like a figure carved in stone.

Chidam was Dukhiram's resort in all matters. When he suggested placing the crime on Chandana's shoulders Dukhi asked, "What will happen to *Bowma*?"[1] Chidam said, "I can save her." The amply-proportioned Dukhi felt completely reassured at his brother's words.

Chidam had told his wife to say that the older wife came to strike her with a knife and she resisted with a cleaver in her hand which struck her sister-in-law by accident. All this was a creation of Ramlochan who instructed Chidam in detail in all the elaborations and proofs that would be needed in favour of the story.

The police began their investigation. Everyone in the village by now firmly believed that Chandana had murdered her sister-in-law. Every witness proved that. When the police asked Chandana she said, "Yes, I killed her."

"Why did you?"

"I just couldn't stick her."

"Did you have a quarrel?"

"No."

"Did she come to strike you first?"

"No."

"Did she torture you in any way?"

"No."

People were taken aback to hear such a reply. Chidam became extremely perturbed and interposed, "She is not telling the truth, the older wife first..."

The Inspector shut him up. But the usual procedure of questioning brought out the same answer, again and again – Chandana refused to admit to any aggressive intent on the part of the older wife.

Such an obstinate woman was rare! She was inclining towards the gallows with all her strength and nothing was

[1]Address for a younger brother's wife.

succeeding in pulling her back. Chandana was mentally telling her husband, "You, I am leaving, I would rather embrace the gallows with my fresh youth – let that be my last bond with the world."

Arrested and to be sent to prison, stained with disgrace, Chandana, a rather unoffending, small, fickle and humour-loving village housewife, left – before the eyes of all her acquaintances – her home for ever, walking on the familiar village road, by the ground where the Chariot festival took place, through the market place, then by the end of the village pond in front of the Mazumdar's house and finally past the post office and the school building. A crowd of children walked behind her and the village women who were her friends kept looking at police-led Chandana as she passed – some of them through a gap in their head covering, some from their doorways, some hiding behind trees; all shuddered in shame, abhorrence and fear.

Chandana admitted her guilt to the Deputy Magistrate as well and it never transpired that the murder had anything to do with any torture dealt out by the older wife. The day Chidam appeared before the Magistrate as a witness he began crying with hands pressed together, "Please, Sir, my wife is not guilty." The judge rebuffed him, stopping his passion-ate outburst and began questioning him; whereupon Chidam revealed the true details one by one.

The Judge didn't believe him: for the chief witness – a gentleman – Ramlochan, had said, "I came into the scene soon after the murder: the witness Chidam disclosed all to me and then clinging to my feet asked, 'Please tell me how I can save my wife.' I said nothing for or against. The witness asked me, 'If I say that my elder brother when refused food struck his wife in a rage, will my wife be saved?' I said, 'I warn you, you wicked man, do not utter falsehood in a Court – there is no greater sin than that...'" and so on.

Ramlochan had concocted a few stories to save Chandana. But when he found her adamant he considered, "My God, I do not wish to be charged with false evidence. It is best to say just the little bit I know." So he said what he knew and didn't just let it go at that either. The Deputy Magistrate committed her to trial at the sessions court.

In the meanwhile life in the world around carried on with its cultivation, marketing, joys and sorrows. And as on previous years *Sravan*[1] downpour continued falling on the fresh paddy fields.

Police came to the court with the accused and witnesses. In the Munsiff's Court a lot of people were seated in front, awaiting their own case. A lawyer had come from Calcutta over the sharing of a pit beyond someone's kitchen[2] and there were thirty-nine witnesses present on the side of the defendant. Umpteen human beings had come there eager to settle with hairsplitting accuracy the accounts that they considered ought to be in their favour and they believed that there was nothing more important than that in the whole world. Chidam was looking through the window, his eyes fixed, at the busy, everyday world and everything there appeared to him like a dream. There was a cuckoo calling from a banyan tree in the compound – it was above all law, above this Court.

Chandana said to the Judge, "Tell me sahib, how many times do I have to say the same thing?" The Judge tried to make her understand, "Do you know the punishment for the crime you are admitting to?"

Chandana said, "No."

The Judge said, "It is death by hanging."

Chandana replied, "I beg of you sahib, hang me and be done with it. Do what you like but I cannot bear to be questioned any more." When Chidam was brought to the Court Chandana turned her face away.

The Judge said, "Look at the witness and tell me who he is."

Chandana covered her face with her hands and replied, "He is my husband."

[1]See footnote 1 p. 48
[2]Disputes often occurred because of unclear property demarcation lines.

Question – Does he not love you?

Answer – I should doubt it.

Question – Do you love him?

Answer – Yes, I love him very much.

When questioned Chidam said, "It is I who committed the murder."

Dukhiram fainted when brought in as a witness. Regaining consciousness he replied, "Sahib, it is I who committed the murder."

Question – Why?

Answer – I asked for food, she didn't give me any.

After a lot of cross-examination and listening to other witnesses the judge came to the clear conclusion that these two brothers were admitting guilt only to save a woman of their household from the dishonour of being hanged. But Chandana kept to the same story from the police to the sessions court without so much as a word of difference. Two lawyers, voluntarily and zealously, tried to save her from a sentence of death, but they had to admit she had defeated them.

The kind-hearted prison doctor in the jail asked Chandana before she was going to be hanged, "Do you wish to see anyone?" Chandana replied, "I would like to see my mother once more."

The doctor asked, "Your husband wants to visit you, should I call him?"

Chandana observed, "What nonsense."

Sunshine and Clouds

Yesterday it had been pouring down in buckets. This morning the rain stopped, and pale sunlight and scattered clouds began writing, in turn, their own signatures over the field of near-ripe oush[1] paddy. The wide, dark backdrop assumed the colour of glistening mud through the touch of the light and immediately afterwards appeared soft and pleasant under the shade of the clouds.

While there were only two actors, sunlight and cloud, each playing its part on the stage of the sky, there were countless dramas taking place on the stage of the world down below.

With the lifting of the curtain – to stage the drama of a rather ordinary human existence – a house in a village by the roadside could be seen. It had only one brick-built room and by its two sides ran a decaying brick wall, encircling a few mud rooms. From the road one could see a bare-bodied young man in the room, through the bars of the window. He was seated on a bedstead and frequently fanning himself with a palm-leaf fan held in his left hand, trying to remove both heat and mosquitoes, while engaged at the same time in reading a book that was in his right hand.

Outside on the village road a girl dressed in a striped sari was walking up and down in front of the room, finishing up,

[1] Variety of paddy that ripens in the rainy season

one after another, the *kalajams*[1] held in a fold of her garment. One could see from her face that she knew the young man studying in the room quite intimately, and also that she was trying to draw his attention to tell him that she was quite unconcerned about him, being busy eating *kalajams* without a care in the world.

Unfortunately the man studying in the room had bad eyesight and was consequently untouched by the silent and apparent indifference shown by the girl, at a distance. The girl knew that too, so after fruitlessly strolling for a time she had to use the stone of a *kalajam*, instead of silent disregard, to draw his attention. It was that hard to maintain the purity of one's pride with a man who had bad eyesight!

When one or two stones, thrown anyhow, had struck the wooden door by luck, making a rapping noise, the man lifted his head from his studies. The girl sensed that he had looked up and engaged herself with redoubled attention in selecting ripe *kalajams* from the pocket made with her sari. The man frowned, and by peering, recognized the girl. He left his books, came to the window and laughingly called to her, "Giribala!" Unperturbed and as if unaware of the world around her Giribala kept herself thoroughly busy selecting *kalajams*, while slowly moving on a pace or two.

It was no longer hidden from the shortsighted young man that he was being punished for some unknown offence. He came out hurriedly, asking, 'Why, none for me today?' Giribala paid no attention and after a great deal of searching and examination selected one particular *kalajam* and, totally unconcerned, began eating it.

The fruits came from Giribala's family garden, and the young man was allowed a share every day. But Giribala appeared to have forgotten this, and today her demeanor suggested that she had collected all of them only for herself. But it was not clear why she had to collect *Kalajams* from her own garden and then eat them with such relish at someone

[1]Small, juicy, black fruit akin to cherry.

207

else's front door. The young man then came near and held her hand. Giribala twisted it this way and that, trying to release herself; then she suddenly burst into tears and fled, her *kalajams* scattering all over the ground.

The feeble sunlight and cloud of the morning had settled down in the afternoon with a tired and placid look. While swelling clouds were heaped up at one corner of the sky, elsewhere the exhausted afternoon sunlight was playing on the leaves, on the water in the pond and on every limb of rain-washed nature. The girl from the morning was seen again near the window with bars, as was the young man in the room. The difference was that now the girl had no *kalajams* with her and the young man no book, but of course there were other differences of a deeper and more serious nature.

It was difficult to say what urgent necessity had brought the girl there again and made her hesitate at that particular place. Whatever it was, it was not to converse with the young man inside, her gestures appeared to suggest. Rather, it seemed, she might have come to see whether the fallen *kalajams* had sprouted by now.

But one reason amongst others why this had not happened, was that the fruits had been collected and kept on one corner of the young man's bedstead. While the girl was peering at the ground, seeming to search it anxiously for some imaginary object, the young man controlled his amusement, and kept himself busy selecting a *kalajam* and eating it. When one or two stones dropped near her feet the girl understood that she was being punished for her pride. But was this just? When she had already abandoned all the vanity of her tiny heart and was looking for an opportunity to surrender, it was cruel to create obstacles in her path – it was a task that was hard enough as it was. Realising that she had been found out in her effort to give herself up, she flushed, and was looking for ways of escape when the young man came out and again held her hand.

The girl twisted, trying to release her hand and escape as

she had in the morning, but this time she did not break out crying. Rather, red in the face she turned her head, hiding it behind her tormentor's back and began to laugh with abandon. As she entered the room she behaved as if it was only because she had been defeated and caught, and was being pulled by the hand, that she was going into the room – a jail with iron bars.

As the play of light and shade in the sky is of little consequence, the play of these two human beings on earth was equally inconsequential and transitory. However, considered from another point of view, the play of light and shade in the sky is not insignificant, nor is it just a play, only seeming to be one. The short history of these two unknown human beings on a lazy, rainy afternoon may, similarly, appear of no account amongst thousands of events on this earth, but that is not so either. The same age-old immensity of fate that is adding eon to eon through infinite time, in a significant and unwavering manner, was also sowing the seeds of lifelong happiness and misery that morning and afternoon, in and through the apparently inconsequential tears of that girl. Nevertheless the sensitive pride of the girl would appear rather meaningless to a possible onlooker, as it did to the young man, the hero of this tiny drama. It was not easy for him to fathom why the girl appeared annoyed one day, while showering affection on him on another; why she sometimes increased his allowance of *kalajams*, while stopping it altogether another time. The young man could find no reason why, on certain days, she put all her thoughts, feelings and skill to please him, while trying to hurt him on others, engaging in that task with all her puny strength and hardness of heart. Nor was it clear to him why her hardness became greater when she failed to hit him, while when successful, it melted in a thousand streams through tears of repentance, and then flowed in as great affection.

The insignificant history of this unimportant light-and-shade play is recounted below.

People in the village were busy, as usual, with faction, intrigue, sugar-cane cultivation, false lawsuits and jute trade, except for Sashibhusan and Giribala who delved in to feelings and discussed literature. No-one felt any anxiety or curiosity on that score, as Giribala was only a ten year old girl while Sashibhusan, an M.A., had just gained his degree in Law. They were neighbours.

Giribala's father had, at one time, owned a lot of leased-out land in the village. Bad times forced him to sell it all and accept the post of a tax collector under a foreign landowner. The job was in the same district as his residence, so he did not have to move.

Sashibhusan had passed his Law examination but he made no effort to find himself any work. He did not bother to mix with people or even say a few words in the village meeting places. His bad eyesight meant that he had problems in recognising even the people he knew and when he looked at anyone carefully he had to frown, which appeared like insolence to others.

Whilst it may be fine to remain on one's own amidst the sea of humanity in Calcutta, it is taken to be impudence in a village. When his father gave up, and finally engaged his idle son to look after their meagre property in the village, Sashibhusan had to put up with a great deal of harassment, jeering and insults from the villagers. There was another reason too for the harassment. Sashibhusan loved peace, which made him unwilling to marry. Parents with marriageable daughters took this unwillingness as over-bearing pride and so were unable to forgive him.

The more Sashibhusan was pestered the more he retreated into his cell. His usual occupation was to sit in a corner with a few bound English books on his bedstead and read them as fancy took him – this amounted to all the employment he had, as the property looked after itself, one could say. It has already been mentioned that the only person he had any relationship with in the village was Giribala.

Giribala's brothers were being educated at school. Back at

home they would sometimes ask their ignorant sister questions about the shape of the world, the relative size of the sun and the earth and the like, and when she gave the wrong answers they corrected her mistakes with utter contempt. If the idea that the sun was bigger than the earth appeared 'not proven' to Giribala and she could summon up enough courage to question it, her brothers showed yet more scorn; 'Our books say so and you dare . . .'. Giribala was silenced by the revelation that a printed book said so; it was proof enough and she had no difficulty in accepting the book's verdict as final. Her deepest desire was to be able to read books, like her brothers. At times she would sit down with a book and turn over the pages, and pretend to be reading. The small, black printed letters looked as if they were guarding the main gate to some mysterious domain, with various signs raised high on their shoulders; they did not answer any of Giribala's questions. The book, *Kathamala*,[1] did not reveal one word about its tiger, jackal, horse or ass to the curious girl and *Akhyanmanjari*[2] with all its stories looked at her like someone vowed to silence. Giribala pleaded with her brothers to teach her; they turned a deaf ear to her requests. Sashibhusan was her only help in the matter.

To begin with Sashibhusan was as an unfathomable mystery to Giribala as the books, *Kathamala* and *Akhyanmanjari*. The young man sat alone on a bedstead, surrounded by books in a small room with a window fixed with iron bars – by the side of the road. Giribala would grab hold of a window bar and look with amazement at this strange, bent-backed man absorbed with his books. She decided that he was much more learnéd that her brothers, comparing the respective numbers of their books; this was a surprise of the highest order. She had no doubt that Sashibhusan had finished reading *Kathamala* and similarly important text books; she was reduced to silence, being unable to fathom the

[1] A book of animal stories for children.
[2] A book of old tales adapted for children.

211

limits of his learning, as she watched him turn over the pages of his books.

In the end the wonder-struck girl managed to draw the attention of Sashibhusan despite his bad eyesight. One day he opened a bound book with pictures and called to Giribala, "Come and have a look at the pictures." She ran away.

But the next day she stood again outside the window, clad in a striped sari, and with silent and solemn attention continued to watch Sashibhusan studying. He called again, and again she ran away, breathless, with her plait bobbing behind her.

Such was the manner in which they were introduced. Their intimacy grew after a time, and it would require historical research to ascertain when she first entered the room – being promoted from her place outside the window – and found her place on the bedstead amidst the books.

Giribala began studying with Sashibhusan. People would laugh to hear that the master not only taught his young pupil the alphabet, spelling and grammar, he read poetry to her, with annotations, and asked her opinions on the subject. God only knows what the girl understood, but there is no doubt that she enjoyed it all, as her own mind helped to supply some wonderful pictures that were drawn half out of understanding and half from incomprehension. She would normally listen with her eyes wide open, but would occasionally ask irrelevant questions or bring in some unrelated topic. Sashibhusan never stopped her – it gave him real pleasure to hear this little critic's praise, criticism and gloss on some world-famous poetry. Giribala was his only sympathetic friend in the whole neighbourhood.

When Sashibhusan first knew Giribala she was only eight years old, now she was ten. In those two years she had learnt both the English and Bengali alphabets and could manage to read one or two easy books. For Sashibhusan also those two years in the village had not been entirely dull and lonely.

*

However Sashibhusan did not get on well with Giribala's father, Harakumar. There was a time when Harakumar used to come to Sashibhusan, M.A.,B.L., for consultations over his law-suits. But this M.A.,B.L. holder was not much interested and freely confessed his ignorance about matters of law (despite his degree). Harakumar took that as sheer deception. Two years were spent in this fashion.

Then a need arose for the rent collector to discipline an insubordinate tenant. He wanted to file various lawsuits simultaneously in different district courts and pressed Sashibhusan for advice. Sashibhusan, far from giving it, said a few unpalatable words in a calm but determined manner; this did not please Harakumar. When he failed to win any of the cases against the tenants Harakumar became convinced that Sashibhusan was helping them. He pledged himself to seeing that such a man was driven out of the village.

Sashibhu began to notice that cattle entered his fields, fire broke out in his lentil plots, arguments arose over his boundaries, his tenants refused to pay their taxes, threatening to take him to court instead, and rumours spread abroad that he would be beaten up in the dark and his residence burned down. At last peace-loving Sashibhusan decided to run away to Calcutta.

Preparations for this were under way, when a tent was set up in the village for the visit of the Junior Magistrate sahib, whose name was Joint. The whole place was stirred up by the presence of his armed guards, constables, servants, dogs, horses with their grooms, sweepers and the like. The village boys, half curious and half afraid (like a pack of foxes following a tiger) began wandering round the establishment of the white man.

It was Harakumar who was supplying the sahib's people with chickens, eggs, milk, butter and other edibles, the cost coming under the heading of 'hospitality'. He was happy enough to supply more food than the Magistrate sahib could consume, but when one morning the sahib's sweeper demanded four *seers*[1] of clarified butter for the dog, this appeared to him to be excessive. He advised the sweeper that even though the sahib's dog could no doubt digest a good deal more clarified butter than a native dog, such a quantity of the stuff was not good for its health. The clarified butter was refused.

The sweeper went and told the sahib that he had gone to the rent collector to find out where to get meat for the dog, but he had contemptuously driven him out, in front of everyone, because of his low caste. The sahib too had been subjected to disrespectful words.

The white sahib was naturally not sympathetic to the caste pride of a Brahmin tax collector. Over and above that his daring to insult his sweeper made it impossible for the sahib to contain his anger; a servant was instantly despatched to order him to appear before the Magistrate.

The rent collector began reciting the name of God in great trepidation as he came and stood before the tent. The sahib came striding out of the tent, making a snapping noise with his boots, and asked in a loud voice and an alien intonation, "Why have you driven away my sweeper?" Harakumar hastily put his palms together and submitted that he could never have had the impudence to drive away any sweeper who belonged to the sahib's retinue; only, when he was asked for four *seers*[1] of clarified butter for the dog he had, at first, objected mildly for the sake of the animal's well-being, before sending people to collect the stuff from various places.

The sahib asked who had been sent and where. Harakumar instantly poured out names just as they occurred to him, whereupon the sahib sent people to find out if indeed such and such people had gone to such and such a place to collect clarified butter, making Harakumar wait at the tent until the result of the enquiry.

The investigators came back in the afternoon to report that nobody had gone anywhere to collect anything and the

[1]Roughly equivalent to 2 kilograms

Magistrate was left with no doubt that the rent collector was a liar while the sweeper was telling the truth. He, Joint sahib, was so seized with indignation that he ordered the sweeper to take the rascal by the ear and make him run around the tent. The sweeper lost no time in carrying out the sahib's order, with crowds watching from all sides.

The news spread before much time was lost. Harakumar returned home, took no food and lay down as if dead. His enemies, of whom he had quite a few because of his job, were delighted at his discomfiture. But when Sashibhusan, about to depart for Calcutta, heard the news, his blood boiled and he was unable to sleep all night.

The next morning he went to Harakumar's house. Harakumar abandoned himself to tears, holding his hand. Sashibhusan said, "You must bring a case against the sahib, charging loss of honour. I shall fight as your lawyer."

The idea of fighting the Magistrate sahib was a frightening prospect for Harakumar. But Sashibhusan did not give up easily. Harakumar took his time pondering the matter; but finding that news of the affair had spread everywhere and was encouraging his enemies to rejoice, he no longer found it possible to vacillate. He went to Sashibhusan and pleaded, "My dear boy, I hear you are thinking of going away to Calcutta – for no reason at all – but we cannot allow that. It gives us courage when someone like you stays in the village. In any case you have to save me from this unspeakable insult."

It was through privacy and being alone – away from the gaze of the populace – that Sashibhusan felt secure; but today he found himself in court. The Magistrate heard his complaints and then called him to his private chambers with a show of cordiality. He asked, "Sashibabu, would it not be better to settle this matter in private?"

Sashibhusan kept his frown-adorned, feeble eyesight fixed on the jacket of a law book on the table and replied, "I cannot give such advice to my client. He has been insulted in public;

how can that be settled in private?"

After exchanging a word or two, the sahib understood that it would not be easy to influence this man of little sight and few words. So he said, "All right, babu; let us see what happens." He then went on a tour, postponing the case to a later date.

Joint sahib then wrote to the landlord, "Your rent collector insulted my employee and showed disrespect to me. I hope you will not fail to take proper steps against him."

The landlord, greatly disturbed, summoned Harakumar at once. The latter explained it all from beginning to end, but the landlord remained annoyed. He inquired: "If the sweeper asked for four *seers* of clarified butter, why didn't you give it to him without argument? You wouldn't have had to spend your father's property on it." Harakumar could not but agree that it would not have meant any loss of his ancestral property. He admitted his guilt, saying, "I was under the influence of bad stars – that's why my thinking became warped." The landlord persisted: "And who asked you to bring a case against the sahib?"

Harakumar replied, "Sir, I did not wish in the slightest to file a complaint. You know Sashi in our village; he cannot get himself a case so he forced me into all this trouble, almost without my permission."

The landlord was furious with Sashibhusan. He reckoned that the man must be a good-for-nothing, newly qualified lawyer who was trying to get himself known by creating an issue on some pretext or other. He ordered the rent collector to withdraw the case without delay – thus pleasing both the senior Magistrate and his subordinate.

The rent collector arrived at the house of the Magistrate Joint sahib, with an offering of fruit and drink. The sahib was told that there had been no intention on the collector's part to start a case against him, but that someone called Sashibhusan, a good-for-nothing, inexperienced lawyer in the village had shown this impudence almost without his knowledge. The sahib became as pleased with Harakumar as he was displeased with Sashibhusan. Using Bengali of a literary style and with characteristic mispronunciation, he said that he was sorry that he had punished the collector. The sahib had just passed his Bengali examination and had been awarded a prize, which resulted in his using literary Bengali even in everyday conversation.

The rent collector then submitted that parents would sometimes get angry with a child, while at other times they would indulge him; there was nothing in this for either the parents or the child to get upset about.

Harakumar then duly tipped the servants of Joint sahib and proceeded to the district town to see the senior magistrate. When he heard about Sashibhusan's insolence he remarked to himself, "Ah, that explains it. I was surprised, as I knew the rent collector to be a good man. It was impossible for him to have started a case without letting me know first and trying to settle the dispute in private."

Then he asked the rent collector whether Sashi had joined the Congress.[1] The latter replied without the least hesitation that he had.

The sahib then understood that all of this was part of a plot by the Congress. Many insignificant followers of Congress were looking for opportunities to write articles in *The Amritabazar*, to create trouble for the government. He was critical of the Government's weakness in not giving magistrates enough direct power to crush these tiny thorns. But he remembered the name of Sahibhusan of the Congress.

While the large affairs of the world stridently proclaim their presence, small matters too, with hungry tendrils, do not fail to claim their rights to the world's attention.

While Sashibhusan was earnestly busy with matters like the affair of the Magistrate, sharpening his knowledge of the law from a number of books, practising his speech and questioning imaginary witnesses – getting hot and bothered at the thought of the crowd in the court and thinking about

[1] Political party ultimately to demand independence.

217

the future chapters of this warfare – his young pupil had been presenting herself regularly at his door with her torn *Charupath*[1] and her ink-adorned exercise book, sometimes with fruits and flowers from the garden, sometimes pickles, coconut sweetmeats or scented catechu in a packet of leaves, all gathered from her mother's stores.

For the first few days she did nothing more than just observe Sashibhusan, absent-mindedly turning over the pages of a huge, unadorned and difficult-looking book which he did not appear to be reading with any great attention. Sashibhusan had always, before this, tried to explain bits and pieces from any book he was reading to Giribala. Wasn't there anything at all worth her hearing in that fat book with a black cover? Maybe not – but was the book that important, and Giribala nothing?

Giribala now wanted to catch her teacher's attention, so she started reading aloud, spelling the words as she went along, using a rhythmic tone that kept pace with the rocking movements of her upper body and the swings of her pigtail. When this produced no result she became very indignant with the fat, black book and looked at it as if it was an ugly, hard and cruel man. Every incomprehensible page appeared like a wicked man's face – and they all ignored Giribala as a mere girl. She thought how much she would like to reward a thief who managed to steal that book – she would offer all the catechu she could get hold of from her mother's store. It is unnecessary to tell the reader all the unjustified and impossible prayers that Giribala submitted to the gods – to which of course they paid no heed.

Wounded in her heart, Giribala stopped going with her *Charupath* in hand to the teacher's house for a day or two. But she soon found some pretext or other to return – and looking askance from the road found him standing alone – without that black book – and lecturing in a foreign tongue to the iron bars of the window, with accompanying gestures.

[1] A Bengali Primer for children.

Perhaps he was practising the art of influencing the Judge and trying it out on the bars. Being an inexperienced bookworm Sashibhusan believed that even in these modern commercial days it was possible for words to perform the same kind of great deeds that were done in previous ages by orators like Demosthenes, Cicero, Burke and Sheridan – to shatter injustice by sharp words, to stigmatize oppression and bring down pride. Sashibhusan was practising the art of putting the insolent Englishman, with his pride of political mastery, to shame before the world and making him repent – all this Sashibusan was doing, by standing in a small, dilapidated house in the village of Tilkuci. One doesn't know whether the gods in heaven were amused, or filled with compassionate tears.

Anyway, Sashibhusan's preoccupation meant that Giribala escaped his attention. Today she did not have any *kalajam* with her. She was embarrassed about the previous incident, and since then, if innocent Sashibhusan asked her whether she had any with her, she took it as a subtle joke and, protesting, tried to run away. So, for want of a stone, she had to adopt another trick. She suddenly looked some distance away and called in a loud voice: 'Please Swarna, don't go, I am coming with you.'

A male reader might believe that these words were aimed at a nearby companion, called Swarnalata. But female readers will have no difficulty in grasping that there was nobody in the distance – the aim was near at hand. But, alas, it was misfired. It wasn't that Sashibhusan failed to hear the words, only that their meaning escaped him. He thought that the girl was eager to play and he had no time to spend today persuading her from her games and making her study instead; he was busy himself, searching for arrows that would pierce the hearts he had fixed as his targets. So the small girl's unimportant aim failed – as did the noble goal of the educated man, as readers already know.

Kalajam stones have the advantage that they can be thrown one after the other, and if four miss their target the fifth may be expected to reach it. But one could not ask an imaginary Swarna to wait just for a moment, and then keep standing indefinitely when no one comes. That would naturally create doubts about the existence of Swarna herself. So when that trick failed, Giribala had to depart. Nevertheless her steps were not so energetic as to suggest that she sincerely wished to enjoy the company of someone called Swarna, waiting at a distance. Her gait suggested that she was trying to sense with her back, as it were, if someone was following her. Even when she was certain that no-one was, she kept looking back, clinging on to the merest hope. In the end she gave up, and tearing up the loosely held *Charupath*, scattered the pieces on the road. If there had been some way of giving back what she had received from Sashibhusan, she would have thrown it all at his door, like discarded *Kalajams*. She promised herself that before meeting him again she would forget all she had learnt with him; it would serve him right to discover that she was unable to answer any of the questions he might put.

Her eyes were wet with tears. Although her stricken heart found some consolation in thinking about Sashibhusan's repentance at her loss of learning, she felt great compassion at the same time for the wretched Giribala of the future, forced to become ignorant again entirely through Sashibhusan's fault. Gradually the sky filled up with clouds, as happened every day. Giribala stood under a tree and began to cry from hurt pride, her body heaving with emotion. Many a girl cries like this, every day; it is nothing special.

Readers know why Sashibhusan's legal research and his cultivation of the art of public speaking came to nothing. The law-suit against the Magistrate was dismissed, and Harakumar himself was appointed as an honorary Magistrate on the district bench. He began wearing a dirty official robe and an oily turban and going to the District frequently to pay his respects to the sahibs.

Giribala's curse against Sashibhusan's thick, black book

began at last to take effect; banished to a dark corner, it started collecting layers of dust, dishonoured and forgotten. But where was Giribala now to take pleasure in the book's abandoned state?

When Sashibhusan finally put away his law books it occurred to him that Giribala was no longer paying him visits. He began recollecting the history of the past few days and remembered that Giribala had recently brought him some wet bakul flowers of the newly arrived rainy season, holding them in a fold of her sari. When he had failed to look up even after sensing her presence, discouraged, she had brought out a needle and thread and, head down, had begun threading a garland with the flowers. It was done very slowly and had taken a long time. Eventually it got to midday, when Giribala was due home, and yet Sashibhusan had remained intent on his books. In the end, Giribala had left the garland on the bedstead, and gone away in a down-hearted manner. He also remembered how, as her hurt pride deepened, she had begun, now and again, to walk by his window, but had not entered the room. It was some time now since she had stopped even that walk on the village path in front of his room. Sensitive as she was, her pride did not usually last this long. Sashibhusan drew a deep breath and sat there with his back to the wall, puzzled and entirely at a loss. His books had become distasteful because of the absence of his young pupil and he could proceed no more than a page or two before having to give up any pretence at reading. His writing was disturbed, as now and again, he had to glance at the door and at the path, with eagerly expectant eyes that were waiting for someone.

He feared that Giribala might be ill, but information he obtained in secret revealed that to be baseless. A prospective husband had been found for her; that was why she no longer came out of the house.

The day after she had scattered her torn *Charupath* on the mud-splashed village road, Giribala, having collected various gifts in a fold of her sari was hurrying out of the

house quite early in the morning. Harakumar too was up
early, having spent a sleepless night induced by excessive
heat, and bare-bodied was sitting outside, smoking a hubble-
bubble. He asked her where she was going. She replied, "To
Sashida's house". Harakumar broke into a harsh rebuke:
"Get inside. You are not going to Sashida's house". He had
quite a few disparaging remarks to make about the absence
of shame in his marriageable daughter, soon to be residing in
her in-law's house. Her jaunts outside were thus brought to
an end, depriving her of the opportunity to assuage hurt
pride. So delicacies like mango cakes, catechu, a special
variety of lime and the rest, were put back in the storeroom.
Soon it began raining – flowers dropped from the bakul
trees, guava trees were full of ripe fruit and the ground
around the *kalajam* tree was strewn with ripe *kalajams* some
of which were half eaten by birds. Alas even the torn pages of
the *Charupath* were no longer to be found.

It was the day of Giribala's wedding, and as the *sanai*[1] was
playing in the village in celebration, Sashibhusan, who had
not been invited, was proceeding towards Calcutta in a boat.
  Harakumar had conceived a tremendous hatred for
Sashibhusan since the dismissal of the lawsuit. He knew in
his mind that Sashi despised him, and so found imaginary
signs of it in Sashi's face, looks and behaviour. The people of
the village were gradually forgetting about the insult to
him – only Sashi kept that dreadful episode alive in his
mind. Since Harakumar suspected this, Sashibhusan
became an object of hatred in his eyes. Just to see Sashi made
him feel a shameful constraint followed by a strong sense of
malice. Harakumar resolved to drive Sashi out of the village.
  Uprooting someone like Sashi was not very difficult, so
this particular wish of the landlord's officer was soon
fulfilled. One morning Sashi boarded a boat with his load of

[1]A wind instrument especially played at Hindu weddings

books and a tin box or two. He had only one link of affection with the village and that was being severed with today's ceremony. He had not fully realised before with what strength that gentle affinity had taken hold of his heart. As the boat sailed, the trees in the village took on more and more a far away look, and the music from the marriage ceremony became more and more indistinct. Then sudden tears welled up in his heart, almost suffocating him, and as the nerves in his temples began to hurt with the rush of blood, the picture of the world was obscured before his eyes, like a shadowy mirage.

The boat advanced rather slowly as, although the current was favourable, the wind was against it – and strong. Then something happened on the river to cause an obstacle to Sashibhusan's journey.

A new steamer line had just come into operation from the river port to the District headquarters, and one of these steamers was coming upstream, fluttering its wings and causing a lot of waves. The steamer was carrying the young manager sahib of the new line and a few passengers, some of whom were from Sashibhusan's village.

As it happened, a trader's boat was trying to compete with the steamer. At times it nearly caught up, but then fell somewhat behind. The boatman was seized with the resolve to pass the steamer, and so put up a second sail on top of the first, and even a third small sail. The boat's long mast leaned forward with the force of the wind, and waves on either side began dancing madly and noisily as the boat shot forward like a horse freed of its reins. Then the steamer started to navigate a bend and the boat took a short cut to push ahead of it. The manager was leaning on the rail, eagerly watching the competition. When the boat had reached its maximum speed and had drawn ahead by a couple of feet, the sahib suddenly picked up a gun and fired at the swollen sail. Instantly the sail collapsed, the boat sank and the steamer disappeared round the bend.

It is difficult to understand what made the sahib do this.

We Bengalees are unable to fathom the motives of an Englishman. Perhaps he could not stand the competition from a native sail, perhaps he felt an overwhelming temptation to see the huge swollen sail pierced by a bullet, or perhaps there was something terrifically funny in bringing the proud boat's existence to a sudden end just by making a few holes in its sail – it is hard to know for certain. But what is certain is that the Englishman had faith that he would not be liable to any punishment for indulging his sense of humour; he believed that those who had lost their boat and their lives were not to be counted as human beings.

Sashibhusan's pinnace was near the scene when the sahib fired and the boat sank, so he saw it with his own eyes. At once, he used his own boat to rescue the boatman and the fishermen, but one man who had been grinding spices inside the boat could not be traced. The river swollen by the rainy season careered on with its strong current.

The blood began to boil in Sashi's heart. The law is slow-moving, like a complex iron-made machine, which accepts proof only after weighing it, and then distributes punishment dispassionately; what is missing is the warmth of the human heart. But Sashibhusan found it as unnatural to separate punishment from anger as hunger from food, or desire from enjoyment. There are crimes which, if one sees them with one's own eyes, one must do something about immediately, otherwise the deity dwelling in the witness will keep on troubling him. The heart is then ashamed to find consolation in the thought that the law will take care of the matter. But the law of the machine-driven steamer transported the manager far away from Sashibhusan; I cannot tell what other benefit the world derived from this, but undoubtedly Sashi's Indian spleen was saved, this time.

Sashi returned to the village with the rescued boatman and fisherman. The boat had been carrying a cargo of jute and he engaged people to rescue the goods. He then asked the boatman to complain to the police against the manager.

The boatman refused, saying, "As it is I have lost my boat.

I do not wish to condemn myself on top of that. A case means that first one has to bribe the police, then leave all one's other business to keep coming back to the court again and again; one has to forget about food, and sleep too. And god only knows what dire consequences one has to face if one complains against an Englishman". When he was told that Sashibhusan was a lawyer and would bear all the expenses and that there was every possibility of getting compensation through the court, he eventually agreed. But the villagers who were on the steamer refused to act as witnesses. They said to him, "Sir, we saw nothing. We were at the back of the steamer and the noise from the engine and of the water made it impossible to hear gun fire from there".

Sashibhusan found the attitude of his countrymen thoroughly contemptible and began a case himself in the Magistrates court. As it happened there was no need for witnesses. The manager admitted that he had fired. According to him, a flock of cranes were flying across the sky and the gun was aimed at them. The steamer was then at full speed and had just entered the bend. He had no way of knowing what had got hurt – a crow, a crane, or the boat. There were so many things to aim at in the sky or on the earth that no intelligent man would willingly waste the meanest bullet on a dirty rag.

Freed without question the manager went to play whist in his club, with a cigar between his lips. The dead body of the man who had been grinding spice inside the boat was washed up nine miles away and Sashibhusan came back to the village with a scorched heart.

Giribala was being taken to her in-laws in a decorated boat on the day he returned. Though no-one asked him to be present, Sashi slowly came up to the river bank. There was a crowd by the landing stage, so he stood at a distance. When the boat left the steps and passed him, in a flash he saw the newly-wed sitting with her face lowered, a veil on her head. Giribala had long been hoping that there would somehow be a meeting with her teacher before she left the village; she did not know that Sashi was standing not far away. She did not raise her face, but her cheeks were flooded with silent tears.

Gradually the boat disappeared from view. The morning sunlight kept shining brightly on the water. The papiya bird on a nearby mango tree seemed unable to exhaust its passion despite its repeated, exuberant singing. The ferry plied back and forth, full of people, and women who had come to fetch water began noisily discussing Giribala's journey to her in-laws. Sashibhusan took off his glasses, wiped his eyes and went back to his small room with its window bars by the roadside. He seemed to hear Giribala's voice, once, saying 'Sashida'. Where was she? She was not in his house, nor in the village, nor on the road, but right there in his tear-soaked heart.

Sashibhusan packed again and started for Calcutta. There was nothing waiting for him there, nor was there any special purpose in his journey. So he decided to go by river rather than take a train.

It was the season of full monsoon and all around the land of Bengal thousands of watery stretches, like twisting veins, both large and small, had appeared. The nerves of this soft green land were filled up and there was an abundance of growth everywhere – trees and plants, grass, weeds and bushes, paddy, jute and sugarcane; it seemed to have gone beyond all bounds.

Sashbhusan's boat sailed amidst these narrow, curved stretches of water. The water had by then overflowed the banks, and hedges of kass grass and reed and, in places, cultivated fields, were under water. The village fences, bamboo and mango groves were now standing at the water's edge. It looked as if the heavenly maidens[1] had overfilled the ridges with water, and dug round the roots of all the

[1]Beings who bestow rain on parched earth in Hindu mythology

trees in Bengal to water them.

The soft and glossy woodland was smiling and shimmering in the sun at the start of the journey, but soon it became cloudy and began to rain. Now wherever one looked it appeared depressing and untidy. Like cows crowding up in their narrow, dirty and muddy islands surrounded by water, getting wet standing patiently, with pathetic eyes, Bengal began to be oppressively soaked in water, with a dumb, sad look amidst its muddy, slippery, water-steeped and motionless woods. Women in the course of their domestic duties were going from house to house, getting saturated and shivering in the cold wind of the rainy day, or in wet clothes, drawing water from the tank, after stepping carefully on the slippery steps. Householders were sitting on their verandahs, smoking, and if particularly called upon by duty, going out with shawls wrapped round their waists, shoes in their hands and umbrellas over their heads. It was not among the ancient and sacred customs of this country – a land scorched by the sun and soaked by the rain – to allow an umbrella over a woman's head.

When the rain refused to stop, Sashibhusan, bored with being in an enclosed space, decided to go by rail after all. He found as estuary-like place and had the boat anchored there to prepare for lunch.

The feet of the lame fall in the ditch – it is not only the fault of the ditch, for the lame foot is specially inclined to fall, as Sashibhusan proved that day.

At the mouth of two rivers some fishermen had spread a huge net, holding it up by bamboo; there was room for boats to pass on one side only. They had been doing this for a long time, and paying tax for the fishing rights. Unfortunately this year the police superintendant of the district suddenly decided to come this way. The fishermen indicated the right course as soon as they saw the boat and shouted a warning in good time. But the sahib's boatman was not used to showing respect for man-made obstacles and he took the boat over the net. The prow was able to push over the net but the boat's rudder got caught. It took some time and effort to free the rudder.

The police sahib became red with anger and while in that state, anchored his boat. The four fishermen, seeing him in a temper, bolted in a breathless hurry. The sahib ordered his men to cut down the net. It had cost seven or eight hundred rupees – and they tore it to pieces. After taking it out on the net, the police sahib ordered that the fishermen be seized. When the police constable failed to find the four fugitives, he brought along the first four men he could catch hold of. They declared their innocence and begged for release with folded palms. As the police sahib was on the point of ordering them to be taken along, bespectacled Sashibhusan appeared, breathless, before the boat, having quickly put on a shirt with its buttons undone and making a slapping noice with his sandals. He said in a trembling voice, "Sir, you have no right to tear up the fisherman's net and harass these four people."

The head of police uttered something particularly insulting in Hindi, and instantly Sashibhusan jumped into the boat, and hurled himself on the sahib, striking him, like someone lost to all reason.

He was not aware of what happened subsequently. When he came to, in jail, the treatment he received, I am afraid, induced neither honour in his mind nor comfort in his body.

Sashibhusan's father engaged lawyers and barristers who managed to get him released on bail. Then preparations got going for a court case.

The fishermen who had lost their net lived in the same district as Sashibhusan and under the same landlord. They had even previously come to Sashi in times of trouble to take his advice on legal matters. Those who had been falsely captured and taken to the sahib's boat were not unknown to Sashi either. Sashi asked them to be witnesses but they were beside themselves with fear. Those who lived a domestic life with wives and children could not afford to get into trouble with the police since that meant a total lack of security. No-one had more than one life in his body; what they had lost they had lost. When they were served with a subpeona they saw this as a fresh danger. They protested, "Sir, you are putting us to great trouble." However they agreed to speak the truth after a lot of cajoling.

In the meantime Harakumar had gone to pay his respects to the district sahibs on the occasion of some duty on the Bench, when the police chief said to him with a smile, "*Nayebbabu*[1], I hear that your tenants are preparing to give false witness against the police". This gave the rent collector a start and he said, "Is that so? How did they come to think, these low-born beggars, that they had so much power in their bones?"

Newspaper readers know that Sashibhusan's case had no leg to stand on. The fishermen denied, one after the other, that the police sahib had destroyed their net. He had merely called them to the boat to write down their names and addresses. Not only that, a few men from the village known to Sashi bore witness that they were present at the scene as part of a marriage party and had seen with their own eyes that Sashibhusan had advanced on the police guards without any provocation, solely to make trouble.

Sashibhusan admitted that after he was insulted he had entered the boat and struck the police sahib, but with good reason – the destruction of the net and the suffering of the fishermen.

It was not at all unexpected that judgement in such a case would go against Sashibhusan. But his punishment was rather severe, as three or four accusations were brought against him: causing bodily harm, trespass, obstructing the police in the carrying out of their duties, all of which were fully substantiated.

So Sashibhusan left his beloved books in his small room and went to jail for five years. His father was about to appeal,

[1]Title given to an estate manager.

but Sashibhusan stopped him with the remark, "It is better to be in jail. Iron chains do not lie. But the freedom we enjoy outside is deceptive and so it leads us into trouble. And if you are worried about bad company, the number of liars and ungrateful cowards is limited in a jail by lack of space, compared with the much higher number outside."

His father died a short while after Sashibhusan was jailed. He did not have many more relatives. One brother had a job in the Central Provinces and rarely came home; he was permanently settled there with his family in his own house. The rent collector, Harakumar, used various stratagems to swallow up most of Sashi's ancestral property, whatever there was in the village. Sashibhusan had to put up with a good deal more rough handling than generally was the lot of prisoners. However the long five years at last came to an end.

So, Sashi came out of jail on another rainy day – broken in health and empty in heart – and stood outside its walls. He had found freedom, but there was nobody and nothing waiting outside for him. And as he stood there, alone, homeless and without relatives, the outside world appeared to him a very disjointed sort of place indeed.

He was thinking of where to start – his ties with his previous life having been severed – when a carriage drew up before him. A servant got down and asked, "Are you Sashibhusanbabu?"

Sashibhusan replied, "Yes". The servant at once opened the door and stood there waiting for him to enter. Surprised, Sashibhusan asked, "Where am I supposed to be going?" The servant replied, "My employer has sent for you."

Sashi got into the carriage, as he was finding the curious eyes of the passers-by intolerable. He thought, "There is some mistake somewhere. But as one must start at some point, why not with this mistake?"

Today, the sunshine and cloud were chasing one another in the fleeting play of light and shade. The deep green paddy fields by the side of the road were flooded with rainy season water and looked fascinating. A huge chariot was standing next to the marketplace, and in a grocer's shop not far from it a group of *vaishnava*[1] beggars were singing to the accompaniment of string instruments and drums:

Come back, come back oh Lord, come back
My heart is hungry, thirsty, troubled,
Beloved, come back.

The carriage proceeded and the singing, although growing fainter and fainter, could be heard for a time until finally it disappeared. Sashibhusan took up the theme and began humming the music, adding words to it as he went along; somehow he could not help himself. He stopped only when the carriage entered a walled garden and came to a halt in front of a two-storied building.

He asked no questions and at the servant's indication entered the house. The room in which he sat down had huge glass bookcases all around – full of books with covers of different colours. Instantly the scene released memories of his old life, and he felt as if freed from incarceration in jail for the second time. These gold-washed, many-coloured books looked to him like a familiar and jewel-studded lion gate through which to enter the land of joy.

There were some things on the table as well. With his bad eyesight, Sashi leaned over it and found a broken writing slate, a few exercise books, one near-torn elementary arithmetic book, the *Mahabharata* in Kashiram Das' translation, and *Kathamala*. 'Giribala Devi' was written in thick letters with ink in Sashibhusan's own handwriting on the wooden frame round the slate. The same name in the same handwriting was there in the other books as well.

Sashibhusan now understood where he was and his heart began hammering. He looked outside through the open

[1]See footnote 1 p. 96

window – to see what? A small room with bars on the window, an uneven village road, a young girl in a striped sari, and his own life's passage – peaceful, secure, private.

The happiness of those times had been nothing extraordinary or excessive. Day had followed day unknowingly, doing small duties, feeling small joys, and the tutoring of a small girl amidst his own serious studies was quite an insignificant event. But that isolated life at the end of the village, peace and contentment, admittedly of no great dimension, that tiny face of a young girl – all of these assumed, like heaven, an existence beyond space and time as well as beyond reach, taking their place amidst the shadowy and imaginary forms that belong to one's land of desire. All these pictures and memories of the past, fused with this day's pale light of the rainwashed morning and with the music that was still singing softly in his mind, to become a thing of unparalleled beauty, – melodious and brilliant. The last memory of that sensitive, neglected, hurt girl's face on a muddy and narrow village road, became for him as if something divine, something uncommonly wonderful and beautiful, full of hidden depth and pain, that had been made at the hands of the god of fate himself. The haunting tune he had heard earlier continued playing in his mind along with the memory, making him feel as if an unfathomable sorrow lying at the very heart of the universe had cast its shadow on the face of that village girl.

Sashibusan buried his head in his arms, and among the slates and books on the table, continued to remember things past. After a time, a soft noise reached his senses, and lifting up his head he saw her not far away, waiting silently, with fruit and sweetmeats in a silver dish. The moment he looked up, Giribala – unadorned, clad in white as a widow – knelt down before him to pay her respects. Then the widow stood up and looked with gentle compassionate eyes at Sashibhusan, at his shrunken face, pale colour and broken health. As she did so tears flooded into her eyes and ran down her cheeks.

Sashibhusan tried to ask how she was, but no words came. Suppressed tears took hold of his vocal chords and the words that emerged out of his heart stopped dead in his throat. Then the party of singers we have already met begging from door to door, arrived at the building and began to sing:

"Come back, come back oh Lord, come back.
My heart is hungry, thirsty, troubled,
Beloved, come back."

A Vain Hope

I found Darjeeling covered everywhere with cloud and rain. I felt no inclination to go out; to stay in was even less satisfying.

I had breakfast at the hotel, put on thick boots, covered myself from head to foot with a mackintosh and went out for a walk. Now and again it drizzled and the thick fog and cloud everywhere made one feel that God was, as it were, about to rub out with an eraser the whole picture of the universe, including the Himalayas.

Walking alone along the Calcutta road I felt bored, with nothing to fall back on in this land of cloud, and a fervent desire to grip again with my five senses the wonderful mother earth, so deliciously adorned with sound, touch and colour.

Just then I heard not far away the anguished voice of a woman sobbing. Sobbing is nothing strange in this world of disease and grief, and it is doubtful whether I would have taken notice elsewhere and at another time. But amidst this infinite world of clouds, that sobbing sounded like the only cry left in the whole vanished world; I couldn't treat it as insignificant. I followed the sound and found myself in the presence of a woman in an ochre dress, her golden-brown, matted hair done up on her head, like a mountain peak. She was sitting on a piece of stone on the roadside and sobbing in a soft voice. It did not sound like an expression of recent grief; more like a long stored-up, silently borne exhaustion and fatigue that was welling up, breaking down under the pressure of today's cloud-dark loneliness.

I said to myself, "This is wonderful, just like a make-believe story. I never hoped to see with my own eyes this sight of a *sannyasini*[1] sitting on a mountain peak and crying".

I couldn't make out where she belonged and asked in simple Hindi, "Who are you? What's troubling you?"

At first she did not bother to reply, but just looked at me once with her tearful, glittering eyes from amidst the clouds.

I said again, "Don't be afraid of me, I am a gentleman". She laughed at my remark, and replied in pure Hindusthani, "I have gone beyond fear and the like a long time, and bashfulness and shame too. *Babuji*[2], the *zenana*[3] where I once belonged was such that even my own brother had to obtain permission to enter. I am now unveiled before the whole world."

To start with I was a bit annoyed. My ways and demeanour were all very westernized, like a sahib, but this wretched woman was calling me *"Babuji"* without a thought. I considered bringing the story to an end right there, and with cigarette in mouth, departing noisily, speedily and with pride, like a railway carriage – demonstrating my stiff-upper-lipped westernized ways. But curiosity took the upper hand; I assumed a superior manner and tilting my head somewhat asked, "Can I help you, do you have anything to ask for?"

She fixed her gaze on my face and in a while answered, "I am the daughter of Golam Kader Khan, Nawab of Badraon."

I knew nothing about where Badraon was or the identity of this Nawab Golam Kader Khan, nor did I have any idea what could make his daughter, dressed as a *sannyasini* sit by the Calcutta Road and cry. Truth to tell I didn't even believe

[1]See footnote 1 p. 126.
[2]Equivalent of 'Mr' in Hindi.
[3]Inner apartments exclusively for women in a Muslim household.

all this, but I thought that I wouldn't be a spoil-sport and disturb the flavour of the story just as the plot was thickening.

At once I rendered her a long salaam with a solemn face and said, "Do forgive me, *Bibisaheb*[1], I didn't recognize you."

There were many justified reasons for not doing so. First of all, I had never come across her before, moreover the fog was so thick that it was difficult to find one's own hand and feet.

Bibisaheb took no offence, rather, quite pleased, she indicated a separate stone by a gesture of her right hand, giving me permission to sit.

I noticed that the woman possessed the power to command. I was greatly honoured to have received permission from her to sit down on a rather mossy, hard and uneven stone. The daughter of Golam, Kader Khan of Badraon, Nurunissa or Meherunnisa or Nur-ul-mulk[2], had conferred on me the right to occupy a dirty seat beside her, by the Calcutta road in Darjeeling. When I came out of the hotel with my mackintosh on, such an exalted possibility was beyond my dreams.

Such a story of conversation in seclusion between two sojourners, a man and a woman sitting on stones in the bosom of the Himalayas may immediately give rise to the idea of some recently composed lukewarm narrative poetry, or there may arise in the minds of readers the sound of spring water falling through lonely mountain caves and with it the beautiful melodic-murmers of the *Meghdut-Kumarsambhab*[3] composed by Kalidas. But one must admit that there cannot be many New-Bengal young men who could keep their self-respect intact if they had to sit with a poorly dressed Hindusthani woman, on a dirty seat – with boots and mackintosh on – by the Calcutta road. But that day

[1]Address for a Muslim woman.
[2]Muslim names for women
[3]Romantic narratives

thick fog had covered everything; there was nothing visible that had to be hidden from the world out of a sense of delicacy in openly doing something undesirable – there was only the daughter of Golam Kader Khan of Badraon and I, a budding Bengali Sahib, amidst this infinite cloud kingdom. We two were sitting on two pieces of stone, like two sole surviving remnants, after the destruction of the world. The peculiar humour of this odd meeting revealed itself only to us, nobody else.

I asked, "*Bibisaheba*, who brought you to this pass?"

The daughter of Badraon struck her forehead and said, "How should I know who does all this; who has concealed these immense, stoney and stark Himalayas behind some insignificant fog?"

I raised no philosophic point and admitted it all saying, "That is true, who knows the secret of fate? We are like worms."

I could have argued and not let *bibisaheba* off so easily, had I enough of her language, but the little Hindi I had acquired in the company of door-keepers and servants would not have been enough for me to argue with any degree of clarity – sitting by the Calcutta road – on the topic of fate versus free will, with any daughter of a Nawab, be that of Badraon or some place else.

Bibisaheba said, "The strange tale of my life has found its conclusion today; I shall tell you of it, if it be your order."

Embarrassed I said, "Of course there is no question of order; if you would favour me with your tale, I should be delighted."

Let no-one think that I said exactly these words in the Hindusthani language. I would have liked to, but didn't know how. When *Bibisaheba* was speaking I felt as if the gentle breeze of early morning was waving through a dew-washed, gold-tipped, gentle-green field of corn – at every step there was such ease of politeness and grace, such unobstructed, effortless flow of words! I was answering her in brief, in bits and pieces, and in a most direct manner like a barbarian.

I had never known such complete, unceasing and easy civility in language before. For the first time I realized, while talking to Bibisaheba, the extreme poverty of my own ways.

She said, "The blood of the Emperor of Delhi ran in my father's family. To maintain the pride of that lineage, it was difficult to find a suitable husband for me. A proposal of marriage with the Nawab of Lucknow did come, but my father had not quite made up his mind when fighting broke out between the Government and the Sepoys, on the issue of cutting cartridges by teeth.[1] Hindusthan became dark with cannon smoke."

I had never heard Hindusthani from a woman before, particularly a woman of high status. I could clearly see that this language was aristocratic, although today it was no longer in use. Now everything has become short, reduced, unadorned through the railway-telegraph, pressure of work, and loss of nobility. Just to hear the language of this daughter of a Nawab conjured up before my mind's eye, as if by magic, the imaginary city of the Moghul Emperors amidst this dense fog of Darjeeling, – (now a modern hill-station built by the English – lines of sky-reaching, huge buildings built of white marble; on the streets, long-tailed horses with finely woven mats on their backs; *howdahs* fringed with golden thread on backs of elephants; multi-coloured headdresses on townsmen; wide shirts and pyjamas, made of warm cloth, silk, muslin; curved swords on commerbunds, their upward curves reflected in the silver-threaded shoes; – much leisure, long dresses and profuse civility.

The Nawab's daugher said, "Our fort was on the Jamuna, and the commander of our army was a Hindu Brahmin, Kesharlal by name."

The woman poured the entire music of her female voice, in an instant, on that name, "Kesharlal". I put my stick on the ground, shifted my position, and sat straight.

[1] The soldiers believed the cartridges contained cow fat, beef being forbidden to Hindus. This incident contributed to the first rebellion against the British in 1857.

"Kesharlal was an orthodox Hindu. I used to get up early in the morning – every day – to see, from a window in the inner quarters, Kesharlal steeped up to his breast in the waters of the Jamuna and circumambulating there, offering homage to the rising sun with clasped hands and face turned upwards. Then he would sit near the landing-steps in his wet clothes and concentrated on chanting *mantras*[1], after which he would return home singing a devotional song in *raga bhairo*[2] in his clear musical voice. I was a Muslim girl, but have never heard anything of my own religion, or known the manner of adoration of God according to its ways. Religious ties were slackened amongst our men then, through luxurious and irregular living and drinking; religion was not particularly alive in the pleasure-houses in the inner quarters either.

"Maybe God has given our minds a natural quest for truth, or there could have been some other profound reason, I don't know. But the sight of Kesharlal's *puja*[3] offerings every peaceful morning in the new light of the rising sun on the marble steps by the calm, blue Jamuna, would fill my freshly awakened mind with an ineffable glow of devotion. The Brahmin Kesharlal's fair, lithe and handsome body used to appear to me like a smokeless ray of light through the daily observance of this orderly and controlled ritual; and his glow of virtue would make this Muslim girl's benumbed heart soft with a wonderful sense of respect.

"I had a Hindu maidservant. She used to bow down to Kesharlal every day and take the dust off his feet, which made me both glad and jealous. This servant fed other Brahmins from time to time and offered money due to them on various ceremonial occasions. I gave her money on my own initiative and asked, 'Aren't you going to invite Kesharlal?' She stuck out her tongue in shame[4] and said, 'Kersharlal accepts no

[1] Esoteric words in Sanskrit recited in prayer.
[2] Musical mode sung especially in the morning.
[3] An act of worship.
[4] See footnote 2 p. 90.

food or offering from anyone'. Not being able to offer Kesharlal any sign of devotion, my heart continued aggrieved and hungry.

"One of my grandfathers had forcibly married a Brahmin girl. Sitting in the inner apartments, I used to feel in my veins the flow of her pure blood, and through that connection, imagine a bond of union with Kesharlal, and this appeased me somewhat. I used to hear from my Hindu maid the manners and customs of the Hindu religion in great detail; the wondrous tales of gods and goddesses, the unparalleled history of the *Ramayana* and the *Mahabharata*; and there, in the inner quarters, these tales would reveal to my mind a beautiful picture of the Hindu world. Images and representations, the sound of the conch shell, shrines with golden pinnacles, the use of incense in abundance, the scent of flowers mixed with sandal-paste, the miraculous powers of yogis and sannyasis, the superhuman nobility of a Brahmin, the play of gods in the guise of human beings – all these, together, created for me an unearthly world of magic, very ancient, distant but widespread; and my heart, like a small bird lost from its nest, used to flutter around of an evening from room to room in a huge, ancient palace. The Hindu world was to my adolescent heart an enchanting fairyland.

"Then fighting began between the East India Company and the Sepoys. The waves of revolt reached even the small fort of our Badraon.

"Kesharlal said, 'Now we must drive out the beef-eating white man from Aryavarta'. And once again a play of dice had to be arranged between the Hindus and Muslims for the royal seat in Hindusthan.

"My father Golam Kader Khan was a careful man. Referring to the English by the name of a particular relative[1] he said, 'They are capable of great feats; the people of Hindustan cannot win against them. I don't wish to lose my

[1]"Shala" means brother-in-law – often used as term of abuse.

little fort in uncertain hope; I shall not fight with the Company.' When the blood of the Hindus and Muslims of Hindusthan was boiling over, this business-like calculation of my father produced a sense of shame in all of us. Even my begum mothers were agitated.

"Kesharlal, himself and his army, equipped with weapons, came to my father, 'Nawabsaheb, if you do not join us I shall have to put you in bondage and take charge of the fort for as long as the fighting lasts.' My father said, 'All this upset is quite unnecessary, I shall be on your side.' Kesharlal said, 'I need money from the treasury.' My father did not give much. He said, 'I shall let you have it as and when the need arises.'

"All the ornaments that I possessed to adorn my limbs from head to foot, I tied up in a piece of cloth and sent to Kesharlal in secret through my Hindu maid. He accepted them. The pleasure of it filled my every ornamentless limb with a sensation of delight.

"Kesharlala scrubbed and cleaned rusty gun barrels and old swords, in preparation for the revolt. But one afternoon the District Commissioner with white soldiers in red uniforms arrived, and filling the sky with dust, entered our fort. My father, Golam Kader Khan, had sent the British word of the uprising in secret.

"Kesharlal had such an uncanny hold over the Badraon army that they were ready to die fighting with their broken-down guns and dulled swords.

"The home of my traitor father felt like hell to me. My heart was bursting through regret, grief, shame and hatred, but I shed no tears. I donned the clothes of my coward brother and went out of the inner apartment in disguise, when nobody had time to notice anything.

"When dust and gunpowder smoke, the cry of soldiers and the sound of gunshots were over, the terrible peace of death covered water, land and sky. The sun had set, dyeing the waters of the Jamuna blood-red, and an almost full moon was shining in the evening sky.

"The battlefield was a terrifying sight, strewn with dead

bodies. Any other time I would have felt great compassion, but that day I was looking around, as if in a dream, to find Kesharlal; no other end meant anything to me then.

"After a long search in the brilliant moonlight of the second quarter of the night I found the bodies of Kesharlal and his devoted servant, Deokinandan, a short distance away from the battlefield, on the banks of Jamuna, under the shade of a mango grove. I could see that in a mortally wounded condition either the master had carried the servant, or the servant the master, from the battlefield to this safe place, and then surrendered himself to death.

"First, I fulfilled my long-felt and avid desire for devotion. I fell at Kesharlal's feet and letting down my knee-length hair wiped the dust of his feet with it again and again. Then I took his ice-cold feet to my warm forehead, and the moment I kissed them my long-suppressed tears could no longer be held back.

"Suddenly, Kesharlal's body showed signs of movement and an indistinct but tortured sound of pain emerged from his mouth. I started, and let go of his feet. I heard him say, once, 'Water!', his voice dry, his eyes closed.

"At once, I dipped my garment in the water of the Jamuna and came back running. I began twisting the garment to drip water between his opened-up lips, and tearing off its wet end, bandaged the frightful wound in his forehead – a wound that had destroyed his left eye. When I had thus sprinkled Jamuna water over his face and eyes several times, his consciousness began to return. I asked, 'Any more water?' Kesharlal asked, 'Who are you?'

"I could contain myself no more and blurted out, 'This humble self is your devoted attendant, I am the daughter of Nawab Golam Kader Khan'. I thought that Kesharlal, his death approaching, would take with him this ultimate knowledge of his devotee. Nobody could deprive me of that pleasure.

"The moment he knew who I was he roared like a lion, 'Daughter of a traitor, follower of another religion! You have destroyed the *dharma*[1] that was proper to me, by making me drink water from the hands of a *yavan*[2] just when I am about to die! So saying he struck my cheek with his right palm with great force. I saw black and nearly fainted.

"I was then only sixteen, my very first day out in the world, outside the shelter of the inner quarters. The reddish beauty of my soft cheeks had not yet been stolen by the hot, greedy sunlight of the sky outside. The moment I stepped out I received this first greeting from this world, from the god of my world."

"I was sitting, bewitched, as if in a picture, with my cigarette extinguished. I didn't know whether I was listening to a story, to the language itself or to its music. I sat speechless but the moment had come when I couldn't remain silent anymore; I burst out, "An animal!"

The Nawab's daughter said, "Who is an animal? Could an animal refuse water brought to its lips while dying in pain?"

Embarrased I said, "That is so, he was a god" The Nawab's daughter questioned this too, "Would a god refuse the devout offerings of his follower?" I said, "That is true also", and then kept quiet.

The Nawab's daughter continued, "I felt as if the whole world had come crashing down on my head. Then, after a moment's lapse, I got back my senses and from a distance bowed down at the feet of that pure Brahmin – powerful, severe, cruel and indifferent – saying in my mind, 'Brahmin, you accept nothing; the attention of the lowly; other people's food; the gifts of the rich; youth; the love of a woman – nothing. You are independent, alone, detached, distant; I do not even have the right to surrender myself to you.'

"One couldn't know what Kesharlal felt seeing the Nawab's daughter bend down her head on the ground; but his face showed no surprise, nor any other emotion. Self-possessed he looked at my face, once, then slowly got up.

[1]Religious conduct which forbids acceptance of anything touched by a non-Brahmin

Startled, I put forward my hand as a support, but he refused it and with great difficulty got himself to the landing stage on the Jamuna's bank. A ferry boat was anchored there, but there was no passenger or boatman. Kesharlal got into the boat, released the chain, the boat moved to the middle of the river and gradually disappeared. With hands clasped towards that boat I wished that I could sacrifice this fruitless life, with all its load of heart, youth and devotion, amidst the tranquil, moonlit Jamuna on that soundless night – like a bud dropped untimely from its stalk.

"But I failed. The moon in the sky, the dense, dark line of the wood on the other side of the Jamuna, its water deep and motionless, the top of our fort gleaming bright in moonlight at a distance above the mango grove, everything sang a death song in a placid and solemn chorus. That night the three worlds, its planets, moon and stars urged me to die in one voice. Only one thing, a worn-out vanished boat on the bosom of the waveless and untroubled Jamuna, snatched me away from the eagerly extended embrace of infinitely fascinating death – appearing dignified, enticing, peaceful and cool in that moonwashed night; so I walked instead on the path of life. Like one under a dream-induced illusion I began walking by the side of the Jamuna, through deep *kash* grass, desert-like sands, uneven, toppled-down banks or through woods thick with undergrowth, hard to tread."

The narrator stopped; I said nothing. The Nawab's daughter began again, after a pause. "The events after this are very complicated. I do not know how to relate them clearly and with proper analysis. In those days I was travelling through a dense forest, as it were, and it is not possible now to figure out which way I took, or when. The problem is where to start or finish, which bit to keep or abandon, and how to make the entire story perceptibly distinct so that nothing appears unmanageable, impossible or unnatural.

"But in the days of my life I have known that nothing is impossible or beyond man's capability. It may appear that the outside world would be entirely unmanageable for a girl hitherto living in the inner quarters of a Nawab's household. But this is only imagined. Once you are out, a path is found to walk on; it is not a Nawab's path, but a path nevertheless and men have always walked on it. It is uneven, full of variety, endless, divided in many directions, complicated with joys and sorrows, with hazards and hindrances; all the same it is a path.

"It will not be a pleasure for you to hear the long sojourn of a Nawab's daughter, alone, on this path; and even if it were, I feel no enthusiasm to talk about it. In short I had to go through a lot of suffering and sorrow, insult and danger, yet life did not become unbearable. Like a firework the more it burned the more speed I gathered. As long as I was walking at full speed I did not know that I was burning. Suddenly today, the light of that deepest suffering, which was at the same time my ultimate happiness, has blown itself out; and I am dropped on the roadside, on its dust, like a lifeless object. My journey is over today. My story ends here."

Then the Nawab's daughter stopped. Mentally I shook my head, it just couldn't end here. I broke the silence between us in my broken Hindi, "Excuse my impertinence, but if you tell me the end of the story in a bit more detail the unease of this poor man would lessen somewhat."

The Nawab's daughter laughed and I could see that my broken Hindi was bearing fruit. If I could carry on a conversation in pure Hindi, she would have felt shy with me, but the fact that I knew very little of her language meant a great gulf between us acted as a veil, as far as she was concerned.

She began again, "I would often hear of Kesharlal but never managed to meet him. He joined the group of Tantia Topi, and became part of the revolts which would from time to time break out upon the east, west, south-east and north-west like thunder, and disappear equally as suddenly. I had then became a *yogini*[1] and was studying Sanskrit holy books

[1]Female yogi

with the Guru Sivananda Swami of Benaras whom I addressed as, 'Father'. Information reached him from all over Hindusthan; I used to study Sanskrit treatises devoutly, and at the same time collect news of the fighting with tortured anguish.

"In time, the British Raj smashed this revolt in Hindusthan, trampling it under foot. Then no news of Kesharlal could be had any more. The brave figure from various corners of India who were often in sight in those blood-red days of destruction were suddenly left behind in darkness. I couldn't endure the anxiety any more. I left the shelter of my Guru and took to the road, travelling all the while from one direction to another; from pilgrimage to pilgrimage, to ashrams[1] and temples, but no Kesherlal was to be found. One or two people who knew his name said that he had died either in battle or on Government orders. Something inside me said, 'No, never, Kesharlal cannot die, that Brahmin, that scorching, consuming fire cannot be extinguished. He is still waiting like an upward flame by some inaccessible, lonely altar to receive my self-giving'.

"Though Hindu books talk of Sudras[2] becoming Brahmin through knowledge and tapasya[3] there is no mention whether a Muslim can became a Brahmin; the reason being that there were no Muslims then. I knew that it was a long way to my union with Kesharlal, I had to become a Brahmin before that. Thirty years passed in the process. I became a Brahmin in my heart, and in my outward conduct and customs, in entire sincerity. The blood of that Brahmin grandmother of mine began running through all of me in its purest state. And having mentally established myself with total candour at the feet of that Brahmin of my fresh young days, that Brahmin of the end of my youth, that Brahmin who was the only one for me in the whole world – I gained a kind of haloed grace.

[1]Secluded abodes of spiritual practitioners
[2]Lowest of the four castes
[3]Arduous practices for developing spiritual energy

"During the fighting at the time of the revolt I had heard a great deal of Kesharlal but it was not this picture that was in my heart. What was indelibly printed there was Kesharlal whom I saw quietly floating away, alone, in a small boat in the midst of the motionless Jamuna on a moonlit night. Always I saw that Brahmin sailing over a lonely current night and day and reaching towards some unknown mystery – he had no companion, no attendant, no need of anyone; that pure, self-absorbed man was complete in himself. Even the planets, the moon and the stars watched him in hushed silence.

"Then I heard that Kesharlal had fled from the Government and taken shelter in Nepal. After I lived there for some time I learnt that he had left a long time ago, nobody knew for where.

"Since then I have been travelling amidst mountains. The land was not Hindu. *Bhutias* and *Lepchas*[1] are *Mlechas*[2]. They do not observe proper customs and rituals in their eating and conduct; their gods, their ways of worship are all very different. I was afraid that the purity and cleanliness I had acquired over long practice would become stained. I kept myself away from all unclean associations with great care. I knew that my boat had reached its shore, and that my life's ultimate pilgrimage was not far away.

"What is there to say after that? The end is brief; when the lamp dies a single puff will extinguish it. At the end of thirty-eight years, this morning, in Darjeeling, I saw Kesharlal."

To see her stop there I asked with great curiosity, "How did you find him?" The Nawab's daughter replied, "I saw Kesharlal in a Bhutia neighbourhood, living with a Bhutia wife and her grand-children and, with a cheerless face, gathering corn from corncobs in a dirty courtyard."

The story ended here. I felt I must offer some consoling

[1]Himalayan tribes
[2]Beyond the pale of Hinduism
[3]Mlechhas = beyond the pale of Hinduism

words, "How could he, who in fear of his life had to live for thirty-eight years in foreign company, save his own customs from being contaminated?" The Nawab's daughter said, "Do I not know it? But what a delusion I was under all this time! I didn't know that the Brahmanhood that captured my adolescent heart was merely a matter of habit, of just following custom. I knew it as *dharma*, the right thing to be followed, something beginningless and endless. If I didn't think so, how could I, when merely sixteen, come out of my father's shelter, receive unbearable insult from the Brahmin's right hand in exchange for my mind and body – blossoming, blooming, trembling in devout passion – and accept that, like initiation from a Guru's hand, on my bent-down head with mute and redoubled devotion? What a pity! You Brahmin have acquired a new set of customs, leaving the old ones behind. Where can I find a new youth, a new life in exchange for the youth, the life that are gone!"

The woman stood up and said, *"Namaskar Babuji"*.

Instantly she corrected herself and said, *'Salaam² Babusaheb"*. As if by this Muslim greeting she took her last leave of Brahmanhood, with its crumbling foundations, dust-ridden and broken. Before I could say anything, she disappeared amidst the grey fog of that mountain peak.

I closed my eyes for a moment and saw the whole story, as it were, painted before my mind's eye.

I saw a sixteen year old Nawab's daughter, seated comfortably at a window by the river Jamuna, on a seat decorated with a golden fringe, her concentrated body filled with the passion of devotion; I saw a pilgrimage temple and a *sannyasini* there at the time of evening prayer; and then the hopeless figure of an old woman, bent down by a broken heart full of misgivings. The strange and anguished music of conflicting and contrary blood-streams in a Brahmin-Muslim – melted down in the elegant and perfect Urdu

¹Dhasma
²Hindu greeting
³Muslim greeting

language – began to vibrate in my head.

I opened my eyes and saw that suddenly the cloud had disappeared and the blue sky was basking in soft sunlight. English women in horse-drawn carriages and Englishmen on horseback were out to take the air, and now and again some Bengalis with mufflers wrapped round their necks, were looking at me with amusement from the corners of their eyes.

I got up hurriedly. That story heard amidst the clouds no longer seemed to me true when facing this sunlit, unhidden scene of the world. I believe the suffusion of the mountain fog with my cigarette smoke, had to a large degree created an imaginary piece – that Muslim-Brahmin woman, that Brahmin hero, that fort along the bank of the river Jamuna – perhaps none of these were real after all.